MURDER
AT
•TOMORROW•

MURDER
AT
•TOMORROW•

Kara George

Walker and Company
New York

To my mother and father

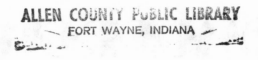
Copyright © 1982 by Kara George

First published in the United States of America
in 1982 by the Walker Publishing Company, Inc.

Published simultaneously in Canada by John Wiley & Sons
Canada, Limited, Rexdale, Ontario.

ISBN: 0-8027-5477-5

Book design by Laura Ferguson

Library of Congress Catalog Card Number: 82-60144

Printed in the United States of America

10 9 8 7 6 5 4 3 2 1

•1•

EDDY O'Brien, *Tomorrow* magazine's 70-year-old mail-room boy, sped on his appointed rounds, a folder stuffed with Associated Press clippings clutched firmly under one arm. First Politics. Then Foreign. Upstairs to Theater. Feet encased in high blue sneakers, bow legs arcing in baggy brown corduroy pants, Eddy's unlined pink face protruded from the top of a green and white T-shirt emblazoned "Kiss Me, I'm Irish."

As he piled the Associated Press clips on desks, he received a few grumbled "thanks." But what could you expect from writers, reporters, and editors who, evidently, did not know the meaning of an honest day's work? From Eddy's observation, members of the *Tomorrow* staff passed their time griping about Exeter Enterprises, the new management, gossiping, eating, drinking, reading, hanging out, complaining, spouting half-baked philosophy, or staring morosely into space. The time devoted to actual writing was a drop in the ocean

No wonder America was suffering from an energy crisis. Waste. Waste. Waste.

Meanwhile, Eddy grew bunions and developed sore arches standing in front of the A.P. machine that, minute by minute, spat out reams of paper. Eddy read the stories, clipped them, and routed them to the appropriate departments. One consolation: Eddy did not have to read *Tomorrow*, America's "think" newsweekly. Give him the betting sheet any day.

Personalities was Eddy's last stop. Editor Felix Magill was tipped back in his chair, feet propped on his desk, reading a book. His round, prematurely bald head gleamed under the fluorescent light. Felix rubbed his substantial stomach, encased in a brown, crew-necked sweater, and emitted an occasional burp. Felix's assistant, reporter Theo Marlow, sat hunched over a paper-strewn desk, red pen in hand.

5

How relaxed. Yet Felix and Theo never gave Eddy a moment's rest. "Watch for any news on Caroline Kennedy." "Where are the Liz Taylor clips?" "Give us anything on Senator Bleep's million-dollar house."

Eddy slapped a hefty bunch of clips into the overflowing basket on Theo's desk and gave her a slow, lewd wink. "Hot news today," he leered. In spite of her endless demands, Eddy counted Theo among the few human beings at the magazine. A slender, long-legged girl with honey-colored hair, a delicate sprinkling of freckles on an up-tilted nose, and black almond-shaped eyes, she was not painful to look at and she occasionally acknowledged his existence.

"Thanks, gray tiger." Theo gave him a broad wink in response. A gratified Eddy returned to the mail room.

Theo leaned back and stretched, pulling away from the Bette Davis clips that littered her desk. What was the exact shade of Bette Davis's blue eyes? Cornflower? Aqua? As part of her reporter's job, Theo checked the minute details that, strung together, lent verity to Felix's Personalities items, giving *Tomorrow*'s readers the feeling they were getting the inside story.

Theo put a story clip from *The New York Times* calling Davis's eyes "sky blue" next to a *Newsweek* story describing the actress's eyes as "aqua" and made a note to consult the library for a Davis bio. Of course, she could call Davis herself, getting the number from Felix's private collection of phone numbers of the famous, but she didn't want to bother the actress for such a small detail, except as a last resort.

A gentle snow pelted the windows. Across the hall in Religion, Emmy Kaufman's teakettle gave a perky whistle. In the "old days," three months ago, before Exeter Enterprises bought *Tomorrow*, bad weather made Theo feel pleasantly safe and enclosed, cozy. Now, with the constant uproar about the new management, the magazine's atmosphere was jittery. And a practical joker's anonymous pranks weren't helping build morale. Theo felt irritation and a vague sense of claustrophobia. She would be glad to leave the office for the cocktail party to launch novelist Samson Cody's latest blockbuster.

Felix sat up, slammed the book closed on his desk, scratched his nose, and said: "Damned bastard. That Sam Cody can really write, even if he is a certified maniac and publicity freak. I keep waiting and praying that he'll fall flat on his face. But his new novel is disgustingly

6

brilliant." Felix's cherubic mouth pursed. "Glad you're going to the Pringle Press party instead of me, Theo. Frankly, I couldn't stand to see Cody's gloating."

"Felix, don't give in to literary envy," Theo said. "A million people would love to have your job—lunch with film stars, cocktails with Prince Charles, a by-line in *Tomorrow* every week."

Behind Felix a burnt-orange wall was adorned with dirt smudges, a Charlie Chaplin poster, and various pieces of paper, curling at the edges, attached by Scotch tape. Paper littered Felix's desk along with a large ashtray, a yellow coffee mug, paper clips, stubby pencils, and inkless pens. More paper was piled on the windowsill, covered by a film of dust, and newspapers flowed off the top of a green metal filing cabinet that stood in the corner of the office. The unending paper seeped into every corner of *Tomorrow*, as relentlessly as the sands that blow across the Sahara.

"Poof," Felix sulked. "Here today, gone tomorrow. Personalities just ain't news with a capital *N*. I knock myself out perfecting items on how an aging movie star is starting a scholarship fund for poodles or Julia Child's preparing a banquet for the President. So I give people a few tidbits to chew over, to enliven their drab conversation. But where does it get me? Anyway, the magazine's going down the tubes along with the Exeters."

Felix warmed to his currently favorite topic. "Do you know what the Exeters do? They turn magazines into whorehouses. Anything for a buck. Their minds are sick, primitive, devoid of any journalistic ethics."

"But Felix, be realistic," Theo interrupted. "*Tomorrow* needed a face-lift. It was stale. Look at the drop in advertising pages and circulation. At least the Exeters are trying to bring the magazine up to date, to make it a money-making venture."

"Yeah, yeah, chasing the almighty dollar. That's the name of the game. Who cares about integrity?" Felix said. A diehard newsman, Felix equated journalism with truth. His office emulated the shabby comfort of a city room. His bow ties and occasional felt fedoras were symbols of a pre-TV era when newsboys shouted "Extra! Read all about it!" from street corners.

"Well, what's the use?" Felix paused. "Anyway, Theo, don't forget to ask Sam Cody to name the living author he most admires and the one he most despises. Question number two: Is it true that he

7

won't allow the book to be made into a TV mini-series unless he can play the part of the family patriarch? Question number three . . ."

"I know, Felix," Theo said, trying not to sound impatient as she moved pieces of paper into neat stacks on her desk. "You want to know his middle name."

"How did you guess?" Felix asked merrily, his mood suddenly changing. He took a puff of a thin cigar, his latest concession to giving up cigarettes. "And Theo, don't forget, exact quotes with the 'ahs' and 'ehs,'—I guess you know what to do."

"I hope so, Felix, after working with you for two years."

"Tonight I am going to go out and get drunk," Felix said. "The hell with Samson Cody."

"Have fun, Felix," Theo said, tucking a notebook into her handbag along with a pen. "See you tomorrow with the Bromo and iced tea." Theo was familiar with Felix's hangover cures. Working so closely with the writers, reporters were almost like office wives. Some became the spinster aunts of newsdom, absorbed into the fabric of the magazine like the constantly whirring wire service machines

Theo left the Personalities office and walked down the connecting stairway to the fourth floor to tell Lotte Van Buren, chief of reporters, that she would not be attending the reporters' meeting at 5:30.

As Theo approached Lotte's office, a shout rang out. "Damn! I will not stand for it," Lotte yelled. The head reporter stepped out into the corridor and looked up and down the hall. Spotting Theo, Lotte grabbed her by the arm and pulled her into her office.

"Look," Lotte said, pointing to the phone. Lotte picked up the receiver and the entire phone came with it. "My phone has been glued together." Lotte's face was red and her large, hyperthyroid blue eyes batted rapidly.

Theo stared at the phone in Lotte's hand. "What a disgusting trick," Theo said.

"It's more than disgusting," Lotte seethed. "It's sabotage. I'm helpless without a phone." Lotte put the instrument down on the desk with a bang.

"It must be the prankster," Theo said.

"Prankster? Ha. Villain is a more accurate word." Lotte jammed a cigarette into a black holder, then fixed a steely gaze on Theo. "Theo, I realize that we have not had the most wonderful rapport lately, but gluing down phones is not a joke."

"Lotte, why would I play a nasty trick like that on you?"

"You were the only person out in the corridor."

"I've been in the Personalities office for the past hour."

Lotte lit her cigarette and puffed at it rapidly. Sleek, fiftyish, with every hair of her dark blond pageboy in place, Lotte was usually unflappable. "It's all so unnerving," Lotte said. "One tends to get a bit paranoiac."

"I'm a professional," Theo said. "I don't glue down phones."

"I see." Lotte stubbed the cigarette out impatiently. "I'll use some solvent and get the phone unstuck. Then I will talk with our publisher Mark Exeter about it. These so-called jokes are strictly gallows humor. Something has to be done." Lotte glanced at her watch. "Theo, will you be attending the reporters' meeting?"

"No. I was coming by to tell you. I'm covering the Pringle Press party for Samson Cody."

"Very well, Theo," Lotte said crisply. "Next time I hope you will give me more advance warning. I like to schedule meetings so that all reporters can attend."

Theo left Lotte's office with relief. Lotte was famous for playing favorites among reporters, and Theo was currently on the "out" list. Nevertheless, Theo felt the accusation about gluing down the phone was undeserved. She stopped in the ladies' room for a last-minute check on her appearance. Lotte's stares and glares made her feel as if her face was smudged and her hair hanging down in strings.

Theo applied more blusher to give her skin a rosy glow, dabbed on a touch of eye shadow, and freshened her lipstick. The simple beige wool dress set off her honey-colored hair, and the $250 boots, a major splurge, lent security. She hurried over to the cocktail party, her mood lifting as she saw the lights and snowflakes drifting down on Fifth Avenue. On a snowy day, the city took on the atmosphere of a school holiday, with New Yorkers complaining but relishing their brief battle with the elements.

The party was at Brentano's Fifth Avenue bookstore. A front window featured a display of Samson Cody's book along with a life-size photo of the famous author with the rumpled face and crown of curly gray hair. Theo sailed through the door, handed her invitation to a guard, checked her coat, and made her way down the stairs. She perked to the cocktail party hum, the crowds of people. Theo thrived on cocktail parties, the animation, the smoke, even the much-touted phoniness. Book publishing parties were the best, laissez-faire operations yielding a surprising mixture of personalities.

At the end of the room, Cody held court, face moving with animation while flashbulbs popped around him. Because his novel was based on a family history, Cody had in tow his small sturdy mother, current wife, one ex-wife, and six children from various marriages.

Theo headed for the bar and ordered a Scotch. "Say, Theo, how goes it?" A blond young man with thick horn-rimmed glasses, Ron Jones, a reporter from *Time* magazine, stood next to her. "I hear Mark Exeter is really shaking things up at *Tomorrow*."

"Maybe it could use some shaking up." Theo laughed, balancing drink, cigarette, and handbag. As she chatted with the *Time* reporter, Theo's eyes roved around the room. There was Shirley Maclaine, a friend of the author . . . a famous lady poet . . . a United Press correspondent Theo had dated briefly until she discovered the secret of his slim wallet: a wife and four kids. Theo's eyes widened. A pair of remarkable green eyes were fastened on her. They belonged to *Tomorrow* publisher Mark Exeter, chatting with a woman writer of suspense novels. Exeter smiled at Theo. Theo smiled back. Did he know who she was? Exeter turned away.

Theo got out her notebook and pen and headed to where Samson Cody held court. Pushing her way through the crowd, Theo marched up boldly to Cody, announced her credentials as a *Tomorrow* reporter, and began firing questions at him. If the newspeople around her resented her monopolizing the author, she didn't care. Theo was out for a story.

An hour later, notebook full of quotes and "color" that eventually would add up to eight lines in *Tomorrow*, she stood in front of Brentano's stamping her feet, hoping the snow wouldn't injure her expensive boots. Perhaps she should have accepted the dinner invitation from the publicity director of Pringle Press.

No cabs. No buses. Somebody joined her on the sidewalk.

Theo looked up.

"Theo. Theo Marlow from *Tomorrow*, isn't it?" Snow settled softly on longish salt-and-pepper hair. In the streetlight Mark Exeter's eyes glittered like emeralds. Theo stared at his cleft chin.

"I saw you at the party, Mr. Exeter," Theo said, smiling up at the publisher. "I was covering it for 'Personalities.' "

"One of the best sections in the magazine," Exeter answered with gusto. "Looking for a cab?"

"Yes, but without much luck," Theo said. "I'm thinking of making a run for the subway."

"Why go riding on the subway on this wonderful snowy night?" Exeter said. "I have a better idea. I never touch food at cocktail parties and I'm starving. Why don't you join me for dinner?"

Theo hesitated for a split second. She would be dining out with the "enemy," and the publisher of *Tomorrow*, to boot. According to the rule books on how to succeed, it was not an advantageous move.

Exeter raised one eyebrow humorously, impatiently. "I promise you, Theo, my table manners are flawless," he said.

"I would love to have dinner with you."

"Good," Exeter said. He put a hand under her arm. "Come on. The restaurant Le Pont Neuf is French, only six blocks away, and unknown to anyone at *Tomorrow*."

"Sounds wonderful," Theo said.

Snow fluttered down deliciously, like confetti on New Year's Eve. In the distance Theo heard singing and laughter. Mark Exeter was so close to her that she could smell his expensive after-shave lotion.

A sudden gust of wind blew them closer together, both slipping on the sidewalk and then regaining their balance as Exeter took a firmer grip of Theo's arm.

"Theo," Exeter said, "the snow and you make me feel like dancing."

Theo felt the party was just beginning.

•2•

THE overly cheerful voice of WOR Radio's John Gambling slammed into his right ear as Nick Nicoletti opened his left eye to see, staring down at him, a gigantic green eye surrounded by yellow murk. "Oh, no," he groaned, staring at the wet, paint-encrusted canvas. Had he done that? Maybe he should completely forget about painting and stick to the private-detective business. As he pulled himself up, the lingering taste of brandy brought back the evening before, the drinks at Fanelli's. What started as a casual pause at his favorite SoHo hangout had strung out until three in the morning, courtesy of running into Germaine, a successful sculptor, sometime girlfriend, and downstairs neighbor. Germaine, inspired by her tenth glass of red wine, had perpetrated the eye, and for that he felt better. Nicoletti watched snow falling outside his window as John Gambling announced, "It is 8 A.M. and sunny in New York." So what did John Gambling know? And what did Germaine know about painting?

Nicoletti poured himself into the shower and considered his appointment with Mark Exeter, the publisher of *Tomorrow*. Unlike most potential clients, Exeter had sounded neither embarrassed, excited, nor furtive when he called. Exeter was cool, businesslike, and to the point. Nicoletti was curious. Most people hired private detectives when they were at the end of their rope. A desperation move. Usually Nicoletti had more business than he needed and was in the fortunate position of being able to turn undesirable cases away. His first case, seven years ago, tracking down the murderer of an heiress, had made him an instant celebrity.

Nicoletti was perfect "material" for the press: magna cum laude graduate of Cornell University; former all-American football player; a failed, one-time painter. Six feet tall, solidly built, with a mane of curly black hair, a craggy, strong bony face graced by a beaklike Italian nose, he was photogenic to boot. Today Nicoletti avoided public-

12

ity, finding that in his line of work having one's picture in the papers wasn't always a plus.

As he got out of the shower, drying himself with a beach towel, the phone rang. Padding out and picking up the black receiver, he heard the raspy voice of Mario, the florist: "So do I send them or don't I send them? I didn't hear from you, but I remembered the date, so I got them from the market this morning, special. Twelve American Beauty roses."

Nicoletti glanced at the calendar. It was his wedding anniversary. Every year, in spite of the divorce, the dozen American Beauty roses went to Daphne, and he couldn't decide if he did it for love, guilt, or plain old slob sentimentality. For the first time he had forgotten the date.

"Sure, Mario, and thanks for remembering."

"Listen, kid, you don't have to send them. Anyway, you've been divorced for four years, and I'm doing a really classy funeral this afternoon where I can work those red roses nicely into the arrangement."

The idea of Daphne's roses adorning a funeral bier didn't appeal. "No, Mario, why break tradition? How's business?"

"Terrific, kid. Yourself?"

"Good, Mario, good."

"Okay. So I'll send the roses with the usual card, a simple, unmushy note that reads 'With love, Nick.' "

"Maybe you better skip the love. Just Nick."

"You're learning, kid. See you."

As Nicoletti got dressed, carefully selecting gray trousers, navy-blue blazer, pale blue shirt, red and blue striped tie, he thought about Daphne: long-stemmed roses for the all-American girl, college sweetheart, wife. Daphne had stuck with him through thick and thin—the Marine Corps, the job at the advertising agency when he discovered he wasn't a corporate type, his "finding-himself" period, a job as Art reporter at *Tomorrow* magazine. That job was the brainstorm of ex-Cornell-roommate and friend Felix Magill, Personalities editor at the magazine. Nicoletti liked meeting and interviewing the Great Artists of Today and at the same time felt frustrated playing the observer. He wanted to be a painter, always had. When he visited artists' studios, the paints, turps, easels seemed to him wonderful toys of the imagination. He wanted to play; instead, he reported for *Tomorrow*.

Tomorrow. *What does Mark Exeter want?* Then the two years in

13

Florence, Italy, studying, painting, living on pasta, wine, and love. Glorious years if not for the certain knowledge that he was not a Matisse or Rembrandt. Patient Daphne.

Back to New York, living in an apartment in his parents' house in Greenwich Village while Daphne nursed her dream of a split-level in suburban Scarsdale. Trying to "go straight." Working for an insurance company. Ugh! Which led to a temporary job as an insurance investigator. Nicoletti found he liked the careful, intricate investigative process, standing outside of society and looking in, almost an artist's stance. And it appealed to his sense of adventure, of looking below the surface of human activity, of, sometimes, helping to see justice done. He announced to Daphne that he was getting a license and hanging out his shingle as a private eye. That tore it.

Being married to a gumshoe was more than Daphne could take. She needed security, stability, respectability. End of marriage. Did he still love her? Maybe. Could they live together again? No. Particularly because she had recently wed a Wall Street lawyer. Word came through the grapevine that the new husband was too respectable, even stuffy, and Daphne was chafing at the bit. Did people ever get what they wanted?

Nicoletti had a couple of things he wanted: his loft in SoHo—his painterly palace filled with a few pieces of comfortable, worn furniture, Picasso etchings, a small Matisse. And there was the uptown office, Private Eyedom, where at 10 A.M. publisher Mark Exeter would appear to spill his tale.

Nicoletti grabbed a raincoat off a chair, shut and locked the heavy door, and headed down the wide staircase. He rang the bell on the next landing.

"Who the hell is it?" At 8:30 A.M., Germaine was her most strident.

"Your lover."

Bleary-eyed, long hair tangled, wearing a man's shirt, a cigarette dangling out of her mouth, Germaine came to the door. Her cocky grin broke through the dissipation. "Lover? My stomach still hurts from the giggles. But it was sweet, what I remember of it."

"You paint terrible eyes."

"That's why I'm a famous lady sculptor. I do some things better than others." Germaine gave him a quick peck on the cheek. "When are you going to pose for me?"

14

"When I'm older, ravaged, and ready to sit still for immortality."

"I'll hold my breath," Germaine said. "Bye. Enjoy."

Nicoletti went down the stairs and out the door. So he did not have a wife, or even a lover. To compensate, there was occasional friendly lovemaking with a comfortable woman like Germaine and occasional passion—strange for him, the dedicated romantic who was all or nothing, madly in love or not interested.

But life evolved differently than one anticipated. On this February day, with a gray, snow-filled sky caressing New York's smudged streets, he felt good, sensing possibilities in the air. He went down into the subway, stopped to buy *The New York Times*, and headed for the office uptown, ten minutes and a world away.

He went up on the elevator in the building on Fifty-fifth Street and Madison Avenue. Close enough to the Fifty-seventh Street art galleries so that he could take an occasional stroll to them, his office had a respectable, smart address. Down the hall was a lawyer's office, across the hall, a public-relations firm whose claim to fame was representing Robert Redford. Opening the office door, he heard rock music playing on the radio. His angel-faced secretary/assistant was dancing blithely around the reception room, humming, cavorting, blond ringlets bouncing. The face, Botticelli; the body, Renaissance sculpture.

"Hello, Rocko," Nicoletti said, taking his coat off. "Practicing for a part in the chorus line?"

Rocko clicked off the radio. "I went to this really fantastic disco last night with a dynamite girl I met in the lobby at the New School. Hair down to here," Rocko said, gesturing. "And can she dance. I mean that's the way to her heart. So she taught me this new number. Dada dada dada. And I've been practicing. How we met was by the elevator when I asked her, 'Have you learned much from your class in Eastern philosophies?' And she said, 'That was last semester. I'm into aerobic movement now.' "

Rocko sat down at his desk. Wearing a fine gold chain around his neck, open-necked shirt, tweed jacket, tailored French blue jeans, and cowboy boots, Rocko looked distinctly "now." The unstudied chic was the result of hours spent studying fashion magazines and persistent trips to Bloomingdale's. Rocko was the younger brother of a friend, and Nicoletti initially hired him to "keep the kid out of trouble." As it turned out, Rocko was the perfect assistant.

For instance, Rocko relished the divorce cases Nicoletti found so repugnant.

An insatiable satyr, with an unquenchable interest in sex, Rocko was expert at getting to know straying wives and the girlfriends of straying husbands. With his sweet, innocent smile, who could resist him? Recently he had enrolled in the New School to broaden his mind, spurred to intellectual activity when he discovered there were five women students to every man.

"How are your studies going?" Nicoletti asked.

"Exciting. That's the only way to describe them," Rocko said. "Stimulating. I never realized how intelligent I was until now. Also, I find I have a talent for bullshit. I'm great in discussions. As one lecturer said, I have an oblique, original point of view."

"Ech," Nicoletti said. "Callow youth." He went into his office, dominated by a large, sleek rosewood desk. A collection of circus posters brightened the walls. Supple leather chairs and a deep burgundy carpet completed the furnishings. His office was masculine, uncluttered.

He called through the door: "I'm expecting Exeter at ten, so let's try to look businesslike. And maybe get those letters out to the lingerie company on the West Coast." On his last case, he had tracked down an industrial spy who was stealing secrets on a new bra construction and giving them to a rival company for a tidy sum. The sleuthing was successful, and a large fee was in the offing, but he felt vaguely guilty about the case. Was the no-back bra really a find?

With half an hour to spare, Nicoletti got out the file that Rocko had put together on Mark Exeter and went through it.

Newspaper clips ballyhooed Exeter as "the British press baron," scion of multimillion-dollar Exeter Enterprises, owner of thirty magazines and newspapers around the world. There were *Time* and *Newsweek* stories about his first New York acquisition, *Tomorrow*, America's "think" newsweekly, that speculated whether Exeter's commercial taint would destroy it. Photographs of his marriage to glamorous actress Vanessa Wills. More stories about his talent for turning failing publishing properties around. His educational background was impeccable: Eton, then a degree at Oxford University. Stints working for his father's newspapers around the globe. Exeter had a mixed press: people admired him or hated him in varying degrees.

At precisely five minutes to ten, Rocko buzzed Nicoletti on the intercom. "Mr. Exeter is here." Nicoletti stood up to greet the publisher. Mark Exeter was tall, lean, tanned, and wearing a blue pinstriped double-breasted suit with a gray cashmere scarf tossed casually around his throat. He looked "to the manor born," although his father had worked in a print shop before amassing his empire, and his mother had once run a fish 'n chips shop in London. Exeter's large green eyes met Nicoletti's in a direct gaze, and he extended his hand, offering an ingratiating smile.

"I'm happy—I might even say relieved—to meet you," Exeter said.

"Sit down," Nicoletti said, gesturing to the leather chair. "As you probably know, I'm a *Tomorrow* alumnus. I worked for the magazine for a year as a reporter in the art department."

"Yes, I'm aware of that," Exeter said. "That's why I thought you would be quite perfect for the job. Point of curiosity, why did you leave? Most people stay forever at *Tomorrow*. Seem to regard their jobs as happy sinecures."

"Maybe that was the problem," Nicoletti said. "It was too safe."

"A man who likes risks. Good. That's my philosophy," Exeter said. Exeter appeared completely poised, seated with one leg crossed over the other, trousers riding up to show silk socks. "Tell me, do I appear to be the ogre press lord that the press depicts me as?"

"Not on first appearance," Nicoletti answered.

"And you don't appear to be the type of detective who keeps a bottle of Old Overshoes in the top drawer and spends his time watching neon signs flickering across the street." Exeter paused. "I've long been a fan of fictional detectives, but I never thought I would be consulting a real one."

Nicoletti encouraged him. "Coming to me is like consulting a doctor or lawyer. Whether I take the case or not, anything you tell me is in strictest confidence. The only other person who would be privy to the information, if I do take the case, is my assistant, Rocko."

"Oh, yes, the, er, receptionist." Exeter took out a pack of cigarettes, offered it to Nicoletti, then lit a cigarette with a sleek, gold lighter. "This is it. I am actually coming to you with two problems and you seem tailor-made to help me solve them. The first is my wife, the actress Vanessa Wills. If you follow the gossip columns, you know we are separated. At any rate, I am more than amenable to a divorce and prepared to make a healthy financial settlement. But Vane is demanding that she get half of my Oriental-art collection. Claims to have helped build it, which is a lot of poppycock. The girl might have other talents, but what she knows about art you could put on the head of a pin. Now this is the sticky part. . . ." Exeter took a quick puff on the cigarette. "Vanessa's in New York, trying out for some film roles. To fill her time, I hear she's been engaging in some rather kinky sexual scenes."

Exeter's voice was precise. "I've known about Vanessa's high jinks, her occasional flings, for some time and chose to ignore them. We British are not as puritanical as you Yankees. Nevertheless, since she specializes in playing ethereal women, Joan of Arc and the like, I don't think the publicity would do much for her image. What I want you to do is get me the information, the *who, what, when*, and *where* on her newest fun and games. I would use the information as a lever to get her to back down on the art collection demand." Exeter paused, frowning. "It wouldn't come out in court. I hope it doesn't sound like blackmail. My lawyer advised me that it was my best recourse."

"I see," Nicoletti said, appraising the publisher. The shark was beginning to surface, he thought. "You should know that although I would direct the investigation, I never personally involve myself in this type of case. Rocko, my assistant, would do the actual legwork."

"He seems well equipped for the job," Exeter retorted.

"And what's the other problem?" Nicoletti asked.

"This is more of an annoyance than a serious problem, but it's beginning to eat into the morale of my staff at *Tomorrow*. Some prankster has been doing strange things, leaving obscene notes in typewriters and playing other practical jokes. For instance, Lotte Van Buren, head of reporters, found the receiver of her phone glued down. She was extremely upset."

"How long has this been going on?"

"For the past month, not long after Exeter Enterprises acquired *Tomorrow*," Exeter answered. "As I said, it gives a bad tone to the operation. I have my hands full as it is trying to whip *Tomorrow* into shape—taking what was a floating cocktail party atmosphere and making the slightest changes casts me in the villain's role. *Tomorrow* is journalistically brilliant. But it is not a money-making proposition. I want the magazine to reach its potential. Working in a tainted atmosphere doesn't help. I thought you could track down the culprit."

"Have you been a victim of any of the pranks?"

"Of course." Exeter reached into his pocket and pulled out a folded piece of paper. "I found this on my desk Friday. The prankster doesn't discriminate about what days he plays his tricks, but he always does something particularly unsettling on Friday." Exeter handed the note to Nicoletti.

Nicoletti read the careful typing:
CHINESE PROVERB SAYS LIFE A RIDDLE.
SOME RIDDLES SHORTER THAN OTHERS.

"Inane," Exeter commented. "If it were only myself, I would ignore the ridiculous business. But the women staffers in particular are disturbed. Frankly, Lotte Van Buren is in a black humor, and she's the last person I want offended."

"Nobody wants Lotte against them," Nicoletti said, remembering the superefficient head reporter with nerves of steel who could dig up anything from an obscure Dante quote to the price of eggs in Mongolia. Nicoletti paused, looking at the publisher. "Exeter, these pranks might be more serious than you think. Sounds like somebody has a vendetta against the magazine."

"It's a sorry business," Exeter said. "Will you take the case, or rather, cases?"

"Yes," Nicoletti said. "But I'd like to be able to move around the magazine without arousing suspicion. I hear *Tomorrow* is starting a new department called Crime. Perhaps you could bring me in as a consultant on it."

"Excellent idea," Exeter said. "I'll tell our editor, Eli Patterson, about it."

"How is Patterson?"

"Electric. Magnetic. Totally mad. Erratic. Do you know him well?"

"No," Nicoletti said. "He arrived at *Tomorrow* at about the same time I was leaving."

"Now that I've unburdened myself to you, I almost feel as if the problems are off my mind," Exeter said. "You'll want a retainer, I suppose."

"One thousand dollars. There's a daily fee and expenses, but my rates are standard."

"I'll have an office set up for you at *Tomorrow*," Exeter said. Exeter took a check out of his pocket, swiftly filled it in with a silver pen, and handed it to Nicoletti. "I'll look forward to working with you," Exeter said.

Nicoletti took the check and put it to the side of his desk. "I hope you realize, Exeter, that certain risks are involved when you hire a private detective."

"Such as?"

"The information I uncover isn't always pleasant."

Exeter cocked one eyebrow, his mouth twisting slightly to the side. "I'm a man who prefers to deal with known quantities, regardless of the dimensions," he said.

"Good," Nicoletti answered.

"And, by the way, will you call me Mark? And may I call you Nick? Formalities can get in the way." Exeter's smile oozed charm.

"Of course," Nicoletti said.

Exeter left.

So this was the dangerous Mark Exeter, the feared press baron, who, as he exited, left a whiff of expensive cologne behind him. Tonight Nicoletti was meeting Felix Magill, *Tomorrow*'s Personalities editor, for dinner. Felix was sure to have more than a few views on Exeter.

Nicoletti sat down at his desk and stared out the window, where, rather than a neon sign, the awning of a health club called out to fitness addicts.

In spite of Exeter's elegant manners, Nicoletti sensed ruthlessness behind the Bond Street facade. He also felt trouble ahead, that deeper dangers than Exeter hinted at roiled beneath the surface at *Tomorrow*. Why? Maybe it was the man's personality. He was both protective of the *Tomorrow* staff and critical. "A floating-cocktail-party atmosphere," he termed the magazine. An unusual man, who unemotionally accepted his wife's so-called high jinks until he could use them for his own self-interest, to protect his Oriental-art collection.

Nicoletti picked up the intercom. "Say, Rocko, come in here. I have a new case that I think is going to be right up your alley."

•3•

SHIVERING in the snow, Rocko stood in the shadow of a massive apartment building on East Sixty-fifth Street watching the door of the town house across the street. He occasionally glanced at his white moped parked by the curb. If actress Vanessa Wills didn't appear soon, his ears and some other parts of him would be frozen off. He should have worn a hat, but vanity would not permit it. Hats made him look idiotic; not wearing one was part of his new independence.

How many goofy, woolen hats, usually hand-knit, had his mother made him endure? He would run out of the apartment in New York's Little Italy and hide them or lose them, but Mama always came up with a new one. Things were different now, working for Nicoletti, a guy he could respect. Nicoletti possessed brains, looks, independence—unlike most of Rocko's relatives, minor Mafia figures who ran "fronts" like dry-cleaning establishments and candy shops. Dumb clucks.

Rocko loved his job and its challenges, relished the divorce cases Nicoletti despised. Why was he so interested in sex? Occasionally, he wondered if he were sick. Maybe someday he would become a regular square Joe, your twice-a-week-sex guy, but it was hard to imagine.

Snow was falling now in beautiful, chubby flakes; Rocko caught a snowflake on the tip of his tongue. The door across the street opened. There she was, Vanessa Wills, a slender, red-haired woman with a magnificent model's face, hollow cheekbones, and white skin, wrapped in a mink coat with legs encased in high boots. She smiled up at the man with her, a skinny guy with a black beard and mustache. Rocko moved towards his moped as the couple got into a silver Audi. Rocko got on his moped, souped up to go more than thirty miles an hour, and, keeping a discreet distance, followed the Audi through the snow-filled streets.

Ten minutes later Rocko stood at the bar at the Entre Nous Disco, sipping ginger ale and watching Vanessa Wills with her bearded companion. She wore a white satin jump suit that revealed every curve of her slender, shapely body. Could that gal move! Of course, dancing in a disco with some guy who looked like a poet, or maybe a priest, did not put her in the criminal category or make her a sex fiend, as her husband Mark Exeter claimed. Patience, Rocko, patience. Isn't that what Nicoletti said? Keep your eye on your man, keep your distance, and wait. Waiting was the private eye's game.

"Wow. Wow. Wow," Rocko said under his breath, keeping time to the music. Vanessa Wills moved as if her bones were made of liquid, a hip lurching to the left, breasts arcing to the right. Pow! She wasn't hard to keep your eyes on and, in fact, was the center of attention. "Famed British actress seen in New York disco with mysterious man," the gossip columnists would report. Which was maybe why she and her date exited from the dance floor and headed for the coat check.

Five minutes later, Rocko was back on his moped, following the Audi. It drove west and up Broadway, stopping in front of an old hotel that housed an occasional out-of-town salesman and The Pleasure Palace, New York's notorious new swingers' club.

Vanessa Wills and companion parked the Audi and went in the door. Rocko locked up the moped and entered a brightly lit lobby. An elderly gentleman with a sour face and yellow teeth perched on a wooden stool by the elevators. He eyed Rocko shrewdly. "Pleasure Palace? Elevator to the left. No men without dates."

Rocko shrugged and rang for the elevator. He got on, pushed the self-service button, and shuddered down to the lower level, getting off to see a blue neon sign announcing The Pleasure Palace. An athletic-looking young man in a close-fitting spangled T-shirt stood by the entrance where a more discreet sign read ADMISSION, $50.00 PER COUPLE.

"Sorry, buddy," the guard said to Rocko. "No guys without gals."

Rocko reached into his wallet, fished out *two* fifty-dollar bills, and handed them to the guard.

"Dressing rooms inside," the guard nodded towards the door. "The club's on the other side." He handed Rocko a locker key and a towel.

Five minutes later, with only a towel wrapped around his naked body (he took the dress-code clue from others in the locker room), Rocko stepped out into The Pleasure Palace. In the steamy atmosphere, the result of vapors arising from a heated Olympic-sized pool, mirrored walls reflected a fantasy world of naked men and women. Hitching his towel, Rocko took a slow look around. Incredible. He set out to explore the nooks and crannies of The Pleasure Palace in search of Vanessa Wills and to experience the flesh-filled scene.

In the whirlpool, eight people were submerged, beatific grins spreading across their faces as the warm, bubbling water massaged them and they massaged each other while making eye contact across the water. Tempted to plunge in, Rocko moved on to search for Wills.

Walking into the steam room, he gasped as the hot, wet air hit him and gasped again as the sight of two men making love to one woman, writhing bodies glistening with steam and perspiration in the pale blue light, emerged through the murk. He stepped closer. A second woman was observing and giving stage directions to the trio. She was a skinny blond. No beard or Vanessa Wills. As Rocko moved closer, the blond turned to him: "Care to play with us, honey?"

Enticing, but Rocko shook his head no and left the steam room. His own body was dripping with excitement. He moved along to a postage-sized dance floor with whirling lights, "The Pleasure Disco." One couple occupied the floor. To a vibrant beat, a girl with a red flower in her dark hair, dressed in spike heels and a black G-string, danced with a muscular, heavy-bellied man wearing only a French sailor's cap. The couple gyrated frantically, his large hands wrapped around her buttocks, her hands entwined around his neck. Before the dance ended, the man picked the girl up in his arms, carried her to a chaise on the side, where they made love while the multicolored lights swirled over their bodies. The man thrust slowly, surely, as the girl responded with ecstatic movements, crying out: "Ay, yah, yay."

Agog, Rocko watched for a moment. Was voyeurism really his scene? He looked into the room next to the disco. Like a sexy cocktail party without clothes, men and women lay on mats on the floor, talking, making love, and inviting each other to dally. Rocko saw entwined arms and legs, like an illustration from *Playboy*. He needed time out. He found an empty chaise by the pool and lay back, stretching his muscles, breathing deeply, trying to get his own sexual impulses under control. He had never seen another couple make love, unless you wanted to count his peeking through the keyhole to watch his brother Carlo making out with his nearsighted fiancée. Strictly a turnoff.

Then Rocko spotted her, Vanessa Wills, naked, a magnificent body and not one stitch of clothes. No coy towel-wrapping for Vanessa Wills. In the company of "the beard," she strolled around the pool with the same grace she might give to a walk in an English garden. Rocko half-closed his eyes and lay back on the chaise watching her.

"Mama mia," he said to himself. "Pay dirt." He fingered the gold pendant around his neck that disguised a microscopic camera.

"The beard" plunged into the pool, and Vanessa Wills kept strolling, at a saunter, towards Rocko. Through half-closed eyes, Rocko saw her looking towards him. Was it his imagination? No. She was definitely watching him. He trembled from excitement, groaned inside.

What should he do?

She stopped next to him and stared down with violet eyes.

"Darling," she said with a distinctly British accent. "You have the most enchanting curls. Goldilocks."

Rocko stood up. "God, you're beautiful." The tremor in his voice wasn't faked. He threw off the towel that was wrapped around him and tossed it on the chaise next to him.

They kissed. Everything felt moist, liquid, glowing, flowing. Steam, music, glittering mirrors, water, limpid bodies surrounded them, enclosed them.

Taking Vanessa Wills's hand in his, Rocko led her to the dance floor. Later they explored The Pleasure Palace together.

That night, Rocko learned something new about himself. Love in a crowd with a beautiful stranger was a heavenly experience.

"I tell you, Nose, the guy is a real son of a bitch." Felix Magill leaned across the table in the back room of Fanelli's, pouring out his feelings to his old college buddy, Nick Nicoletti. "Exeter can only drag *Tomorrow* down. He's destroying the spirit of the place."

Felix waved his glass at the waiter for another drink and continued.

"You know, Nose—hope you don't mind if I call you that—I'm drunk and glad of it. Afraid to open my mouth at *Tomorrow*. That place has become a damn jungle."

Nicoletti sipped his beer. "Felix, nobody was ever afraid to open his mouth at *Tomorrow*, particularly you."

"Yeah, yeah," Felix said, lighting up his long cigar and missing at the first try. "Boy, I miss those Lucky Strikes, great coffin nails that saw me through life's crises as well as cover stories."

Felix looked morosely into his bourbon and water. "Remember, Nose, when I was going to be a great playwright and you were going to be a painter? Everyone I meet these days becomes something else than he planned. A would-be actor becomes a radio announcer. An aspiring radio announcer ends up as an insurance broker and occasionally grabs the mike at the Lion's Club . . . Maybe that's why I hate Exeter so much, because all he was ever planning to be was a publisher and that's what he is."

"Ever ask him what he wanted to be, Felix?"

"Ask him? I talk with the bastard as little as possible," Felix said. "It's all true about his mixture of the naked and the deadly. Do you know that he insists on changing the Personalities department over from black-and-white to four-color pictures? And he wants at least one sexy shot an issue—the old boobs-and-bum formula. Disgusting. Depraved."

"You always liked gorgeous girls, Felix."

"But not in living color," Felix answered. "Don't you understand? The *copy* is the color. That's the *Tomorrow* philosophy. Anyway, my reaction to Exeter is mild compared to Eli Patterson's. If Exeter keeps introducing his innovations into the magazine, I think Patterson will quit."

"If Patterson quits, where will that leave you?"

"I'll leave with him. All of Patterson's people will walk out the door together, thumbing our noses at Exeter Enterprises en masse." Felix thumped the table, causing his drink to teeter. He pulled it back and took a gulp. "We've talked about it."

Nicoletti was familiar with Felix's rantings. "Felix, as one of your oldest friends . . ."

Felix interrupted. "My oldest friend . . . best friend I have . . ."

Nicoletti continued. "What are you going to do if you leave *Tomorrow*? Newspapers are folding, and I don't see newsmagazines springing up. Let's face it, you're a newsman. Would you be content writing for *Backpacking*, let's say, or *Sail*?"

"Don't care," Felix said. "I'll leave and write a book giving the nitty-gritty about Exeter Enterprises. Newspapers, they're vanishing like the dinosaur." Felix waved his arm to order another drink. "I tell you, the opportunities for a seasoned newsman are practically zero. Does anyone care about experience? No. You've got these millions of eager journalism school graduates who were turned on by the Woodward-Bernstein Watergate exposé all thinking they're going to be heros. Nowadays, when some kid makes a phone call and gets the spelling of somebody's name right, he calls it investigative reporting. La-di-da. Half of them wouldn't know a story if it hit them between the eyes. Furthermore, they're illiterate. Dickens? They saw the movie *Great Expectations*. Give me the good old days when a newsman did his job, got drunk, fell asleep with his socks on, and was back on the job at 8 A.M." Felix raised a new glass of bourbon and water in salute. "Gone are the days of the raffish, rowdy newsmen," Felix slurred. "But I'll drink to them."

Felix and Nicoletti clinked glasses.

"Furthermore, I'm tired of the weird pranks and funny notes at the magazine," Felix intoned, swaying in his chair. "Never happened before the Exeters arrived."

"Do you have any idea who might be playing the tricks?"

"Dunno," Felix said. "Figure it must be some creepy kid who thinks he or she is being funny, or maybe is a little nuts. One of the trainees, pardon me, interns. How I dislike that word. It's a newsmagazine, damn it, not a hospital. Anyway, I haven't been the recipient of one of the strange billets-doux yet. Maybe Exeter is leaving them around. Maybe he's trying to frame somebody."

"Who would Exeter want to frame?"

"Patterson, maybe, to get him out of the magazine," Felix said. "Who knows? Anyway, I'm glad you're going to be in the office for a while, consulting on the new Crime department. Crime was Patterson's idea," Felix said. "And the story to kick off the new department looks big."

"What's it about?"

"An exposé of Brandon Motors, America's largest producer of gas guzzlers," Felix answered.

"Brandon Motors? It's like exposing mom and apple pie."

"I worked on the story," Felix answered. "It's powerful. A bombshell."

"What did you find out?"

"Brandon's big honchos not only spy within their own ranks. They spy on other corporations."

"Is that news? That's the story of American business in action."

Felix burped. "It's news. Patterson uncovered something big, dynamite."

"What?"

"He wouldn't tell me. It's under lock and key. Only Patterson knows." Felix slurped his drink. "But Patterson isn't a guy given to hyperbole." Felix pursed his mouth and ran his hand over his bald head. "My intuition and tenth bourbon tells me it's concerning fuel, energy, gasoline. Big. Timely. On target."

"What do you think Exeter will do when he learns the dimensions of the story?" Nicoletti said. "You told me he was trying to pull Brandon advertising into the magazine."

"A problem," Felix answered. "Dunno. Under the old publisher, Hendricks, no amount of advertising bucks could influence editorial. Exeter is a different ball game. A publisher isn't supposed to mess around with editorial the way he does. He's supposed to give speeches at luncheons. Stay in his place."

Nicoletti motioned for the check. "From my one meeting with Mark Exeter, he seems to know his place—on top of the heap."

"Even the mighty fall," Felix slurred, his bald head gleaming innocently, his voice dejected. "He'll get his."

Nicoletti got the check, reached into his pocket, and paid. "Let's drink to *Tomorrow*," he said. "May its exposés increase."

Nicoletti and Felix finished their drinks.

"Amen." Felix hiccuped.

Nicoletti and Felix tumbled out of Fanelli's and slogged their way through the snow back to Nicoletti's loft. Felix collapsed on the couch and broke into a rumbling snore.

Nicoletti draped a blanket over Felix and called his wife on Long Island to let her know Felix was safe and sound.

Gazing over at the murky green eye on the canvas, Nicoletti remembered his meeting with Exeter. Exeter's eyes were clear and cool and green, but, like the painted eye, unfathomable.

Tomorrow would be his first day at the magazine under the guise of editorial consultant. It was ten years since, with the exception of Felix, he had spent much time with the *Tomorrow* crew. Perhaps the differences would be revealing.

Down in Germaine's apartment, Nicoletti heard music, laughter, an occasional shout and thump. Germaine, a perennial party giver, was holding a gathering to celebrate the snow.

He locked the door behind him, pocketing his keys, and went down the stairs.

"Nick," Germaine cried, flinging her arms wide. "Welcome. Join the fun. We thought you'd never come."

•4•

THE party's over, Nicoletti thought, tossing his coat on a shaky, old-fashioned rack in a windowless cube at *Tomorrow*, his temporary quarters at the magazine. *Tomorrow*, still maintaining its intellectual counterchic with spotted walls and antique wire-mesh in and out baskets firmly in place.

Fine soot covered the top of the gray metal desk. Opening the bottom left-hand drawer, Nicoletti was greeted by a forlorn-looking pair of black galoshes. He opened the middle drawer, where a few pencils rattled around, along with a half-eaten package of Life Savers, three bobby pins, and a map of France. Did the office's last occupant fall for the owner of the bobby pins and elope with her to Europe? Good luck, Nicoletti thought, pondering the office worker's compulsion for leaving souvenirs—a love letter, a résumé, a dated office diary— behind when evacuating.

As he walked down the hall to Exeter's office, he heard the thrum of typewriters and the jingle of the coffee-wagon bell, sounds of the magazine coming to life. Jane, secretary to Mark Exeter and also Eli Patterson, sat at her desk in the area separating the two offices. A blond girl with an egg-shaped face and long white teeth, she flashed Nicoletti a grin. "Hi there," she said. "Go right on in." Exeter's door was open.

The publisher was setting up a small projection screen on a tripod on top of the bookcase in the precise spot where, Nicoletti remembered, the old publisher had kept a dart board. In Exeter's office, change was very much in evidence.

The office was elegantly decorated, with a collection of Japanese prints on one wall and a large, carved antique desk graced by a Chinese bronze equestrian statue.

Exeter looked up as Nicoletti entered. "Hello, Nick," he said. "Are your temporary quarters adequate?"

"If I were sentimental, they'd give me pangs of nostalgia, ' Nico-letti said. "That office hasn't changed in ten years."

Exeter quirked an eyebrow. "Decor is the least of the magazine's problems," he said.

"I came to tell you that I spoke with my assistant Rocko this morn-ing, and I think the first case we discussed—or rather your problem—could be on the way to being resolved. We should have a report for you tomorrow."

Exeter looked up from his fiddling with the screen. "Fast work," he said, presenting Nicoletti a glowing smile. "I like a man who at-tacks a problem head-on." Exeter stood back to look at the screen.

"Now, if I could see that collection of prankster's notes, I can get started on the second problem," Nicoletti said.

"Mmmmn, Eli Patterson is arriving for a meeting in about two seconds. I'd like you to sit in on it with us. You might have some in-put, as a former *Tomorrow* reporter and disinterested outsider."

At that moment, Eli Patterson burst into the room, scattering ashes from a stubby cigarette. Slightly gap-toothed, with crackling blue eyes and curly sandy hair that frizzled around his head, Patterson was not conventionally handsome. His face was puckish-looking, with a broad, turned-up nose covered with fading freckles. He was barrel-chested, with slender, almost nonexistent, hips, and his rolled-up shirt sleeves revealed strong, muscular arms. Compared to the smooth Exeter, Patterson gave the impression of reckless, feisty flamboyance.

He pumped Nicoletti's hand vigorously. "Glad to see you," he said. "Hear you're going to lend your expertise to the new Crime de-partment." He turned to Exeter. "Exeter, do we have a story! The Brandon Motors piece is a killer. We're going to knock them dead at *Time* and *Newsweek*. I think we can go with it this week."

Hands thrust in his pockets, Exeter walked over to stand behind his desk. "Eli, I still don't quite comprehend how Brandon Motors' activities can be billed under Crime."

"I told you," Patterson said. "We're planning to cover everything in this department, not just cops-and-robbers' stories." Patterson's blue eyes snapped and his jaw thrust out.

"Well, enough of this discussion," Exeter said. "Why don't you both sit down. I want to show you the concept for a new advertising campaign. According to a recent demographic study, *Tomorrow*'s

493,000 readers are definitely educated and upscale. But they possess one fatal flaw. The magazine's readers are old, with the median age fifty. However, this campaign will counteract the geriatric image."

Exeter turned off the lights and switched on a slide projector. A picture of a handsome young couple, packs on their backs, greeting a saffron-robed monk flashed on the screen. The snow-capped Himalaya Mountains filled the background. The deep, resonant voice on the tape recorder began: "Meet Betty and Bill. They read the 'new' *Tomorrow*. They're young, adventuresome, aware of *their* tomorrows. In *Tomorrow*'s Isms columns, they learn about the age-old art of meditation in Tibet. Travel tells them how to take a flying, backpacking junket halfway around the world and still have money for serious camera equipment. If you're a 'now' person, read the 'new' *Tomorrow*, the magazine for people with a future."

The presentation droned on in the overheated room, showing apple-cheeked Betty and Bill in a variety of youthful, energetic situations. Finally it was over. Exeter switched on the lights and moved around to the front of his desk, leaning against it with ankles gracefully crossed.

"What do you think?" he asked.

Patterson stubbed out a cigarette, lit another one. "I think it's rather droll, as a matter of fact," the editor said. "The Bobbsey twins in the Himalayas. The Bobbsey twins go dancing. But what's with the 'new' *Tomorrow*?" Patterson continued. "These Madison Avenue admen are a bushy-tailed bunch. Don't they know the magazine doesn't have a Travel department? And what the hell is Isms?"

Exeter sat down at his desk and folded his hands in front of him. "Isms is a new department that will replace Religion," the publisher said. "It will cover everything from EST to the pope. Cults. Things that young people are into."

Patterson threw back his head and gave a short, barking laugh. "You can't be serious. We'll be the laughingstock of the news world," Patterson said. "*Isms* is hardly even a word, unless you talk in crossword-puzzle-ese."

"We will popularize the word," Exeter said tersely.

"Totally, I think the new concept stinks," Patterson retorted. "You better hire a new ad agency."

"It's more than a concept," Exeter answered forcefully. "It's a directive, a blueprint for changing the magazine. We must attract

31

young readers. They are the people major advertisers sell to. Young people buy cars, clothes, indulge in hobbies, travel. This is not a joke, Eli."

"I'm not laughing," Patterson said.

"And there's another broader change I want to see in the magazine. I want *Tomorrow* to be more people-oriented," Exeter said.

"People-oriented?" Patterson fumed. "We do tremendous reporting on people. We've been a model to other magazines."

"Yes," Exeter answered. "But you don't publish all the relevant information. For instance, you had the story on Ted Kennedy's affair with the Paris model, but you didn't use it."

Patterson shifted restlessly in his chair. He leaned towards Exeter. "I believe a person's private life remains private unless it infringes on the public interest. That is a journalistic ethic."

"Passé," Exeter said with a wave of his hand. "Today everyone's life is an open book."

"Listen, Exeter," Patterson protested. "If you turn this magazine into a gossip rag for teenyboppers, we're going to lose every reader we ever had . . including the ones polkaing in senior citizens' homes."

"That remains to be seen," Exeter said. His thick eyebrows drew together in a straight line. "I want you to have a dummy copy of the 'new' *Tomorrow*, with the new departments and approach in two weeks, Eli. I know you will bring all your brilliance to bear on the job."

Patterson stared silently at Exeter. He crumpled a pack of cigarettes in his hand, the crackle a raw explosion.

"One more thing, Eli," Exeter said, his voice low and firm. "Starting this week, I want to see every line of copy for approval before it goes into the magazine."

Patterson's hands shook as he lit another cigarette. "Approving copy isn't the publisher's job, Exeter."

Exeter's voice was cold. "You might find my actions unconventional, but I'm here to shape up the magazine. That's what I intend to do." Exeter's intercom buzzed. "Now I have another meeting."

Patterson glared at Exeter, got up, turned on his heel, went into his office across the hall, and slammed the door, hard.

"Emotions run high on this magazine," Exeter said.

Nicoletti walked over to Exeter's desk. "Trying to change a journalist's code of ethics is like attacking his religion," Nicoletti said.

Exeter's tone was dry. "The purists of the print world, all unrealized Hemingways."

Nicoletti felt as if he had just witnessed round one of a prize fight. "Do you have that collection of the prankster's notes?" he asked.

"Ah, yes," Exeter said, handing him a manila envelope. "It's all there, and I hope to heaven you can get to the bottom of the bloody bother." Exeter's mood suddenly swung from vindictive to charming. "What did you think of the presentation on the new *Tomorrow*, Nick?"

"Clever," Nicoletti said. "Slick."

"We'll talk later," Exeter said abruptly. "Let me know if you have any questions about—that," he said, gesturing to the manila envelope in Nicoletti's hand.

Nicoletti left Exeter's office and returned to his gray cubicle. Watching Mark Exeter "do a job" on Eli Patterson offended his sense of fair play. And why did Exeter make Nicoletti witness to the scene? Yet, as much as he disliked Exeter's tactics, his crude way of handling people, some of the ideas for the "new *Tomorrow*" had merit, even imagination. Some.

Getting emotionally involved in a case wasn't his job. He sat down at the desk and opened the manila envelope, a Pandora's box of nastiness.

The notes leaned more to obscenity than wit. One was aimed at Religion reporter Emmy Kaufman. "Chubby, you are too fat to make love. Otherwise I might join you among your needlepoint pillows." Another, to a Foreign-department writer, said: "Drop that typewriter, plagiarist. Keep stealing stories and WATCH OUT." A note to the publisher warned: "Beware, Exeter, you could be *x*-ed out. Ha Ha." The notes were carefully typed on yellow copy paper. Included in the bundle was a list of the prankster's other tricks: cutting the Art editor's gallery invitations into tiny pieces; stealing the Politics editor's private phone book (it was later returned); and gluing down Lotte Van Buren's phone receiver. A clever kook, Nicoletti mused, observing that the notes and tricks had one common denominator.

Weird. Weird. Weird.

As Nicoletti stuffed the material back in the envelope, a familiar figure, Eddy, the mail-room boy, appeared in the doorway.

"As I live and breathe," Eddy cackled. "Nick Nicoletti. I hear you've come a long way, got your own business, not like the rest of us working slaves."

"I thought you'd be retired by now, Eddy," Nicoletti said. "Living it up at the track in Miami."

"Working is a hard habit to break after putting in thirty years with *Tomorrow*," Eddy said. "But I'll be leaving shortly, heading for Hawaii. I hear the girls are luscious," Eddy winked. He walked into Nicoletti's cubicle, leaning confidentially towards him and lowering his voice. "Don't like the funny business going on around here." Eddy shook his head ruefully. "Lotte Van Buren was in hysterics this morning. Walked in and found her phone wire cut."

"Phone wire cut?" Nicoletti said. "Two days ago, somebody glued her phone down. Pretty sadistic."

Eddy popped his eyes melodramatically. "Probably done by some young punk who smokes dope. I blame it all on the bad influence of television."

"Have you had any pranks played on you, Eddy?"

"Me? No," Eddy cackled. "I move too fast. Who could catch up with me?" Eddy scratched his head. "To tell the truth, Nicoletti, I'm probably not important enough to have a trick played on me. Well, work to be done. If I don't do it, nobody else will. See you around, Nicoletti."

Nicoletti watched the gnomish Eddy scamper down the hall. He put the manila envelope filled with hate notes in the drawer. Then he walked down to Lotte Van Buren's office.

A young telephone repairman with gear hooked in his belt was shuffling out as Nicoletti went in. Lotte was seated at her desk, chair swiveled to face the wall, with one hand resting on the telephone while with the other hand she dabbed at her eyes with a handkerchief.

"Hello, Lotte," Nicoletti said. "I hope I'm not barging in on you at a bad moment."

Lotte swiveled quickly in her chair. "Nick Nicoletti." Her voice was low, and she offered Nicoletti a radiant smile with trembling lips.

She stood up and grasped his right hand in both of hers. "Heaven must have sent you my way."

"Not heaven, Lotte, Mark Exeter. I'm consulting on the new Crime section."

"Close the door, Nick. Sit down. It's wonderful to see you again, even under these circumstances." Wearing a well-tailored beige suit with a colorful scarf at the throat, Lotte looked, as always, smart. Her thick-lashed blue eyes fluttered rapidly.

"I was sorry to hear about your divorce, Nick," Lotte said.

"So was I. How is Joe?"

"Joe? We were divorced five years ago," Lotte said. "Still friends, fortunately. I'm remarried now, and happily." Lotte sighed. "Marriages come and go but this magazine was always the constant in my life."

Lotte gulped. She looked at the phone again, back at Nicoletti. A sob broke from her throat and tears streamed down her face. "Please forgive me, Nick. This is so unlike me. I don't think I've cried since I watched a television rerun of *My Foolish Heart* three years ago." Lotte dabbed at her face with a handkerchief and blew her nose. "I am angry with myself for being rattled. I've always considered myself unshakeable."

"I heard that your phone was glued down two days ago," Nicoletti said. "A rotten trick."

"Yes. I was able to handle that. I tried not to take it too seriously. But when I walked in this morning and found the phone wire cut, I felt threatened, physically threatened. As if someone were trying to cut off my right arm." Lotte paused. "Nick, you worked here. You know that a reporter is *lost* without a phone. With that black instrument, I can call the President's press secretary or the Louvre in Paris, anyone, anywhere. Without it, I'm powerless."

Lotte picked up a pair of scissors and handed them to Nicoletti. "I believe this was the—may I say—weapon. The scissors are first-rate, from Germany. I get them sharpened periodically. I use them to clip newspapers and magazine articles. Could never stand a dull blade. You know what a fussy person I am."

"What time did you find the wire cut?"

"At 10:15 when I arrived. It could have been anybody, Nick, and it could have been done this morning, or last night, after I left. I was going to yoga class and left immediately at six. Half of the magazine was here later than that." Lotte looked up at Nicoletti, her eyes sad. "At first the notes and pranks were a joke. Now they are taking on an ugly life of their own."

"Do you have a likely candidate in mind? Someone you've argued with?"

"Not really," Lotte answered dully. "Look, Nick, you know I'm a demanding boss. In over thirty years at *Tomorrow*, I have offended a number of people by asking for perfection. But there's no individual I would single out as an enemy. This person must be deranged, a Jekyll and Hyde," Lotte erupted in hysterical laughter. "Oh, Nick, remember how everyone used to gripe. Now I don't know what we griped about. From a distance, the old *Tomorrow* looks idyllic. Change is hard."

"How are you faring with the new management, Lotte?"

"All right. I spent weeks doing an in-depth report for Mark Exeter on how the reporter/writer system works. Aside from that, I won't complain. Exeter Enterprises was inevitable. Hendricks, the former owner, poured money into the magazine to keep it afloat, but it couldn't go on. He's in his late eighties. Aside from introducing colored photographs into Personalities, the Exeters haven't made any drastic changes yet. . . ." Lotte's voice trailed off.

"But things are different."

"Oh, so different," Lotte sighed. "I'll be frank. A magazine achieves a certain balance. It's a community with a life-style, an ethos. There's been the beginning of disintegration with the new management," Lotte said. "Yet, I feel hopeful. Perhaps we need change. I follow a wait-and-see policy."

"Lotte, have you ever considered leaving *Tomorrow*, going to another magazine?" Nicoletti asked.

Lotte blinked, puffed at her cigarette, and smoothed the cover of a magazine on her desk. "What a question, Nick!" Lotte said. "It simply wouldn't occur to me to work for another magazine."

"Why not?" Nicoletti said. "People do it all the time."

"I've built my career at *Tomorrow*," Lotte said. "You might call me the chief architect of the reporter system, Nick."

"And that's a solid achievement," Nicoletti said.

"I hope so, Nick," Lotte answered. "I like it here. If the prankster was found, I think the sun would shine again." Lotte frowned, then continued, almost gaily, "Let's have lunch sometime. I've found this marvelous Portuguese restaurant where you bring your own wine and, well, you could almost swear you were in Lisbon."

"We'll do that, Lotte," Nicoletti said. "My office is right down the hall. If you get rattled again, come down and ventilate."

"Thank you, Nick. It's reassuring."

Nicoletti went back to his cubicle, shrugged on his raincoat, and headed for the elevator. Down on Madison Avenue, he took deep gulps of fresh, cold air and watched the lunch-hour crowd slogging up Madison Avenue, stepping over snow banks and blinking in the sunlight.

He couldn't wait to get back to his own familiar office, put his feet up on the desk, and have a cold beer. After a few hours at *Tomorrow*, it loomed like an oasis of tranquility. *Tomorrow* was a mass of raw nerves and hysteria. That was the beautiful part about painting. You gazed at Rembrandt and got communication, ecstasy, emotional contact, and no grief. People were different, intricate and demanding.

Yesterday he awoke wondering what Mark Exeter wanted. Now he knew part of the answer to that question. Mark Exeter wanted too much. Of everyone.

Back in his private-eye lair, Nicoletti went to the small refrigerator, pulled out a chilled bottle of Heineken's beer, and uncapped it. Rocko was out to lunch. Nicoletti needed a couple of hours of silence and nonhuman contact. Time to chew over *Tomorrow*.

Was Exeter's blueprint for the magazine a brilliant scheme or would it put America's "think" newsweekly out of business? Exeter was a man of many colors. Charming. Witty. Cold. Tyrannical. Like a lighting technician, he seemed able to switch emotions on and off, the traditional riddle within an enigma.

And the prank player, cutter of phone wires, who was he or she? A careful, observant person. A clever schemer. The notes seemed to cry out and say: "Look at me. I'm somebody. I have power over you. I can make you cry. I can frighten you, throw you off balance. I am not your ordinary jokester. I am somebody to be reckoned with." One thing was certain: the prankster played jokes at random but could be counted on to perpetrate one of the tricks on Friday night, deadline night at the magazine. And Friday night would be the key to unmasking the prankster's identity.

Nicoletti flipped through the Exeter file that Rocko had placed neatly in the middle of his desk. Rocko offered a report of his activities at The Pleasure Palace with Vanessa Wills, phrased in "tough-guy" detective language with no details omitted. A note attached to the report said: "Photographs being developed." There was plenty of ammunition here for Exeter to get actress Vane Wills to back down on grabbing for the Oriental-art collection. Exeter seemed able to get what he wanted, hang on to what was valuable, and discard people and objects he found unnecessary.

Nicoletti put the file to the side of his desk, dropped the beer bottle in the wastebasket, put on his coat, and locked the door behind him.

Down on the street, he hailed a cab and told the driver, "Metropolitan Museum of Art." Extravagant, maybe, but the Metropolitan was one of Nicoletti's favorite retreats.

At Seventy-second Street he decided to walk the rest of the way, left the cab and went over to Fifth Avenue.

Central Park was enchantingly cloaked in snow, a few birds pecking at the ground, trees delicately etched in black and white. A couple strolled hand in hand down a path. Nicoletti looked closer. The woman was Vanessa Wills, her red hair pulled back and fastened by a scarf to reveal the famous bony facial structure. Her companion fit Rocko's description of her date the evening before, a "skinny bearded guy who looked like a priest or a poet." Rocko had hit the nail on the head. The man was Byron Manos, *Tomorrow*'s Religion editor, a former Greek Orthodox priest, a poet with two slim volumes of verse to his credit. He was slender, with enormous, burning coal-black eyes. He looked like a monk on a Greek island, a monk who occasionally popped into The Pleasure Palace.

The couple stopped, dropped hands, and seemed to be engaged in an argument. Wills shook her head as if saying "no." Manos put his hands palms up in a gesture of "why?" Then he reached out and put his arms around her. They stood embracing, filling the winter landscape with warmth. Nicoletti looked away and kept strolling up the street. Did Exeter know that Manos was involved with Vanessa Wills? And if he did? The magazine was incestuous, with layer upon layer of relationships flourishing in an atmosphere of controlled chaos.

In the Metropolitan, Nicoletti paused in the gallery filled with brilliant banners and medieval armor, brave forms ready to do battle, to fight for life and principle, to follow bold leaders into the fray. Nicoletti contemplated people's brief, fragile ambitions, the lengths they would go to towards the realization of a goal. The limits. Yes. The absolute limits.

Friday would be deadline night at the magazine. Gazing at the gleaming armor, Nicoletti planned the scheme to help identify the prankster. Nicoletti would give Eddy O'Brien a night off at the fights and let Rocko play copyboy.

Nicoletti looked forward to Friday night with eager anticipation.

•5•

IT was a Friday night with a difference. Word spread about Exeter's plan for the "new" *Tomorrow* and a doomsday frenzy filled the air. Battle lines formed. Staffers who wanted to keep their jobs kept silent or backed Exeter. Why not a "new" *Tomorrow?*" The majority lined up behind editor Eli Patterson. If Patterson did leave *Tomorrow* (unlikely—Exeter *needed* him, the smart money said), his troops would follow.

Nicoletti sipped a beer in the back-of-the-book department, where, at 9 P.M., with stories written and waiting to be edited, it looked more like a party than a working organization. The traditional Friday-night drinkfest had begun, but tonight it was a full-scale hoopla. Bottles of gin, bourbon, Scotch sat boldly next to ice and plastic glasses on the large table where "interns" clipped newspapers in the daytime. Writers and reporters slurped, jostled, and speculated, filling and refilling glasses. A tall blond poured steadily from an enormous jug of martinis.

The art-department cartoonist put the finishing touches on a sketch. Mark Exeter, dressed in a gorilla costume, strangled Eli Patterson with one paw, waved a copy of *Tomorrow* aloft in the other. In a balloon billowing out from Exeter's mouth, the words were scrawled: "Bloody fun, I think I've won." The cartoonist Scotch-taped the sketch to the wall over the drink table. "Cheers!!!!" Irreverence, that was *Tomorrow*'s style.

Two reporters warbled off key, "Bull dog, bull dog, bow wow, wow. Eeeeeeeeee-liiiiiiii Patterson."

A slender writer with a pockmarked complexion turned to a petite reporter in skintight jeans: "I'd invite you out for a drink to unwind, but unfortunately I'm already drunk."

Nicoletti left the merry throng and walked down to Personalities.

Felix Magill sipped from a tall, mahogany-colored drink and puffed on a thin cigar. Theo sat with her feet propped on the rim of a wastebasket, holding a glass of red wine. She looked exhausted, with dark circles under her eyes.

"Welcome, Nick," Felix said. "Come fill the cup of sorrow and regret. Celebrate the imminent end of a magazine."

Nicoletti stood in the doorway and took in the tableau. "What I always liked best about you, Felix, was your talent for understatement," Nicoletti said. "Anyway, who's talking about the end of a magazine?"

"Me," Felix said, belligerently. "If Patterson deserts this sinking ship, we've got nothing. Nobody to fight Exeter."

"You fight him," Theo said. "I'm sick and tired of this whole business. Why not stop the gloom-and-doom talk. Let's try and pretend we're rational adults."

"Speak for yourself, Theo," Felix said with a shrug. "Tomorrow and tomorrow and tomorrow creeps," Felix quoted solemnly.

Emmy Kaufman, the plump, pretty Religion reporter, crossed over to Personalities from across the hall. Constantly on diets, Emmy sipped a glass of white wine and crunched a celery stick. Her mass of carrot-colored curly hair and round ingenuous brown eyes gave her the look of a mature Orphan Annie. On her feet Emmy wore slippers, to run more swiftly on errands for her boss, Byron Manos.

"Isn't it awful how one man has the power to destroy a magazine," Emmy said in a soft voice. She sat down in the "visitor's chair" next to Theo. Looking sad and perplexed, Emmy continued. "I don't think Byron will accept Exeter's idea about changing the Religion department to Isms. I think he'll quit." Usually a teetotaler, Emmy looked rather dazed as she sipped her white wine.

"Don't be a twit, Emmy," Theo said. "Byron won't just *quit*. At least half of this brouhaha is booze and bravado."

"It's a fight between good and evil," Felix said.

"Well, not *everyone* hates Exeter," Emmy said, "according to the latest report from the horse's mouth."

"How so?" Theo asked.

Emmy's wine appeared to be fizzing straight to her head. "He seems to be carrying on simultaneous affairs with not one, but two, women at the magazine."

41

"Big deal," Felix said. "He can sleep with a giraffe, for all I care, as long as he leaves *Tomorrow* alone."

"Which women?" Theo's voice was cold.

"The exotic new reporter in the Foreign department and Mary, Medicine's all-American girl."

"And where did you get this piece of intelligence?" Theo asked.

"Lotte Van Buren, of course," Emmy said. "Please don't repeat it. I'm sworn to secrecy."

"When does the creep have time for all the romance?" Felix said with disgust.

Theo looked, almost with desperation, at Nicoletti. "I can understand why you left this magazine ten years ago." She turned to Emmy. "Don't people ever get tired of gossiping about Mark Exeter?"

"Really, Theo," Emmy exclaimed, her eyes wide.

"Frankly, I'm sick of it," Theo said. "I thought this was a magazine, not a holy crusade." She grabbed her handbag, jumped up, and ran out the door, grazing Nicoletti's arm as she made her exit.

"I hope I didn't offend Theo," Emmy said innocently. "Maybe I should go after her."

"Nah, leave her alone," Felix said. "She's been acting strange for the last couple of days. Ever since she received the bouquet of flowers after the Samson Cody party."

"Oh?" Emmy's forehead wrinkled. "The violets?"

"Yes," Felix said, nodding towards a wilting arrangement that sat atop the green metal filing cabinet in a glass vase.

"Fading," Emmy said plaintively. "Poor Theo. Perhaps something went wrong."

"Don't count on it," Felix answered. "I expect her to be back in five minutes, having exorcised the demons. Anyway, I can't think about romantic dalliances. I have my mind on more important things," Felix said. "Survival."

Suddenly Rocko appeared rushing down the hall, his hands overflowing with copy. Since he was a quick study, Rocko's substituting for Eddy on a hectic Friday night had hardly caused a ripple at the magazine. Now he was all business. "Eli Patterson wants you to come down to his office," Rocko said to Nicoletti.

Nicoletti excused himself from Emmy and Felix and went down

the back staircase to Eli Patterson's office. Shirt sleeves rolled up, tieless, Patterson sat behind a scarred wooden desk. Unlike Exeter's chic office, Patterson's lair was stark, workmanlike, decorated with books and a few personal possessions.

As Nicoletti walked in, Patterson looked up with bloodshot eyes.

"Hello, Nicoletti," Patterson said. "Want to close the door?"

"Sure," Nicoletti said. "What's on your mind?"

"This," Patterson said, pushing a slim blue box across the desk to Nicoletti.

Nicoletti picked it up. It was a child's pencil box. Nicoletti lifted the lid. Inside, he found neatly sharpened pencils, but in the compartment usually reserved for an eraser, there were fish hooks. A neatly typed note inside the box read: "Goodbye, Patterson. Catch the Big One. Don't let the Big One catch you."

With ashes spilling down his shirt, Patterson looked frazzled, nervous. "It's the last straw," he said. "So completely creepy. As a private detective, what do you make of it, Nicoletti?"

"When did you receive it?"

"Tonight, in the interoffice mail."

"So it could have been sent this afternoon."

"Yes," Patterson said. "Possibly."

"It looks like a gift from the prankster," Nicoletti said. "But why a pencil box?"

"I always edit in pencil. I suppose that's the reason," Patterson said. "But what's the weirdo trying to tell me? That I'm going bye-bye?" Patterson reached out for a glass on his desk and took a gulp.

"No, I don't think so," Nicoletti said. "It sounds as if the joker is leaving."

"Thank God for little favors," Patterson said, taking another gulp of his drink. "Nicoletti, my nerves are shot. . . ." Patterson dropped his conversation with Nicoletti as Mark Exeter, unannounced, opened the door and walked quietly into the office. Exeter's hands were thrust deep in his pockets. He nodded to Nicoletti, stared down at his well-polished shoes, and looked at Patterson. The two had not spoken since yesterday. Patterson lit a cigarette, ignored Exeter, and resumed going over the copy in front of him.

"Eli," Exeter said.

Silence.

"Eli, Parker Johnson just called from Detroit."

Silence. Horns beeped outside the window. Dim laughter trickled down from the party upstairs.

Exeter addressed a spot on the wall over Patterson's head. "As *Tomorrow*'s ad manager, he had just taken the advertising director of Brandon Motors to dinner. Brandon agreed to run their advertising campaign in *Tomorrow*. It's a great coup."

Patterson looked up. "Congratulations," he retorted dryly.

"I want you to kill the cover story. The piece is an exposé of Brandon Motors. They'll drop a potential one-hundred-thousand-dollars' worth of advertising in the magazine." Exeter exploded his bombshell quietly, calmly, without a trace of emotion.

Patterson stared back at the publisher. Now deadly silence filled the room.

"No," Patterson said firmly. He got up and came around from the back of his desk, waving the story in Exeter's face. His harlequin mouth was drawn in a taut line. Every freckle stood out in his pale face.

"The story stays," Patterson shouted.

"For God's sake, Eli, why do you have to make everything so difficult?" Exeter asked. "It won't be killed forever. We'll run the story at a later date."

"A year from now? Oh, no, Exeter."

Nicoletti watched the two men, fascinated at Exeter's ability to be impervious to the emotions he provoked, at Patterson's absolute inability to reach for a compromise.

"Either the story stays or I go," Patterson seethed.

"Then I am afraid you will have to go." Exeter's voice was low and perfectly even.

Patterson flung the copy down on his desk, walked over to a tall gray metal filing cabinet, unlocked it, and pushed it over on the floor. It fell with a loud crash, drawers gaping open to spew out an avalanche of paper.

"There's your Brandon Motors story," Patterson shouted. "Do whatever you want with it. Burn it." Patterson grabbed his jacket off the back of a chair, stuffed his cigarettes into his pocket, and walked up to Exeter, his fists clenched. "You're not killing a story, Exeter. You're murdering a magazine."

Ignoring Patterson, Exeter walked over to his desk and picked up the copy for the Brandon Motors story. "I'll keep this," he said, his eyes dark and chilly. He walked past Patterson and back into his office.

Patterson stared after him. "Son of a bitch," Patterson said under his breath. "I'll get him. I'll get the bastard yet. I'll get him, Nicoletti." Before Nicoletti could answer, Patterson was on his way down the corridor, head high, pained eyes focusing straight ahead, a general forced to desert his troops.

Nicoletti stood in Patterson's smoke-filled office, looked at the paper heaped on the floor, the background on Brandon Motors, spilling out of the overturned filing cabinet. The pencil box, the prankster's present, sat on the corner of Patterson's scarred desk. Nicoletti picked it up and walked back to his cubelike office, put the pencil box in the drawer next to the manila envelope, and locked the drawer. He sat for a few minutes, thinking.

Then Nicoletti went back upstairs. The party had become more boisterous. Most of the *Tomorrow* staff—Felix, Byron Manos, Theo, even Lotte Van Buren—were gathered by the clipping table. To music from a tape recorder, a few of the *Tomorrow* staffers were dancing. As Nicoletti moved towards Felix, a sudden hush fell over the gathering.

Mark Exeter walked through the crowd and stood by the clip desk. He held his hand up for silence. "I have an announcement to make. I thought it only fair to tell you before rumors started flying. Eli Patterson quit tonight." Gasps. "He quit over my decision to delay running the story on Brandon Motors." Indrawn breaths. Shiftings from foot to foot. A sob from a tight and impressionable intern who harbored a severe crush on Eli Patterson. "We need a new cover story. I know you won't let personal feelings interfere with professionalism." A smothered guffaw.

Exeter frowned. He spotted Felix in the crowd. "Felix, you have a story on America's ten top models scheduled for next week. Can we go with that piece?"

Felix's face and even his bald head were a bright red. "It's only half-written. We just got the interview with the top model yesterday."

Exeter switched from tough to persuasive. "We have a magazine to get out, Felix," Exeter said. "Can you do it?"

Felix hesitated. "Yes, I can do it," he said.

"Good," Exeter said. "If you need any help, ask Lotte Van Buren. I'll be downstairs in my office." Exeter turned and left, eyes following him as he went down the stairs.

"I'll do the story," Felix said. "But I'll do it for *Tomorrow*, not Exeter. I'll hand in my resignation along with the final copy." He looked at Nicoletti. "Be happy you're not a journalist tonight." Felix turned to Theo. "Come on. Let's sober up. We have a cover story to write."

The news of Patterson's resignation reverberated through the magazine like an earthquake tremor. Somehow the issue would be put together, composed of equal parts Scotch and professionalism. Tears flowed, glasses were filled and emptied, pacts were made, and résumés were brought out of bottom drawers.

At 1:30 A.M. Nicoletti left the magazine and hailed a taxi to take him to Fanelli's. He found his favorite spot at the bar, sat down, and ordered a brandy and soda. Sipping his drink, Nicoletti felt dissatisfaction and a gnawing anger as he remembered Mark Exeter's forcing Eli Patterson to resign.

It was not unusual for an editor to fight with management, quit, and be back at work in the morning. Temperament was a magazine tradition. But tonight's bitter confrontation between Exeter and Eli Patterson reeked of finality.

Nicoletti ordered another brandy and soda. Things seemed wrong, tilted, out of line. After the frenetic atmosphere of *Tomorrow*, the raucous chatter of the artists around him was almost soothing. Nicoletti sipped the drink slowly.

Leaving the bar, Nicoletti walked back to his loft. Stars twinkled between the huge twin towers of the World Trade Center. The streets were quiet, and, mellowed by the brandy, Nicoletti attempted to sense logic and order in the universe.

In the loft he flung off his clothes, got into bed, and saluted the murky green eye on the canvas a "good-night." He turned off the light and fell into a deep sleep.

At 7 A.M. the phone rang.

Barely awake, Nicoletti picked up the receiver.

The voice was a slow, deliberate monotone with a heavy cockney accent. "This is Alexander Exeter. You were hired to find the evil-doer at *Tomorrow* and you failed. My son, Mark, has been brutally murdered. I hold you responsible."

·6·

MARK Exeter's corpse was inelegantly sprawled on the floor of his office at *Tomorrow*. The body was prone, right arm stretched out, left knee drawn up as if to ward off pain. His head was turned to the side, revealing the ugly wound in the back of his head. Exeter's skull was brutally bashed. Dried blood streaked his face and ran down into the man's silky, monogrammed shirt.

Looking down at the lifeless body, Nicoletti felt a twinge of guilt. When he was alive, Exeter's trademark was an impatient vitality. Could Nicoletti have prevented Exeter's death? A policeman energetically drew a chalk line around the body while another man dusted the office for fingerprints. Two orderlies dressed in white lounged outside the office with a stretcher, waiting to cart Mark Exeter's remains away.

Police Detective Sgt. Arnold Ajax, a cheerful-looking young man with a round, ruddy face and the muscular build of a wrestler, tapped a small notebook with a pencil. Nicoletti was glad to see his familiar face.

"This murder's a doozy, Nicoletti," Ajax said enthusiastically. "We're sitting in precinct headquarters at 6:30 A.M. catching our breath from the usual Friday night madness. A prostitute's been stabbed. A wife says her husband is trying to kill her. A gay liberationist says he's been raped. Your run-of-the-mill urban crime. Anyway, at 6:30 A.M. the phone rings and it's this chick. She says: 'Mark Exeter's dead. Murdered. In his office at *Tomorrow*.' And bang, she slams down the phone. So we come flying over here with the medic and sure enough, the guy is done in. Not a breath of life in him. But the strange part of the murder is, one: a neatly typed note is sitting in the middle of Mark Exeter's desk. It reads, 'Forever brother, hail and farewell.' It's signed with the initial E."

"I think that's a famous quote from an old Roman poet," Nicoletti said. "Catullus. It was a favorite on tombstones."

"How do you know this stuff, Nicoletti?" Ajax asked.

"I spent two years in Italy."

"Okay," Ajax said. "It seems the killer has a literary as well as a morbid bent. The second strange thing is the positioning of the murder weapon, that bronze statue. Must weigh twenty pounds. It was placed on top of the desk, rather than dumped on the floor where you would expect the killer to drop it."

Nicoletti looked over at the antique Chinese statue, sitting in the precise spot it occupied when Exeter was alive. "That's exactly where Exeter kept the statue," Nicoletti said. "How do you figure the murder took place?"

"How I see the murder is this," Ajax said. "The killer walked up behind Exeter, picked up the statue, conked him on the head and knocked him out, and continued bashing until he was dead. He or she held the horse by the rump and murdered Exeter with the sharp head of the horseman. You see, it's covered with blood."

"What time do you think Exeter was killed?" Nicoletti asked.

"The body was still warm when we arrived, but the office was overheated. One more example of energy waste. We figure the killer struck any time from 2 A.M. on," Ajax said. "Another crazy aspect of the killing. *Tomorrow* was like Grand Central Station half the night. People all over the place. In fact, one of them is here right now."

"Oh?"

"After finding the body, we went looking for the girl who reported Exeter's murder and, possibly, the killer," Ajax said. "Upstairs, I hear snores. I walk into this room and find this bald guy snoring away on a cot. I wake him and tell him Mark Exeter's been murdered. He says, 'Good old Exeter, anything for a laugh' and asks me to make the questioning brief because he has to get back to writing a cover story. Name's Felix Magill."

"The Personalities editor," Nicoletti said.

"What's with the sleeping rooms? There are two of them," Ajax asked.

"Sometimes writers and reporters work around the clock," Nicoletti said. "The rooms are so they can conk out when they're tired."

"You seem to know this place well," Ajax said. "And I see by the sign-out sheet that you were here last night. Doing what, Nicoletti?"

"Consulting on the new Crime section," Nicoletti said. "Mark Exeter hired me."

"I see," Ajax said. "Well, do you notice anything different or out of place in this office?"

Nicoletti looked around. With the exception of the body on the floor, it looked the same as the evening before. He glanced across the hall into Eli Patterson's office. The filing cabinet lay on its side on the floor, but the papers that spewed out of it when Patterson pushed it over were gone.

"Did you take anything out of Eli Patterson's office?" Nicoletti asked, gesturing across the hall.

"Nothing," Ajax said. "Everything is like we found it. That filing cabinet was lying on its side with the two drawers empty."

"Those drawers held the background on an important story that set off a blowup between Exeter and Patterson," Nicoletti said. "The material is missing."

"Things don't look good for this editor, Eli Patterson," Ajax commented. "After ascertaining that Mark Exeter was dead, I called his father, Alexander Exeter. He keeps a suite at the Waldorf. I informed him of the crime and the old man was here in ten minutes. A strange bird. He takes one look at the note on Exeter's desk signed 'E.' and his face goes gray. He says: 'That's Eli Patterson. He's the killer. I want him arrested.' "

Two orderlies piled the remains of Mark Exeter on a stretcher, covered the body with a blanket, and left the office.

"And?" Nicoletti asked.

Ajax said: "I thought the old man might be raving, but I better check the situation out. I talked to Larry, the night watchman, who sits by the door downstairs. He said Eli Patterson left the office about 9:30 P.M. last night, mad as hell. Then, at 3:15 A.M., he shows up completely drunk and insists on going upstairs. Larry tried to stop him, but Patterson threatened to deck him, or worse, if he won't let him up into the building. So the guy let him go up."

Ajax continued: "About fifteen minutes later Patterson comes back down and walks out or, should I say, weaves out, with a shopping bag. Patterson stopped by the door to light a cigarette and Larry looked in the bag. It was full of paper. Maybe that was the story background you were just talking about, Nicoletti."

"Possibly," Nicoletti said.

Ajax continued: "Anyway, Patterson was the last person to enter the building last night. I sent a car around to his apartment to pick him up so he could answer a few questions. New York's finest doesn't jump to conclusions. The doorman at his building says he arrived about 4 A.M., carrying a shopping bag in his left hand. His right hand was bloody. He went up to his apartment, came down about half an hour later with a suitcase and the shopping bag. He had cleaned off his hand. He mumbled something to the doorman about 'I won't be around for a while,' grabbed a taxi, and took off. It looks like he skipped."

"He quit his job last night," Nicoletti said. "He could be going any place, burning his bridges. That doesn't mean he killed Exeter."

"The alarm's out for him," Ajax said. "We'll know more when the fingerprinting's done and the lab has gone over things."

"What about the girl?" Nicoletti asked. "The woman who called to report the crime?"

"She wasn't here when we arrived," Ajax answered. "And the watchman didn't see her leave. We're looking for her. She could be the killer. People do bizarre things—like report their own crimes—under severe stress."

"Where's Alexander Exeter now?" Nicoletti asked.

"He said he'd be in his office on the thirtieth floor," Ajax said.

"I'll go up and present my condolences to him," Nicoletti said.

First Nicoletti went up the stairs to the fifth floor, where, at 8 A.M. in the shallow morning light, the magazine looked gloomy and deserted. Plastic glasses and bottles overflowed from wastebaskets, remnants of the party the night before. The cartoon of Exeter strangling Eli Patterson was in place on the wall. Down the hall, Nicoletti heard the persistent tap-tap-tap, tappety tap-tap of a typewriter. Felix working on the cover story. Nicoletti walked down to the Personalities office.

Hunched over his typewriter, Felix looked up as Nicoletti walked in. Felix didn't stand on ceremony. "I've already talked to the cops, Nick," he said, lighting yet another cigar in the smoke-filled office. "I'm sorry I can't take credit for killing Exeter. It couldn't happen to a more deserving guy."

"The police are going after Patterson," Nicoletti said.

"Yeah," Felix said. "Naturally. Patterson killed him, didn't he?"

"I don't know," Nicoletti said. "I don't think so."

"Why?"

"I can't see Patterson standing in back of Exeter and bashing at his skull," Nicoletti said. "I could see him beating him to a pulp straight on. Or maybe strangling him."

"Mmmm," Felix said, puffing his cigar.

"Go back to your cover story, Felix." Nicoletti left Felix and walked to the elevator that took him to the thirtieth floor, the penthouse suite. The elevator doors opened directly on to a large, sparsely furnished room. At the end of the room was a sleek teakwood desk. Alexander Exeter sat behind it, staring out the window. His head was huge, made larger by the effect of a puff of white curly hair surrounding it. Pouches hung under his large green eyes, surmounted by bushy white eyebrows.

Stepping across what seemed to be miles of tan-colored carpeting, Nicoletti stood in front of Alexander Exeter.

"Mr. Exeter, I'm Nick Nicoletti. You called me this morning. Our conversation was rather abrupt. Please accept my sympathy on your son's death."

Alexander Exeter turned his enormous head to look at Nicoletti. His face was stony, cold and ravaged. Spoken heavily in a cockney accent, each word seemed dragged out with lead weights attached to it.

"You extend sympathy? You've got a rare sense of humor, Nicoletti."

"Your son had a rare life-style. He made a lot of enemies."

"If you knew your business, Mark would be alive today. He paid you to find the sod who was playing tricks at the magazine and you missed. It was Eli Patterson. Eli Patterson killed my boy and he'll hang for it."

"You could be hanging the wrong man. What makes you think Patterson killed your son?"

"I know he did it, that bloody rotter. The great romantic press. Journalists. Vultures, every one of them. Give a newsman a job on a two-penny paper and he'll cut out his mother's heart to get a story. If he doesn't have enough imagination to fabricate it."

"What does that have to do with murder?"

"Eli Patterson is one of your by-your-leave artsy-smartsy dilettante weaklings who couldn't stand it when Mark killed his brilliant exposé. He murdered Mark for that."

"For a man who controls some of the biggest newspapers and magazines in the world, you seem to have a low estimate of the news profession—Eli Patterson in particular," Nicoletti said.

"It's the bloody egos I can't abide, spewing their rubbish and poppycock," Exeter expounded. "I began my career with a garage print shop when I was a lad. Printing. That's honest work. You have to know dollars and cents and ink and paper. You carry your lunch pail and maybe take a pint after quitting. No four-martini lunches as drunk by Mr. Eli Patterson, editor-in-chief of *Tomorrow*."

"Patterson quit last night. Your son's dead. What will happen to *Tomorrow* now? Will appoint a new publisher and editor?"

Exeter's pouchy face was ashen. He stood up, placing working man's hands on the desk for support.

"None of your bloody business, Nicoletti." He glared at Nicoletti. "I'll probably sell it. *Tomorrow*'s brought me nothing but hardship and grief. It will always remind me of my son's brutal end."

"Mark paid me for a week's work," Nicoletti said. "That work isn't done yet. I plan to find his killer."

"Don't think you'll get a shilling from me. I know your type. Want to catch the glory. Get your picture in the papers."

"Not quite," Nicoletti said. "Any detective who is instantly recognizable is out of business. If you don't object, I'll work out of the office I was using at the magazine."

Nicoletti thought he caught a glimmer of interest in Alex Exeter's eyes. Then it faded. "Do whatever the hell you want, I don't care." Exeter's cold green eyes, the only apparent physical link between him and his son, flashed. "Just leave me alone."

Nicoletti turned and walked to the elevator. Waiting for the elevator, Nicoletti felt venom-filled eyes boring into him.

"Wait," Exeter said.

Nicoletti turned.

"Find the killer. Find him," Exeter clenched and unclenched his fists. His voice faded. He sat down, put his head between his hammy hands, and wept.

Nicoletti got on the elevator. He was determined to find Exeter's killer. He knew where he was going to start. Head thrust against the February wind, Nicoletti walked over to the Wentworth Hotel on New York's West Side near Times Square.

•7•

THE old stone heap with its gaudy neon sign announcing Light Housekeeping was down at the heels but respectable, sheltering has-been actors and younger ones during hard times.

A plump lady with black sausage curls, dressed in a violently patterned dress, sat at the receptionist's desk in the small lobby, sucking a lollipop.

"Eddy O'Brien, please," Nicoletti said.

"Eddy O'Brien. Room 452," she said musically, offering Nicoletti a practiced, Cupid's bow smile.

"Don't bother to announce me. I'll go right on up."

"Have it your way, dearie," she said, returning to the candy.

Nicoletti rode on a trembling elevator that groaned as it rattled its way up to the fourth floor. The hallway smelled of strong disinfectant. Locating room 452, Nicoletti gave several loud knocks.

"Coming, coming," Eddy's sleepy voice came from behind the door.

Eddy wore a red flannel nightshirt with the emblem "Gramps" embroidered over the pocket, and white wool socks. He brushed a hand through his silver crewcut; his eyes were watery with sleep.

"Nicoletti," Eddy's watery eyes widened. "I hadn't expected visitors quite this early, but come on in."

Nicoletti walked into the room. The toys caught his eye immediately: a miniature railway on the desk; a monkey with brass cymbals on a wooden box; a collection of miniature cars. Photographs and memorabilia covered the walls.

A small refrigerator, a hot plate, television set, and a chair completed the decor. Two suitcases and a large paper carton sat on the floor.

Walking in, Nicoletti almost tripped on a stuffed giraffe.

"Interesting toy collection, Eddy."

"I had a deprived youth. All work and no play. I like toys, and when I find one that appeals to me, I buy it." Eddy pressed a button on the toy monkey, which burst out singing "When Irish Eyes Are Smiling," automated arms clanging cymbals in time with the music.

"Wonderful, Eddy, but enough."

Eddy turned the monkey off. "The toys are an old man's indulgence. At Christmas I pass them along to the Sisters of Charity to give to needy children. Just a little fun."

"Some fun isn't worth it, Eddy. Mark Exeter is dead. Murdered in his office. His skull was bashed in."

Eddy's eyes popped. He looked like an aging elf, a worried one. "Murdered?" he asked in disbelief, sitting down on the edge of his narrow bed. "I can't say I loved the man, but on the other hand I didn't expect to see him murdered. Well, the best-laid plans of mice and men . . . who did it?"

"The police suspect Eli Patterson."

"Eli Patterson. A violent man, yes, a strong possibility there." Eddy got up and began making his bed. "Can't stand an unmade bed. Sordid appearance."

"The police are looking for Patterson," Nicoletti said. "They found a note on Exeter's desk. It said, 'Forever brother, hail and farewell,' and it was signed with the initial E. Eddy, what time did you go back to the magazine last night, after you left the fights?"

Eddy whirled around. His mouth quivered. "Why would I want to go back to that slave camp in the middle of the night?"

"Because you're the prankster. You left the note on Exeter's desk, not Eli Patterson."

Eddy shook his head. "Saints preserve me. What gave you that idea, Nicoletti."

Nicoletti pointed towards the suitcases. "Where were you going, Eddy?"

"To visit my grandson in California."

"For a weekend? Is that why you also gave a good-bye gift to Eli Patterson, a pencil box, sent through the interoffice mail in the afternoon?"

"You're a suspicious man, Nicoletti," Eddy said, tsking-tsking and blowing his nose.

"I think you were planning to cut your ties with *Tomorrow*," Nicoletti said.

"So what else is new?"

"I set you up last night, having my assistant Rocko sub for you as the copyboy. It's the first Friday night in a month that a dirty trick wasn't played, unless you want to count the sentimental gift to Eli Patterson of a few pencils nicely sharpened in the mail room."

"A thoughtful gesture, Nicoletti," Eddy said.

"You're the only person who could have played the dirty tricks," Nicoletti said. "You've been with *Tomorrow* for thirty years, have the run of the magazine, know people's routines, when they're in and out of their offices. You've learned their Achilles' heels, their weak points. That Emmy Kaufman is sensitive about being overweight. That Lotte Van Buren regards her phone as an extension of herself."

"Lotte Van Buren. Slave driver is what I call her," Eddy said. "She's been running me ragged for years."

Nicoletti leaned against the door. "You don't understand what I'm saying, Eddy. I know you're the prankster. I don't think you're the murderer. The police might have different ideas, particularly after they dust for fingerprints."

"The law? Fingerprints?" Eddy sat down on the bed and smoothed the blanket with his hand, an old man's automatic gesture.

"Who saw you go back to the magazine last night, Eddy?"

"All right, Nicoletti, stop hammering at me," Eddy said. "I did go back to the magazine last night, and I did leave the note. But I didn't kill Exeter. Nobody at the magazine saw me."

"How did that happen?"

"I knew that at approximately 2:30 A.M. on Friday night Larry, the night watchman, would leave his post by the door and go down the hall to the phone booth to call his wife. I stood across the street and waited for Larry to disappear. Then I slipped in the door and took the elevator upstairs."

"Then what?"

"A light was coming out of Exeter's office. I decided to wait a few minutes, to see if Exeter would go to the men's room, or the like. Sure enough. He came and went upstairs to the Back-of-the-Book department. I left the note and skedaddled."

"So at 2:30 A.M. Exeter was still alive. Are you sure the man you saw was Exeter?" Nicoletti asked.

"Positive. I heard his voice. He was talking to someone upstairs."

"Did you recognize the other voice?"

"No. It was probably a woman. Exeter had more women than Carter had liver pills."

"You went to a lot of trouble to leave a crank note, Eddy," Nicoletti said. "It doesn't quite wash."

"It was going to be my grand exit from *Tomorrow*," Eddy said. He pointed to the two suitcases. "I wasn't going to California. I was flying to Acapulco tonight, know a nice lady who has a shop and a little house there. I made a lot of money on a bet at the fights last night. I decided to take early retirement." Eddy got up and put a windbreaker on over his flannel nightshirt.

"How about a cup of tea? Planning to have one myself."

"No, thanks, Eddy."

Eddy filled the teakettle with hot water from the sink spigot, set the kettle on the hot plate, and sat down on the bed with a sigh. "Sit down, Nicoletti. Take a load off. You won't catch a killer any quicker wearing out your arches. I take good care of my feet—comes from having been a dancer, you see."

"Dancer?"

"Didn't you know? As a youngster I was a star. Danced with my sisters and brothers in a vaudeville act, Eddy and the Five Little O'Briens, we were billed. Headliners. I was the brains behind the outfit." He gestured to a faded picture on the wall. "Sure! I got to be a big money-maker. The act split up, but I kept dancing across the country, married a lovely girl, and had two kids. Then the Depression came along. It all soured. I was broke."

The teakettle whistled. Eddy put a tea bag in a white mug, poured in water, and twirled the tea bag around. "That's when I mixed up with a bad crowd and pulled the bank caper." Eddy sipped the tea, lost in thought.

"I went to prison, lost my wife and kids. I came out of prison a broken man with most of my talent in my feet and not much left, at that. Hendricks, the old publisher of *Tomorrow*, offered me a job in the mail room. He was a humanitarian. He looked past my prison record and saw a person in need."

"Did you enjoy your job at *Tomorrow*?" Nicoletti asked. "Enjoy! I spent thirty years running and fetching for an ungrateful lot at that magazine," Eddy said. "I put up with plenty of nonsense, being treated like an idiot. Eddy, do this. Eddy, get that. The magazine couldn't have functioned without me. But what thanks did I get? I stayed out of loyalty to old man Hendricks, over and above the fact that it's hard for an ex-con to get employment."

"Then the Exeters came along," Nicoletti said.

"Yes. The British bandits took over. I decided to leave, for sure. I wanted to shake *Tomorrow* up before I retired, to let them know Eddy O'Brien wasn't so dumb after all," Eddy said. "But what was the point of the pranks if nobody knew I played them? So I decided to leave the note signed 'E.' so they'd all know it was old Eddy. I looked the quotation up in *Bartlett's*, 'Forever brother, hail and farewell.' I thought it both fitting and gracious." Eddy couldn't resist a cackle.

Nicoletti looked out the window and saw a lone derelict, wearing a blanket tied with a rope, ambling down the street, pausing to rummage in a trash can. New York teemed with lonely, unrecognized people driven to desperate acts.

"The pranks weren't so funny, Eddy," Nicoletti said. "You're a possible murder suspect."

"I suppose the cops will find out about my prison record." Eddy looked at the faded pictures on the wall. "And to think that I supported capital punishment." His blue eyes were sad. "If I hadn't left that note, I could be headed for mañana land. What do I do now, Nicoletti?"

"Go to the cops. Tell them you're the one who left the note for Exeter signed 'E.' "

Eddy's small hands flapped. "They'll have me up the river in no time flat."

"Don't be melodramatic, Eddy," Nicoletti said. "You're not tall enough to bash Exeter on the head with a statue, unless you stood on a chair." Nicoletti watched Eddy. "You owe it to Patterson. Your note helped make him the top murder suspect."

"I'll go, Nicoletti," Eddy said. "Seeing as you're not giving me much of a choice. I suppose they have TV in prison now. I'll catch up on some of those golden oldies I appeared in—musical comedies—before they give me the juice."

"They won't," Nicoletti said. "On Monday I want you to go back to work."

"*Tomorrow* won't let me come back after they learn about the pranks."

"Nobody has to know, Eddy," Nicoletti said. "I'll talk to the police."

"Why should I go back to *Tomorrow?*"

"You have big eyes and ears, Eddy," Nicoletti said. "You might be able to help solve this crime."

Eddy practically beamed. "My mother always said, one thing about Eddy O'Brien, he certainly isn't dumb." Eddy's chest seemed to inflate. "I know that magazine like the back of my hand. Okay, Nicoletti, I suppose I can take a few more weeks of torture after thirty years at *Tomorrow.*"

"But no more pranks, Eddy."

"A part of the forgotten past."

Nicoletti looked around the room. "What were you planning to do with all the toys when you went to Mexico, Eddy?"

"Pack them in that cardboard carton and ship them to my grandson, a lawyer in California. He has kids. He's the only one who gives me the time of day. Sent me this nightshirt."

"Gramps," Nicoletti read the inscription. "Nice." Nicoletti opened the door, then turned around, scribbled an address on a piece of paper, and handed it to Eddy. "That's precinct headquarters, Eddy. I want you there in fifteen minutes. Ask for Sergeant Ajax."

"I'll be there."

Nicoletti left Eddy's room and took the elevator down to the lobby.

So Eddy O'Brien considers himself an unsung hero of Tomorrow *magazine. Amazing, people carrying their egos like hidden, gleaming chalices.* Fishing two dimes out of his pocket, Nicoletti used the first one to call Police Detective Sgt. Arnold Ajax.

"It's looking bad for Patterson," Ajax said on the phone. "The prints on the murder weapon match the prints on a glass on Patterson's desk. We've sent out a nationwide alarm to pick him up."

Nicoletti stood at the pay phone in the lobby of the Wentworth and watched the receptionist, who offered him a coy smile. Nicoletti spoke into the phone in a low voice. "Ajax, I have some information that concerns Eli Patterson. An old-timer at the magazine, Eddy O'Brien, is coming over to talk with you about that note on Exeter's desk signed 'E.' But I'd appreciate it if you could keep what he tells you out of the paper."

"Will do, Nicoletti," Ajax said.

Nicoletti hung up the phone and looked at his watch. It was 10 A.M. He used the second dime to call Mark Exeter's widow, actress Vanessa Wills.

"I would *love* to talk with you," Vanessa Wills said breathlessly on the phone. "I must talk with someone or I'll go mad."

Ten minutes later Nicoletti rang the doorbell of the town house on Manhattan's posh East Sixty-fifth Street. Vanessa Wills opened the door. She eyed him with startled recognition.

"Please come in," she said. Her voice was clear and bell-like. "Didn't I see you near the Metropolitan Museum yesterday? Of course. I wouldn't forget a face like yours. That Roman nose. Such character. So masculine. Let's go into the library. There's a cozy fire there. And I do find books reassuring on distressing occasions." She kept up a steady stream of chatter as she flowed down the hall in front of him.

Nicoletti followed her into the library. A fire crackled in the grate. Vanessa Wills's wavy dark-red hair cascaded down over her shoulders. Devoid of makeup, her porcelain-white face was startling in its beauty. She wore a long, embroidered purple wool caftan that reflected her violet eyes.

"I suppose you've been told about . . ." Nicoletti began.

"Yes. Sit down. That leather chair is comfortable. I'll fetch us coffee and brandy. It's early but . . ." She left the room and returned with a tray. Her hands trembled slightly as she poured brandy into two balloon glasses, handing one to Nicoletti. She sat down on the floor by the fire with her legs under her, took a deep gulp of brandy, and put her head back.

"Better?" Nicoletti asked.

"Yes. Mark's father called me this morning. He was crying. I feel sympathy for old Alex. Mark was his only son. He built Exeter Enterprises for Mark, so that Mark could go to the right schools, wear the right clothes, meet the right people. Sad." She stirred the brandy in her glass, took a sip, and, avoiding Nicoletti's eyes, looked into the fire. "For Alexander Exeter, Mark's death is a tragedy."

"How did they get along?" Nicoletti lifted a delicate cup, put it down.

"Mark didn't really like his father. They had two things in common, green eyes and ambition. Otherwise they were day and night."

"What did Mark have against old Alex?"

"Mark found his father an embarrassment, the cockney accent, the tacky suits, the penny-pinching. It all reminded Mark that he was not the complete aristocrat. More and more, Alex stayed in the background." She turned her violet eyes on Nicoletti. "I like you. I needed to talk with a man."

"I'm listening," Nicoletti said. "Are you shocked by your husband's murder?"

"No." The actress got up and poked at the fire. "I expected somebody to kill him. I feel that the inevitable has finally happened. That makes me feel bad, dirty somehow, as if I put a hex on Mark."

"Why did you expect someone to kill him?"

"I don't know. Vibes, ESP. In a funny way, Mark and I were close." She sat down. "I like your hands, Nicoletti, strong, artistic." She reached out her hand to touch one of Nicoletti's and then pulled her hand back.

Seated on the floor, Vanessa hugged her arms around her knees and rocked back and forth in front of the fire. "I'm nervous," she said. "Why am I so nervous? If you and I made love, that would calm my jitters." She looked straight ahead at the fire. "But no, I don't suppose you would. You aren't a man to make love casually, easily, are you?"

She clamped her hands together. "I feel I can trust you, Nick."

"Yes." He reached over and enclosed her cold hands in his warm palms.

"A woman killed Mark," she said.

"Which woman?"

The actress clung to Nicoletti's hands. "I need this warmth," she said. She dropped his hands. "Any woman involved with Mark who found out about him."

"That he was unfaithful?"

"That was part of it," Vanessa Wills said, biting her lip. She flung her hands in the air. "Oh, what's the use? Mark was bisexual."

Nicoletti shifted in his chair. "You're a sophisticated woman, Vanessa. I thought bisexuality was admired, rather than despised, in our liberated age. But Mark's sexual proclivities couldn't have made you happy."

She got up and stood by the fire. "It made my life hell. I knew about it before we were married. I thought I could change him. It was a nightmare, his affairs with women, affairs with men. Each time I vowed to leave him, Mark would start courting me again. Flowers, gifts, a weekend in Paris. I was hooked, a Mark Exeter junky. I was on the point of a nervous breakdown. I went to a psychiatrist in London. I asked for tranquilizers. He told me I didn't need them and suggested another cure for my problem. I went to my first 'swingers' party with him—the psychiatrist. He was right. It worked. To me sex is a drug, a narcotic. It calms me down. I need it, desperately, sometimes."

She caressed the fire poker. "So I moved from being addicted to Mark Exeter to a dependence on group sex. I don't think either one has particularly enhanced my life." Her eyes seemed to darken to a deep purple.

"You're a beautiful woman, Vanessa Wills."

"But you won't make love to me, will you?"

Nicoletti reached for her hand. "No. If I did, I might fall in love with you. And you're in love with another man."

"Yes."

"A man who was murdered this morning."

"Yes." Finally, the tears came. Vanessa Wills struggled with wrenching sobs. "So awful," she cried. "I loved him. How can I so bitterly miss a man who almost destroyed me? Why? He was so beautiful. Why such an ugly death?"

Nicoletti put his arms around her, holding her tight while the tears flowed over his brown tweed jacket. She was either the world's most consummate actress or the world's most unhappy woman. The tears began to subside.

"Vanessa, there's one thing I don't understand."

"What?"

"Exeter was an international figure, the tough, forward-driving publisher," Nicoletti said. "Didn't he worry about his offbeat sex life's damaging his reputation—or let's say—image?"

Wills pulled slowly back from Nicoletti. Her laugh was a sharp trill. "Don't be ridiculous, darling," she said. "He didn't care a fig. He set the standards. He set the pace. And he expected the world to run with him."

"But his ethos didn't quite work out," Nicoletti said. "He was murdered." He handed his handkerchief to Vanessa.

"I'm alone, Nick," she said. "Even though Mark and I were divorcing, I found it oddly comforting that he was alive in the world with me."

Nicoletti refilled her brandy glass and handed it to her. "I think I understand," he said.

"Thank you," she said, taking a swallow of brandy. "And thank you for listening. I'm a lady in distress. I won't apologize. After all, I'm human, all too human."

"Vanessa, did you see Mark last night?"

Her bell-like voice clouded. "I know what you're asking. The police asked the same question. Between 2 A.M. and 6:30 A.M. I was at a private party on Central Park West. Extremely private. I can assure you there was more than one witness."

Nicoletti stood up. "What will you do now?"

"Forever?"

"No. Vanessa. Today," Nicoletti said.

"I will be alone, Nick," the actress answered, handing Nicoletti his handkerchief back. "Believe it or not, on the day of her husband's death, Mark Exeter's widow will spend the day in solitude." She smiled. "I'm not making any guarantees about the evening."

Nicoletti closed the door to the town house with relief. The man who fell in love with Vanessa Wills would have to battle with the ghost of Mark Exeter, and in death, as in life, Exeter continued to exert a powerful hold.

After Vane Wills, the hustle and bustle of the precinct house was a tonic. As he walked into Sergeant Ajax's office, the detective, in shirt sleeves, was taking the lid off an aromatic sausage and mushroom pizza.

"Paisano," he greeted Nicoletti. "Join me." He gestured towards a chair next to his desk. "This is the first break I've had all day. Thanks for sending over Eddy O'Brien. At least we know Eli Patterson doesn't write funny notes. We're still looking for him. And we're also questioning everyone who was in the *Tomorrow* building after 2 A.M. We're taking the names from the sign-out book in the lobby."

"Could I see the list?" Nicoletti asked.

Ajax opened the desk drawer, pulled out a lined notebook, and handed it to Nicoletti.

Nicoletti read down the list. A messenger arrived at 2:35 and left at 3:05. Parker Johnson, *Tomorrow*'s advertising director, went in at 2:00 and left at 2:40. At 3:15 Eli Patterson went in and signed out at 3:30. At 4 A.M. Byron Manos signed out.

"Manos looks shaky," Ajax said. "There's a rumor he's in love with Exeter's wife. He's an eccentric guy, from what I hear. Maybe after a few drinks, the back of Exeter's head was inviting. Have a slice, Nicoletti?" Ajax pointed to the pizza he was consuming with gusto. "It's a real pick-me-up."

"I'd rather have the name and address of Larry, the night watchman at *Tomorrow*."

Ajax consulted his notebook and scribbled a name and address on a piece of paper. He gathered a piece of pizza into a dripless fold. "You know, Nicoletti, in books the cops are usually at odds with the private eye. But that's not my point of view."

"Generous of you, Ajax," Nicoletti said.

"You have to make a living, so do I." Ajax popped a piece of sausage in his mouth. "This is a case that will capture the public fancy, be splashed all over the papers and on the six-o'clock news for weeks. But finding the murderer of Mark Exeter is not what being a cop in this city is about. I'm protecting the old ladies who live in rent-controlled walk-ups and get bashed in the head for five bucks. Secretaries raped on their way to the office. Mark Exeter? A millionaire son of a bitch who probably had it coming to him. I want to catch the killer and get back to some real work." Ajax twirled a piece of cheese on his finger.

"It's a beautiful speech, Ajax," Nicoletti said. "I know what a competitive bastard you are."

"Right on," Ajax answered. "Luck."

* * *

Larry Hernandez, dressed in clean khaki trousers and plaid shirt, stood behind the counter of Hernandez Bodega on New York's Lower East Side. The grocery was situated in a neighborhood undergoing the growing pains of change. Glistening new apartment buildings contrasted with tired tenements. Chicly dressed residents walked the same streets as derelicts.

The store sparkled with newness. There were neatly stacked cans and boxes, and the pungent smell of spices in open barrels and of fresh herbs filled the air. *Tomorrow*'s night watchman extended his hand graciously to Nicoletti.

"Mr. Nicoletti. How are you?" Larry was in his early thirties, Puerto Rican, an attractive, slender young man with a thin dark mustache. He introduced his wife, Maria, who responded to Nicoletti with a shy smile.

"Nice place," Nicoletti said, looking around the grocery. "Yours?"

"Si, yes, Mr. Nicoletti," Larry crossed his fingers. "We hope."

"Larry, do you have a minute? I'd like to talk with you privately."

"Certainly, certainly," Larry said. "Maria, you take care of things."

Gesturing with his hand, he led Nicoletti to the back room of the store. Larry perched on a wooden carton. "I know why you are here. The murder of Mark Exeter."

"Yes," Nicoletti said. "I want to ask you a few questions."

"A sad thing. A bad thing. I am from San Juan, Puerto Rico, and so is my wife, Maria. I love this city, New York, but it is hard for us. Some crime happens and, the first thing, the police are questioning Puerto Ricans."

Larry shook his head ruefully. "Maria and I, we have two children. We are determined to be good citizens. I work three jobs, the factory in the day, *Tomorrow* three nights a week, and on weekends this grocery." Larry smiled. "I plan to become a capitalist. Anyway, never have I had a run-in with the police until this morning. They questioned me almost until I didn't know what I was saying. But I want to help. I can't believe Mr. Exeter is dead. He had everything. Sometimes I would look at him and feel terrible envy. But no more. Now I am glad to be alive." Larry paused. "A drink? A Coke? A beer?"

"No. Thank you, Larry. I'll make it quick. First, the messenger who arrived at 2:35 A.M. Did you know him or her?"

Larry rubbed his hand across his chin. "No. He was a young boy, thin, wore a cap, had a mustache. He said he had a 'rush' for Mr. Exeter. I phoned Mr. Exeter and he said to send the fellow right up."

"All right, Larry, now tell me about Eli Patterson."

"He left the magazine early in the evening. Then after three in the morning he showed up drunk and crazy. I didn't want to let him go upstairs, but he was so mad and threatening me, I couldn't stop him. He said, 'There is unfinished business, something I left behind." About ten minutes later, he was back carrying a shopping bag. It was filled with paper, all typed. I thought, why should a man come drunk to pick up a heap of paper in the middle of the night?"

"Was his right hand bloody?"

"I don't know," Larry said. "I looked at the shopping bag and then he was gone."

"And the advertising director came in just before Patterson and left before he left?"

"Yes. He had just come in from a trip to Detroit."

"And the last person to leave the magazine was Byron Manos? Did he seem strange in any way?"

"No. He looked sleepy."

"And after that?"

"After? Nobody came in or out, until the police arrived." Perspiration dripped down Larry's face into the collar of his carefully pressed shirt.

"Larry, working three jobs must be exhausting."

"It is, Mr. Nicoletti. I tell you, I only hope that I can quit the factory and the magazine and make a success of the grocery store. Put my full-time energy into it."

"But for that you need money. You couldn't afford to lose a job now."

"No."

"Larry, do you ever doze off on Friday nights, maybe lock the door and take a nap?"

Larry's face was scarlet. "Never. I am alert on the job."

"Larry, I'm not the police. Nothing you tell me goes on the record."

"I am ashamed," Larry admitted with relief. "Yes, I locked the door after Mr. Manos left. I did not intend to fall asleep but I was very tired. I woke up when I heard the police sirens." Larry shook his head. "If the big man, Alexander Exeter, found out, I would lose my job. But nobody could come into the building. The only people who had keys were Mark Exeter and Alexander Exeter."

"But somebody—the murderer—could go out."

"Yes," Larry said.

"It's all right, Larry," Nicoletti clapped him on the shoulder. "Thanks for being honest with me. I won't tell Alex Exeter about your siesta. Good luck with the store."

It was 2 P.M. A dim sun was breaking through the clouds. A perfect day for a drive through the New Jersey countryside to visit *Tomorrow*'s advertising director, Parker Johnson.

Nicoletti got his compact car out of the SoHo garage and drove to a gas station by the Lincoln Tunnel to fuel up. As he sat absorbing gas fumes and watching the attendant move in slow motion, he considered what Felix had said about the Brandon Motors exposé.

Concerning fuel, the energy crisis.

Big.

·9·

A gleaming maroon station wagon pulled up in front of Parker Johnson's fieldstone house as Nicoletti turned into the long driveway. Princeton, New Jersey, acme of middle-class ambition. To live in Princeton, one had to be wealthy, successful, socially pedigreed, or intellectually elite. Parker Johnson made the grade in at least one category, evidenced by the house with leaded windows and weathered door with bright brass knocker. To the left of the house burbled a brook, spanned by a rustic wooden bridge. Even with his allergy to suburbia, Nicoletti recognized the American fairy tale come true as he eyed the *Tomorrow* advertising director's holdings.

He pulled his car up in back of the station wagon. A ruddy-faced man got out of the wagon, followed by two blond teenaged boys and a fluffy white sheep dog. Reaching into the back, the boys hauled out enormous, overflowing grocery bags and walked towards the back of the house, the dog yipping merrily behind them.

Nicoletti emerged from his car and walked up to the square, hearty-looking man who stood puffing a pipe, giving Nicoletti a quizzical, expectant glance.

"Parker Johnson?" Nicoletti asked.

"Yes, yes indeedy," Johnson answered with vigor. His teeth clamped down on the pipe as he mustered a half-smile. "What can I do you for?" Johnson had a full face, receding hairline, gray eyes framed by horn-rimmed glasses. He wore a tweed jacket with leather patches at the elbows, knit navy shirt with red alligator insignia, and gray slacks. "Lost in the neighborhood?"

Nicoletti extended his hand. "No. I'm Nick Nicoletti, a private investigator. Sorry to intrude on your Saturday afternoon, but I'm making some inquiries into Mark Exeter's murder. I thought you might be able to help me."

Johnson pumped Nicoletti's hand. "Tragic business, isn't it?"

Johnson's voice was mellow and resonant, a voice suited to making advertising presentations, a sincere voice that could elicit one hundred thousand dollars in advertising from Brandon Motors. He paused for a moment, as if considering whether to turn Nicoletti away from the door, then planted his feet more firmly in the driveway. "As soon as I heard the news on the radio this morning, I called the New York police and told them all I knew. The quicker the killer is found, the quicker we can get *Tomorrow* back on the track. I don't see what new information I can give you."

"Maybe nothing," Nicoletti said. "I was working on a case for Exeter when he was murdered. You might help put my mind at ease."

"Yes," Johnson answered. "Exeter mentioned you. Well, come in." Johnson turned the key in the front door. "Just coming back from marketing. Amazing what it costs to feed a family of six—seven counting the dog—these days. I'm one of the lucky ones. I can afford it for the moment."

They stepped into the living room. The room was a mélange of copper lamps, needlework pillows, fresh flowers in crystal bowls. A large stone fireplace stretched the length of one wall. An antique spinning wheel stood by the fireplace, and two small blond girls were stretched out on the floor, energetically working in coloring books.

"Sally! Sally dear," Johnson bellowed. "I'm home."

"I'm in the kitchen, Pook," a woman's voice trilled back. "I'm baking a cake. A new recipe from the natural-foods cookbook."

Sally entered the room. Slender and petite, she had pale brown hair tied back with a yellow band.

Johnson introduced her to Nicoletti, explaining that he was a private investigator. Her hand was cool and her forehead puckered. Would this man introduce ugly murder into her Utopia? "Isn't it awful about Mark Exeter?" she said. "Such a waste of potential. I was absolutely shocked. So ironic. Pook had just invited him to speak at the Williams College reunion this year and he accepted."

She turned to her husband, looking up at him like an adoring teenager. "Dear, did you turn in the cans at the ecology center?"

"Right-o."

"And you got the endive and London broil?"

"Right-o."

"Very good," Sally Johnson said. "I'll leave you two men to talk."

71

Johnson glanced over at the grandfather clock, ticking in the corner.

"Nicoletti, how about talking while we jog? I started jogging two months ago, and if I don't get in my Saturday run, I feel out of whack all week."

"Why not," Nicoletti answered. "Probably get some of New York's soot out of my lungs."

Johnson opened a closet door, got out a pair of running shoes, and sat down to put them on.

"Beautiful home, Parker," Nicoletti said, glancing up at the beamed ceiling.

"It's the culmination of a dream for Sally and me," Johnson said, huffing slightly as he bent over his shoelaces. "We've only lived here a few months. Bought it shortly after I took the job at *Tomorrow*."

"Do you think Exeter's death will affect your job?"

"Six of one, half a dozen of the other. Depends on Alexander Exeter, I suppose. The advertising game is a high-risk business. That's why I love it. I appreciate the challenges."

Nicoletti followed Johnson out the door to the gravel driveway, where Johnson jumped up and down, warming up, then loped down the drive towards the woods in back of the house. "So, Nicoletti, how can I help you?"

Nicoletti ran easily beside him. "There was a lot of traffic at the magazine last night. I'm trying to find the last person who actually saw Exeter alive. I see that you checked into the magazine at 2:00 and left forty minutes later."

"Right-o," Johnson said as they ran through the woods. "You're on the ball, Nicoletti. I returned from Detroit elated, as you can imagine, after selling Brandon Motors one hundred thousand dollars' worth of advertising pages in the magazine. I told Brandon I'd send them more background on plans for the 'new' *Tomorrow*. Driving back from the airport, I decided to go up to the office and pick up some material, work on the letter to Brandon this weekend." Johnson was panting heavily. "Unusual for me. My philosophy is work hard and play hard. But you don't play fast and loose with one hundred thousand dollars' worth of advertising."

Johnson's face was pink and perspiration dripped down it. "Lost an inch off my waist in a month, Nicoletti. Jogging is great exercise."

"Did you see Exeter last night?" Nicoletti asked.

"Yes. He was one hundred percent alive. I stopped by his office. We had a drink to celebrate pulling Brandon Motors in as a *Tomorrow* advertiser."

"What was his mood?"

Johnson panted heavily. "I was riding so high from selling Brandon I didn't particularly notice. He seemed fine."

"Did he say anything about Eli Patterson's resigning?"

"Yes. But in an offhand way. Didn't seem concerned." Johnson's face was beet-red, and his breath came in gasps.

"Johnson, I'm not an experienced runner like you. Do you mind if we slow down for a while?" Nicoletti asked.

"Can do," Johnson said with relief, stopping and leaning against a tree for a moment, taking deep gulps of air.

Nicoletti picked up a white birch twig and examined it. "Johnson, is it possible that Exeter was having second thoughts on the Brandon exposé? That he was considering running it? And that you went back to the magazine to talk him out of it? And took the background on the story with you?"

Johnson wiped his face with the sleeve of his shirt. He didn't flinch. "I admire your imagination, Nicoletti. The answer is 'no.' "

"Did you know what the exposé was about?"

"No idea, Nicoletti. Didn't even try to find out. I didn't want it to prejudice my sales presentation."

The two men strolled up the path.

"One hundred thousand dollars is a big piece of change," Nicoletti said. "I suppose you'll make a substantial commission on it."

"Will do," Johnson answered. "And believe me, it will come at the appropriate time. Sally and I plan to buy a camper, drive up to the Williams College reunion this year, and then take a trip through Nova Scotia. My oldest son is entering Yale in the fall." Johnson's breath had returned to normal. "I could be insulted by what you're suggesting, Nicoletti, but I realize you're trying to do your job. Did I murder Mark Exeter because he was planning to run the Brandon Motors story, causing me to lose my commission? Wrong-o. Exeter was my ace. We saw eye to eye. Who knows who the new publisher will be?"

"I suppose it could be you."

"Wrong department, Nicoletti. I'm not looking for that kind of promotion."

"Did Exeter say anything to you last night that might be significant?"

Johnson took deep breaths of the cold, fresh air. "Marvelous air here, Nicoletti," he said. "Since we moved to this place, I realized what the saying 'A man's home is his castle' is all about." Johnson continued to inhale, breathing in as if ingesting ambrosia. "For what it's worth to you, Nicoletti, there's something I remembered when I was comparing cuts of London broil in the supermarket. Exeter was working on a reorganization plan for the magazine last night."

"You mean as part of the 'new' *Tomorrow*?" Nicoletti asked.

"That's an I-don't-know department," Johnson said. "He didn't want to discuss it until the plan was complete." Johnson ruminated. "The man exploded with ideas."

"I suppose you'll miss working with him," Nicoletti said.

"Yes, indeedy," Johnson said. "Mark Exeter made demands on people. He pushed them to reach their full potential. I admire that in a man." They were emerging from the woods. "Anything else, Nicoletti?"

"Did you see anyone else at the magazine last night?"

"Not a soul."

"Eli Patterson?"

"No. The police said our paths may have crossed, but the only person I saw was Exeter."

The fieldstone house came into view. "The house was built in 1792," Johnson said, waving a hand. "In the old days, men built things to last."

"It must give you a sense of continuity with the past."

"Yes, it certainly does. I'm a forward-looking man, but old-fashioned," Johnson said, his face suddenly melancholy. He looked earnestly at Nicoletti through horn-rims. "I'll be square with you, Nicoletti. My home, my wife, my children are what matter to me. My job at *Tomorrow*? I give it my best shot, but it's the means to an end. If the magazine turned to dust, I wouldn't cry."

"I have one more question for you, Parker."

"Yes?"

"Why does your wife call you Pook?"

The advertising director chuckled. "When I was prepping at St. Paul's, I was rather slow and deliberate about everything. Ergo, the nickname Pook for 'Poke.' Affectionate, of course. The tag stuck with a few intimates, including Sally." Johnson chuckled deep in his throat.

"Thanks for your help, Johnson."

"Glad to, any time," Johnson answered, looking old and weary. "I hope this murder business will be cleared up in a hurry."

"Right-o," Nicoletti said, getting into his car with a quick wave good-bye.

Johnson stood in front of his house, watching Nicoletti move down the driveway. The two boys played catch on the lawn, the dog chasing back and forth between them. In the waning afternoon sunlight, lamps twinkled on and smoke whispered out of a chimney.

Nicoletti felt the wholesome atmosphere crushing in on him.

As he drove down Nassau Street, the site of Princeton University's Gothic buildings and Tudor shops, Nicoletti considered whether he could have lived the life of Parker Johnson with a wife, four children, one dog, and contentment only occasionally marred by murder.

An image of Parker Johnson panting as he ran down the Princeton path was fixed in Nicoletti's mind. Johnson was a powerful guy, but out of shape. Still, he could have bashed Exeter's head in, rationalizing that it was for the sake of the wife, the kiddies, the sheep dog, and the Princeton holdings, if Exeter planned to rain on his parade.

Nicoletti left Princeton behind, driving through New Jersey's industrial wasteland, where machinery loomed like giant Erector sets. He turned on the radio. "The New York police have issued an alarm for Eli Patterson, former editor-in-chief of *Tomorrow* magazine and a suspect in the murder of Mark Exeter. . . . A new survey shows that asexuality is the newest trend on campus. . . . Gasoline prices are going up again. . . ." Click. Nicoletti turned the radio off.

In the distance shone New York's skyscrapers, turrets and towers, building blocks and neon, a breathtaking world of soot and steel, beauty and horror. Was Mark Exeter's murderer there among the city's eight million residents? Was he or she suffering remorse or pouring an icy-cold martini? Was Alexander Exeter still sitting in his office, pounding his hammy fists at fate?

Nicoletti drove through the noisy, vaporous Lincoln Tunnel and, like a genie emerging from a bottle, was back on the island of Manhattan. As his car edged down Forty-second Street, past pimps, gospel singers, a movie marquee proclaiming *Girls in Love*, Nicoletti relaxed.

For him, New York's endless variety spelled ease, stretched his soul. It took New York to juxtapose the late Mark Exeter, mail-room boy Eddy O'Brien, upward-striving Parker Johnson, the brilliant, erratic Eli Patterson. And the identity of Exeter's killer? Nicoletti felt as if he were standing in front of a large white canvas and making the preliminary, tentative charcoal sketch, unsure of the colors and shadings that would ultimately emerge.

·10·

THE front door of Nicoletti's loft building was open, a Saturday-afternoon tradition to accommodate residents doing chores and weekend shopping. Nicoletti ran quickly up the stairs.

He turned the corner of the last landing. A girl sat at the top of the stairs outside his door, her face hidden behind New York's afternoon tabloid. The front-page headline screamed: "PUBLISHER MURDERED!" accompanied by the subhead "Search for Editor." Photographs of the late Mark Exeter and of Eli Patterson splashed across the page.

Sun from the skylight caught golden glints in the girl's hair.

The paper crashed down.

"I'm glad to see you," Theo Marlow blurted. She wore faded blue jeans, a blue turtleneck sweater, and a tweed jacket. She carried an enormous leather handbag. Her almond-shaped eyes were framed by oversized, pink-tinted glasses.

"Catching up on the news?" Nicoletti asked.

"Damn rag," Theo said, closing the paper and tucking it under her arm. "No wonder newspapers are called fish wrappers. They're already nailing Patterson for murder, and what they're writing about Mark Exeter! It's slime. They're murdering him all over again in print."

"Mona Lisa with a touch of mayhem in her eyes." Nicoletti extended his hand to help Theo up. "Come in and talk with me."

"You don't seem surprised to see me."

"I'm not," Nicoletti said. He unlocked the door to his loft and gestured her in.

Theo walked over to a dilapidated, overstuffed chair and sat down. "I like your loft," she said. "Masculine. Authentic. Not quite finished. It makes a statement about you."

"The intrepid lady reporter. Constantly observing," Nicoletti said.

He tossed his jacket on a chair, cracked a tray of ice cubes, poured Scotch into two glasses, and handed one to Theo. "Cheers," he said, raising his glass.

"Skoal," Theo said, taking a sip of Scotch. She put the glass down. Her eyes were hidden behind the pink glasses. "Nick, I hear you're working on the case, looking for Mark Exeter's murderer."

"Word travels fast at *Tomorrow*," Nicoletti said.

"Yes, anybody who wants to keep secrets shouldn't work there," Theo said. She picked the glass up again and held it with both hands, as if clutching a life raft. "Nick, I just came from police headquarters. I'm the person who found Mark Exeter's body this morning and called the police."

"I thought it was you, Theo," Nicoletti said, rattling ice cubes in his glass.

"How could you know?" Theo sounded apprehensive.

"People interest me, what propels them," Nicoletti said. "I know how dedicated you are to your job. Felix was writing a new cover story. I know you just wouldn't walk out on him. Felix was there all night. Your name wasn't even on the sign-out sheet for people leaving the magazine after 2 A.M."

Theo stared at Nicoletti. She took off the tinted glasses. "You're right, Nick," she said. "I was there all night. I didn't tell the police everything."

"Such as?" Nicoletti said, encouraging her.

"I told the police about working late, falling asleep, walking downstairs, and finding Mark—the body." Theo took a sip of the drink. "What I didn't tell them was that I was seeing Mark, outside of the office." The words came out in an almost defensive blurt.

Nicoletti looked steadily back at Theo. "What are you trying to tell me, Theo? That you were having an affair with Mark Exeter?"

"No," Theo said. "I met Mark four nights ago at a Brentano's party for Samson Cody. I had dinner with Mark that night and saw him the next night and the next. Thursday night, we had dinner at his apartment. Wine. Firelight. Music. It was beautiful, romantic. But something—lots of things—held me back from getting involved with him."

"Self-protection?"

"Maybe," Theo said. "I was a little afraid of him, his power, his charm."

78

"His charisma," Nicoletti said, ironically.

"I'll be honest," Theo said. "We made a date for Friday night, after the magazine closed. I didn't know what I was going to do, but I wasn't going to become part of a *Tomorrow* harem." She paused and took another sip of Scotch. "And that's why it happened, my finding the body." Theo looked nervously at Nicoletti. "Nick, I feel mixed up. Am I babbling?"

"You're sounding absolutely lucid, Theo," Nicoletti said. "Relax. You're talking with a friend." He walked over, got Theo's glass, refilled it, and gave it back to her. "Trust me, Theo. Our talk is strictly private."

Theo took the glass from Nicoletti, her cold hand quickly touching his. She settled back in the chair. "Felix and I were up half the night working on the cover story," Theo said. "About 3:30 Felix said he was going to catch a few hours of sleep. I told him I was going home, that I'd come back early in the morning. Actually, I was planning to go downstairs and meet Mark. Earlier in the evening, Mark sent me a note through the interoffice mail saying he'd see me later." Theo reached into her pocket and pulled out a folded piece of yellow paper.

"And you went to meet him," Nicoletti said.

"No," Theo said. "Not right away. You see, I had all these conflicting feelings. You remember the hysteria last night. The gloom-and-doom party. Emmy's little bombshell about Mark's affairs. Then Mark killing the Brandon exposé. And Eli Patterson quitting." Theo hesitated. "I decided I'd lie down in the other sleeping room for a few minutes, kind of to calm down. That was 4 A.M. I fell asleep. When I woke up, it was 6:30 in the morning. I went downstairs to see if Mark was there. Sometimes, he told me, he worked all night.

"Then I found him. It was ghastly. I knew he was dead. I called the police and ran. Larry, the night watchman, was asleep. He didn't see me."

"Did you see anyone else?"

"No."

"When you found Exeter's body, where was the murder weapon? On the floor?"

"No," Theo said. "On the desk. I didn't touch anything." Theo shivered. "It was awful. I panicked. I couldn't look."

"Theo, were you falling in love with Exeter?"

"I honestly don't know," Theo said. "My feelings have been confused from the start." Theo pushed her honey-blond hair back from her face. "But, Nick, I didn't come here to unburden myself emotionally. This is why I came." She held up the note that Exeter sent her the night before. She handed it to Nicoletti.

He unfolded it. On one side, Exeter had scrawled, "See you tonight, dear Theo. Love." Nicoletti turned the paper over. The other side was covered with scribbling, diagrams, and initials.

"Doodling," Nicoletti said.

"Yes," Theo answered. "Mark did it yesterday. See. It's dated at the top."

"A map to Mark Exeter's unconscious?"

"I don't know."

Nicoletti looked at the meticulous writing and what appeared to be Mark Exeter's private code, initials. " 'N.T.,' " Nicoletti read aloud. "That must stand for 'New *Tomorrow*.' 'R = Isms.' Understandable. Religion section changing to Isms." Nicoletti examined the paper. Exeter had drawn a large pyramid with the initials E.P. at the top, crossed them, and written "W.G." next to them.

"Do you know anyone at *Tomorrow* with the initials W.G.?" Nicoletti asked Theo.

"No," she said.

At the bottom of the page, Exeter had drawn a small pyramid with a wavy line through it. Underneath the pyramid he had written the initials B.D. and crossed them out. Next to the initials, he wrote "$$$$$$$$$." A member of the *Tomorrow* staff being axed to save money?

"Do you know a person with the initials B.D. at the magazine?" Nicoletti asked.

"No," Theo said. "There is no one with those initials at *Tomorrow*. I looked through the interoffice phone directory."

"Interesting, Theo," Nicoletti said, holding up the paper. "May I keep this?"

"Of course," Theo said. "Do you think it has any significance?"

"Maybe," Nicoletti said. "What time did you receive it?"

"About eight," Theo said.

"So if I read Exeter's code correctly, he was planning to fire Patterson. But Patterson quit," Nicoletti said.

Theo's hand tightened on the glass. "It looks that way," she said.

Theo put the drink down, put on her glasses, and stood up. "You're the detective. I'll let you figure the rest out."

"I hope this episode doesn't make you cynical about life and men, Theo," Nicoletti said.

"I'm a reporter, Nick," Theo said. She reached into her handbag and pulled out a notebook. "I'm keeping notes on everything: finding Mark's body, being grilled and fingerprinted by the police. Facts. Color. Quotes. I plan to write a story, a first-person piece. It could be a real break for me as a journalist."

From behind the tinted glasses, Theo gave Nicoletti a defiant look.

"I'm not arguing with you, Theo," Nicoletti said. "From my own experience, I've found one of life's more useful clichés to be 'When life hands you a lemon, make lemonade.'"

Theo put the notebook back in her bag.

"Good-night, Nick," Theo said.

Nicoletti watched Theo walk down the stairs, a slender girl with her head held high, a girl who could find her would-be lover murdered in the morning and show up wearing blue jeans and Chanel Number 5 in the afternoon.

A whiff lingered in his nostrils.

He put the Scotch glasses in the sink and stared at the murky green eye on the canvas. It was ugly. He should turn it to the wall or hide it. But no. He would keep it there.

Nicoletti went to the phone and called Byron Manos, poet and Religion editor of *Tomorrow*.

•11•

NICOLETTI pushed his way through the crowd in the Bells of Hell, a drinking spot on Greenwich Village's West Thirteenth Street. Pretty girls, beards, aspiring artists and writers nursed their drinks at the bar along with the Saturday-night uptown tourists making the downtown scene. The Bells of Hell. Owned by an English professor from Australia. Poetry readings in the back room were his way of challenging the disco boom. The idea appeared to be working, Nicoletti thought, eyeing the assemblage of lost souls and souls discovering each other. He edged his way past the bar and headed for the back room.

A guitar twanged plaintively while Byron Manos, *Tomorrow*'s Religion editor, stood on a raised platform giving forth his poetry. His black turtleneck shirt matched his coal-black eyes. Next to him, a girl in a black leotard danced energetically. The crowd was silent, rapt. It was Manos's voice, Nicoletti realized, that held them, a voice amazingly rich and deep.

"The crazy ladies of New York carry their dreams in shopping bags
Labeled Bonwit's, Bergdorf's and Bloomingdale's . . ."

The poetry and dance went on to the punctuation of the guitar. Nicoletti, standing by the door, caught Manos's eye.

"Waiting for someone to hold the space around them and
Lead them out, out, out, over the rainbow bridge . . ."

The dancer arced her arms and collapsed on the floor. There was a rustle of applause and Byron Manos stepped down, moving through the audience to Nicoletti. He pulled out a handkerchief and wiped his face, dripping with perspiration.

"Nick Nicoletti, *Tomorrow*'s resident private eye. You have the reputation of being a man of artistic sensibilities. Do you feel sullied by your trade? Prying into people's private lives?"

"No," Nicoletti said. "Rembrandt explored men's souls. I try to learn a person's motivation for breaking society's code. Can we talk?"

"I told you on the phone, Nicoletti. I've already talked with the police. What can I add? Do you want the embellishments of poetry, my spurious or prurient insights into Mark Exeter's soul, which antechamber of hell I expect him to land in? Read my book *The Antic Wine*, if you can find a copy. Publishers don't get excited about slim volumes of verse. The authors, they believe, are worthless on the TV circuit. If you can write a novel about prizefighters and throw in some incest in Brooklyn, you've got it made."

"Come on, I'll buy you a drink," Nicoletti said.

Nicoletti and Manos moved to a small circular table in the front of the Bells of Hell and gave their orders to a waitress with long, Rapunzel-like hair.

Manos sounded bored, annoyed. "Yes, I was the last person to sign out of the magazine last night. Until I left, I was in my office, with the door closed, listening to music and writing poetry. When I listen to music at the magazine, I use a headset so I won't disturb anyone. I heard nothing. I saw nothing. I often stay late after everyone has left, listening and writing. It's my escape from documenting the vagaries of modern religion and its secular appeals. At those times I'm as remote as a monk in a Greek monastery."

"When you left at 4 A.M., was Exeter still alive?"

Manos offered him a glassy stare. "Are you asking me to go on fact or intuition? I have no idea. I got on the elevator and left. The only things I noticed were the empty glasses and empty bottles, aftermath of the premature magazine wake."

Manos gulped down his beer, reached into his pocket, and slapped a five-dollar bill on the table, about to make his exit.

Nicoletti picked it up and handed it back to Manos. "I'm buying the drinks tonight," Nicoletti said. "I like your poetry. It's vivid, colorful. Do you like painting, too? I saw you near the Metropolitan last Thursday with Vanessa Wills—in Central Park."

Manos lifted his empty glass, appraised it, and banged it down on the table. His expression was intense, feverish, angry. Nicoletti was invading private territory. "If it is any of your business, I love Vanessa Wills. I love one woman the way I love one God. I left the church to be with her."

"Have you any regrets?"

"None. I was the priest at New York's Greek Orthodox cathedral, considered a brilliant comer, in line to become archbishop. But it was a sham. Catering to the whims of shipowners' wives, who would have fund-raising parties where they sold miniature bazoukis that played 'Never on Sunday' when wound up. Only a few of the truly faithful remained, mainly tiny ladies in black hats and kerchiefs, who would come on Sunday to pray for the departed and make frequent signs of the cross.

"One day Vane came to a service. She stayed after and asked to talk with me. She was troubled. And so it began.

"But I didn't get my job at *Tomorrow* through Vane. Her husband's buying the magazine was a sheer coincidence."

"Did you get along with Exeter?" Nicoletti asked.

"He was a prick."

"What did you think of his idea of changing the Religion department to Isms?"

"One more cheap Exeter shot. Reaching to exploit the new trend of cultism. Today's madness, as lasting as candy wrappers or the latest brand in toothpaste. Today everyone has his own private little formula for salvation. EST. Gestalt therapy. Screaming in corners. Put a nickel in the machine and see what it spits back for you. The age of charlatans. Witch doctors in gray flannel suits. In a better society, they would be outlawed, burned at the stake. But in America they advertise in the best magazines, go on the 'Today' show, and hold their meetings in Lincoln Center." The former priest's eyes burned with fervor. "In the beginning was the end, Nicoletti. Who cares about my views? I'm a voice crying in the wilderness. I should put on a hair shirt and head for the desert."

"You don't believe cults deserve coverage in *Tomorrow*?"

Manos gave a short laugh. "I've already sold my soul. I give them their fair share of ink every week." Manos leaned back against the wall. His white teeth gleamed. "Exeter was a strange cult unto himself. Leading people into a garbage sea with the same authority as a Pied Piper. Promising money, fame, and all the rewards if you would play his game."

"Did you play it?"

"Sometimes," Manos said. "Mostly, I avoided Exeter. I preferred the company of Bach and, if you will forgive me, the poetic muse. Now I must get back for another reading. Shalom."

Nicoletti watched Manos vanish into the crowd, a slim man who kept mountains of rage within him, the type of person who would undergo torture before revealing secrets. Nicoletti's private soul felt tired, bruised, and faintly tainted. Moving to the door, he wondered what Toulouse-Lautrec would have done with the Bells of Hell.

"Jade becomes you, darling," Vane Wills said, fingering the beads that she herself had placed around Rocko's neck with delicate fingers. "You look like an Oriental prince, a blond Oriental prince."

Rocko lay back on the flower-sprigged sheets. He felt drugged, weak, although the strongest thing he had drunk that night was a Coke. Rocko reached for his detective's objectivity, like coming up for air after diving to the bottom of a lake. He glanced around the room at the costumes draped on chairs. He and Vane Wills had spent the evening putting them on and taking them off. She, the slave girl. He, the Tahitian king. He, the queen. She, the servant. Kinky. Far-out. With Vane Wills, it was all exciting, lush, strange, delicious.

"Incredible," Rocko said. "Tonight."

"You're marvelous, darling."

"Vane, what was your husband like, as a lover?"

"Mark? A completely sexual person. He made love frequently, intensely, and with a wide variety of people. He once said: 'Sex isn't a casual thing with me. I love whom I am with at the moment. I care about that person only.' "

"The guy had a wonderful line," Rocko said. "Can I borrow it?"

"You're such a tease, Rocko," Vane Wills said, rumpling his blond curls. "It's true. Mark had tremendous powers of concentration. If he focused on something, he gave everything to it. Oriental art. Magazines. He was the same way with people. He hated dead, sexless people. He couldn't bear to be around them. He only tolerated them if it would be of some advantage to him. Then, he would cut them to the quick."

"Like that?" Rocko said, moving his finger across his throat as if slitting it with a knife, and popping his eyes grotesquely.

Wills giggled. "Oh, Rocko, you do make me laugh."

"Say that again," Rocko said. "Say *laugh*. I love to hear it with an English accent."

"Laugh, laugh, laugh," Vane Wills said, trilling the word out.

"Do you mind talking about your husband?" Rocko asked, running his fingers lightly over Vanessa Wills's thighs.

"Not now, not with you." She pressed herself lightly against him. "Let's play, Rocko," she murmured. "You're so good at playing."

He took off the jade beads and, reaching up, placed them around her neck.

Later, when Rocko left Vanessa Wills's apartment, his legs, encased in eighty-dollar blue jeans, felt like jelly as he walked down the steps of the brownstone. Only two nights ago she was a glamorous, mythical figure. Now she was an amazingly known quantity.

Rocko would collect his wits, he said to himself as he staggered down the street. He walked into a pizza/calzone restaurant. He was starving.

"A calzone with sausage," he said, barely noticing the girl taking his order.

Maybe Vane Wills was what people meant when they used the term *nymphomaniac*. If she was, he liked it.

He chewed the calzone quietly and washed it down with a Coke.

He checked himself out in the mirror. An innocent blond face looked back at him. That was an interesting aspect of sex, Rocko thought. Nobody could possibly look at him and guess how he had passed the afternoon. Or could they? His shirt was on backwards. He beat a hasty retreat to the men's room. He was off to cruise New York's gay bars.

The least he could do is appear respectable.

Rocko's fourth bar of the evening. He was beginning to feel depressed. Men, men, men. Water, water everywhere and not a drop to drink. He walked up to the circular bar at the Golden Boy. Here, the ambiance was Madison Avenue chic, low-key. The men looked like models, actors, or aspirants to the glamour trades. Handsome men with perfect features and the unfinished looks of people off camera, as if they had left their personas behind them in film or photography studios.

A few of the men at the bar sat staring in the mirror, at themselves and at the people entering, seeking the Saturday night connection, their own way out of loneliness. Poor slobs, Rocko thought, warped at their mother's knees. Happiness is a thing called Joe. Still, whatever turns you on . . .

The bartender had a smooth oval face, a turned-up nose, and an amused grin.

He put Rocko's Coke on the bar and leaned towards him, his voice bright with confidentiality. "Stick around here long enough and Quentin Thorndike, the famous playwright, is bound to come in with his entourage. Thorndike used to be gorgeous, but now?" He pointed a thumb down towards the floor. "Drink. Drugs. Stick to the Coke, baby, you'll live longer. Alone?"

"For the time being," Rocko smiled sweetly. He glanced up at the TV set, which was flashing the latest news bulletin about Mark Exeter's murder along with his photograph. "New York should be renamed the big sick apple, huh? Weird," Rocko said. "The publisher Mark Exeter comes here from England, and three months later he's murdered, zap, in his office. Probably by some nut."

"Mmmn," the bartender said, polishing a glass and leaning towards Rocko. "If you want my opinion, I think it was a crime of passion." The bartender raised his eyebrows.

"How so?"

The bartender lowered his voice. "Exeter, the man who was murdered, came here a few times." He leered. "And he wasn't alone."

"Oh?"

"No. A trio." The bartender giggled. "You see, I'm an actor. In fact, I recently got a cameo part in a film with Ava Gardner. God knows, I hope they don't wipe me out and leave me on the cutting-room floor. Anyway, Exeter came in here with a tall, dark, slender, absolutely beautiful man with a beard. And a woman." His voice got lower. "The British star, Vanessa Wills. I would know those bones anywhere."

"That was his wife," Rocko said.

"Well, not to worry. I couldn't tell if the three of them were looking, if you know what I mean, or just taking in the scene."

"Were they friendly?"

"Extremely friendly to each other, laughing and dancing together. The three of them. Taking turns, all three. Yes. Talked. Danced. Terribly intime." He leaned closer to Rocko. "I couldn't tell who was with whom."

"Did they talk with anyone else?"

"Unfortunately we got busy, so I didn't notice." The bartender put the sparkling glass on the shelf. "One thing I did notice, Mr. Exeter might have made millions, but as a tipper, I would call him Mr. Cheap."

"You can't tell a book by its cover," Rocko said agreeably.

"How true," the bartender said, giggling. "My name is Randolph. I'm off at three if you'd like to wait for me. I know a nice little after-hours place."

Rocko put five dollars on the bar.

"Thanks, Randolph. Maybe some other time. Keep the change."

Rocko plunged his hands into his pockets and walked down the dark street enlivened only by the Golden Boy. Vane Wills. Her late husband, Mark Exeter. And, undoubtedly, the third member of the trio was Byron Manos, her date at The Pleasure Palace, the Religion editor of *Tomorrow*.

Wills. Exeter. Manos. Together.

He would give up sex for a while.

Rocko fished into his pocket and found two dimes. He called Nicoletti's number and left a message with the answering service.

Then he called the girl with the long, dark hair he had met at the New School. She was home. Rocko got into a cab and sped downtown.

To each his own escape.

•12•

HER face flushed with exertion, Lotte Van Buren slashed with the sharp stainless-steel knife, reducing onions into a small, meticulous dice on the top of the butcher-block table. Seated on a wooden stool in Lotte's kitchen, Nicoletti watched her with fascination. Lotte attacked any task with almost awesome professionalism.

"I find cooking marvelously relaxing in times of stress," Lotte said. "That's why I've never invested in one of those do-everything food processors. Cutting and dicing and chopping are all part of the ritual." Lotte put down the knife, wiped her hands on a dish towel, and pushed back a stray hair. She wore gray slacks and a red blouse. "If I knew you were coming, I would have dressed for the occasion, Nick," Lotte said. "Can I get you something? Coffee? A drink?"

"I can only stay for a few minutes," Nicoletti said. "I was a few doors away from your apartment and wanted to give you some good news."

"That would be a surprise," Lotte said, pushing the onions aside to make way for mushrooms.

"I've identified the prankster," Nicoletti said. "You don't have to worry about slashed phone wires anymore."

Lotte's large blue eyes grew wider. She sat down on a wooden stool opposite Nicoletti. "Who is it, Nick?"

"I'm sworn to confidentiality, Lotte," Nicoletti said. "But I can assure you, no more tricks."

"But that's utterly absurd, Nick," Lotte said, red spots on her cheeks growing brighter. "Why the secrecy?"

"Trust me, Lotte," Nicoletti said, picking up a perfectly shaped, white, raw mushroom.

Lotte walked over to a dry sink converted into a bar, poured two glasses of red wine, and handed one to Nicoletti. "If I had my way, the prank player would be fired from *Tomorrow* instantly and blackballed from ever working on a magazine again," Lotte said. "He or she is clearly a psychopath."

"The *ex*-prankster is quite sane," Nicoletti said. "Foolish, yes. Crazy, no."

Lotte jammed a cigarette into a black holder, lit it, took a deep puff, and exhaled. "Tell me one thing, Nick," she said. "Is it a member of my staff?" Her eyes batted rapidly. "One of the reporters?"

"No, Lotte," Nicoletti said. "Absolutely not."

Lotte blew smoke out of the corner of her mouth. "That's some relief," she said. "It seems my suspicions were wrong." She walked over to the stove, poured oil into a large frying pan, and, after a moment, dropped in the chopped onions, which hit the oil with a hiss. Lotte stirred the onions slowly with a wooden spoon.

"Whom did you suspect, Lotte?" Nicoletti asked.

The kitchen clock ticked. Violins hummed on station WQXR, juxtaposed against the muffled sounds of traffic honking from the street. Copper pots gleamed.

"Theo Marlow," Lotte said.

"Why Theo?" Nicoletti bit the mushroom and chewed it slowly.

"She has a history of mental illness," Lotte said. "She had a nervous breakdown in college. I'm the only one who knows. She spent several months at Valecliff, a sanitorium near Newburgh, New York."

"How did you find out?"

"An overly confiding dean told me when I was checking Theo's references," Lotte said. "I hesitated about hiring her, but I thought I'd give her a chance."

"Felix says Theo is one of the best reporters on the magazine," Nicoletti said.

"She's overly ambitious," Lotte said, adding mushrooms to the frying pan. "At times she does things I consider irrational."

"What kinds of things, Lotte?"

"She goes beyond the bounds of good taste to get a story," Lotte said. She put a lid on the frying pan and sat down across from Nicoletti. "I've had several run-ins with her over these incidents. Two weeks ago a famous actor switched his phone to an unlisted number after Theo called him four times to get the details on the death of his dog, including the dog's middle name. One call would have been sufficient. I thought she might be having problems again."

"Have you spoken to Theo about this?" Nicoletti asked.

"I put her on warning," Lotte said. "I told her *Tomorrow* has a reputation to maintain." Lotte picked up the wine glass. Her eyes were blinking double time. "It's a horrible feeling, Nick, working with people every day and not trusting them. *Tomorrow* used to be my serene oasis, a port in a storm, a sanctuary, like a cathedral in the Middle Ages." The energy seemed to drain from Lotte's face. "Those days are gone forever."

"Lotte, when was the last time you saw Exeter alive?"

"Last night. Just before I left at 1:30. I went to say good-night. Said I could be reached at home if any problems came up. I always did that."

"So it was business as usual."

"Not quite," Lotte said. She took a sip of wine. "I told him I was thinking of leaving the magazine."

Nicoletti shifted on the high stool. "But, Lotte, just a few days ago you told me you would never leave *Tomorrow*."

Lotte shook her head wearily. "Yes. But after finding my phone wire cut, that night I went home and thought about it. I asked myself what I was doing with my life. Was it worth it? I'm still young enough for a new start. I have talent. A publisher has been after me to write a book about New York's offbeat shops. I would enjoy that. And I was asked to teach a course in journalism at New York University. I could use some time for myself, Nick. My husband travels frequently on business. I would like to go with him more often."

"So you were planning to cut your ties with *Tomorrow*?"

"Don't make it sound so final, Nick," Lotte said. "I was not planning to stalk out the door that night."

"How did Exeter react to your tentative resignation?"

"Coolly. He said we'd discuss it some other time."

"And you went home?"

"Yes, home to my plants and color TV, the late, late show, and a double bourbon on the rocks."

"Lotte, you always checked major stories. What was the big secret that the Brandon piece was exposing?"

"I don't have an inkling," Lotte said, pouring more wine. "Eli checked the story himself. Wouldn't let anyone touch it."

"Unconventional," Nicoletti said.

"Eli Patterson is a far from conventional man," Lotte said, lighting another cigarette. "As regrettable as it is, I have to assume he killed Mark Exeter in a drunken rage." She puffed on the cigarette. "It's a nightmare, Nick."

"Yes, Lotte, but people wake up from nightmares," Nicoletti said, standing up to leave. "And this one will end."

"Will it?" Lotte said. "No publisher. No editor. *Tomorrow* in a shambles."

"Do you plan to stay at the magazine, Lotte?"

"I'm too loyal to *Tomorrow* to leave now, under these conditions," Lotte said. "I'll stay at least until some kind of order is established."

She walked to the door with him, opened it, and paused. "I'm glad you came by, Nick. My husband, Bob, is in Dallas at an advertising convention. It gets lonely sometimes."

Nicoletti pressed her hand. "Good-night, Lotte. Thank you for the wine and the conversation." The door closed and Nicoletti heard the double lock click behind him. He walked down the carpeted stairway out to West Twelfth Street and strolled towards SoHo.

Theo Marlow, a mental patient. A picture of bravado and honey-blond hair flashed across his mind. Perhaps in today's society, only the sane people were capable of nervous breakdowns. The others walked around in secure loony bins of their own fashioning.

Theo Marlow looked out at the back windows of the brownstone apartment building facing hers across two small yards. On the fourth floor, a party was in progress. On the second floor, she could see Lotte Van Buren's shadowed figure moving about her kitchen.

She took the last soggy tissue, wadded it into a ball, and heaved it into the wastebasket. The crying was over. She opened a desk drawer and took out a wooden box, repository of her favorite possessions. Lifting the lid, she picked up the silver bell made from aluminum foil, her initials painted on it with nail polish. She held it tenderly in her palm. She kept it as a reminder of the months spent in the psychiatric hospital in the mountains. At Christmastime the patients had decorated a tree. Sixteen-year-old Dickie made each person an ornament. "You have happiness in you," Dickie told her. "You make me feel like bells ringing."

The months in the hospital counted as the bleakest time in Theo's life. But it was a time of growth. She remembered the black depression that sent her there. The affair with the married professor. The horrible aftermath. And the hospital.

Would she spend her life drawn to impossible men?

Theo put the silver bell back in the box. She took out a small, exquisitely carved, jade elephant Mark gave her after the evening of snow. She caressed it in her hand. It was cool. She thought about meeting Mark, walking to the restaurant. What she did not count on, plan for, was Mark Exeter's impact on her. It reminded her of her first trip to the Caribbean, leaving New York on a bitterly cold day and arriving in Jamaica to a blast of heat and beauty and saying: "Wow, I didn't know this existed." Mark made her feel extraordinary and alive.

She was older now, wiser, tougher, stronger than at eighteen. The elephant went back into the box next to the silver bell. Mark Exeter was dead.

She glanced back up at Lotte's window. The man with her looked like Nicoletti. Nicoletti. Kind and strong. Or was he? Or was he like most men, mini-Henry VIII's who would gladly lop your head off when you no longer suited their purposes?

Sunday. Thud. Plonk. Through Dr. Blume's window, the sounds of volleyball players on the lawn created a steady rhythm. In the distance Nicoletti saw the blue-brown mountains of the Hudson Valley.

His back to Nicoletti, Dr. Blume stood at the window, looking out at the patients of Valecliff Sanitorium cavorting on the lawn. The psychiatrist turned to Nicoletti. He was a man in his early fifties, casually dressed in sweater and khaki pants. A bulbous red nose gave his face a comical W. C. Fields look.

"Theo Marlow was my patient," the psychiatrist said. "I know she's working as a reporter at *Tomorrow*. When I read about the murder of the publisher, Mark Exeter, naturally I was concerned. Then this morning the report came over the radio about Theo's finding the body."

"If you could answer some questions about her, you might help eliminate Theo as a murder suspect," Nicoletti said.

"I see," Blume answered, tapping his fingers together.

Nicoletti watched the window curtain flapping in the breeze. In the pseudocheerful atmosphere, he sensed pathos clinging to the walls, seeping under the doors. People came to Valecliff when they fell off the edge of the everyday world, bruised souls to be patched and mended, sent out to function in a topsy-turvy society.

"I still see Theo occasionally," Dr. Blume said. "She drops in every six months or so for a consultation. I believe Theo is fond of Valecliff. That she had a positive experience here."

"What brought Theo to Valecliff?"

Dr. Blume rubbed his lip with his finger. "A combination of things. Youth, certainly. Did you know that the rate of mental illness has drastically risen among our young people?"

"What was the immediate reason?"

"Acute melancholia, or, to put it in simpler terms, severe depression."

"Brought on by a broken love affair?"

"Intuitive of you, Mr. Nicoletti. Did Theo tell you?"

"Not in so many words."

Dr. Blume scratched his head. "She fell in love with a history professor at her college. It was a sub-rosa affair. Kept under wraps because he told her it wouldn't 'look good.' We kiss in the shadows, and all that. He was a persuasive fellow and Theo swallowed his line. She was only a freshman. Secret meetings in his room. Locking his office door in the afternoon. Intimate smiles exchanged during a discussion of the causes of the decline of the Roman Empire." Dr. Blume put his feet up on his desk, folded his hands, and seemed to be dreaming of distant love affairs.

"And what happened?"

Dr. Blume pulled himself back from his revery. "Theo learned he was married. His wife lived in a town sixty miles away, stayed there because of her law practice. He spent the weekends with the wife, telling Theo he was visiting a sick mother." Dr. Blume raised his eyebrows and snorted. "College professors. Notoriously promiscuous. Too much time on their hands; attractive, admiring young students all around them"

"And then?" Nicoletti prodded, wondering if Blume picked up his meandering style from his patients.

Blume blew his nose vigorously.

"When Theo learned the truth, she tried to kill him—symbolically," Blume said.

"What did she do?"

"She tore his office apart, threw his books off the shelves, ripped pages out of them, dumped the desk drawers on the floor, shredded the manuscript of a scholarly study to bits." Blume paused and twiddled his fingers. "A symbolic killing, Mr. Nicoletti, going after what was closest to him. When he found her taking his office apart and tried to stop her, she heaved a crystal ashtray at his head. He carries the scar over his right eye."

"And?"

"Theo was raised on a steady diet of sunshine and optimism. Taught not to show her feelings unless they were positive, happy. When she realized that she was capable of murderous rage and violence, she was plunged into a severe depression. Overwhelmed with guilt. That's when she came here."

"She had a nervous breakdown," Nicoletti said.

"You might call it that, yes. We helped Theo realize that she was not a monster but a flesh-and-blood person, a woman who earned her rage." Dr. Blume took his feet off his desk and began to string paper clips together. "I have told you this, Mr. Nicoletti, in confidence, not to tag Theo as a murderer but for the opposite purpose. At Valecliff she learned to deal with feelings that were long suppressed, to confront the bogeys, to bring them out of the dark. She's an extremely intelligent and mature young woman, Mr. Nicoletti. I give her a complete bill of health."

Driving back to New York, Nicoletti tried to picture self-contained Theo Marlow smashing books around the history professor's office. Once, in a rage, his ex-wife had torn through his studio, dumping canvases and paint tubes on the floor. But she didn't follow the act with a nervous breakdown.

Women.

More than one psychiatrist in Nicoletti's experience had given a patient a clean bill of health and sent him or her out to wreak havoc.

He liked Theo; he didn't want his feelings to get in his way.

•13•

STRIDING into *Tomorrow* on Monday morning, Nicoletti felt a tingle of excitement in the air. As he tossed his coat on the teetering rack, Felix Magill, his bald head gleaming in the light, burst into the gray cubicle.

"Nose, I've got the answer," Felix said. "I know who killed Mark Exeter. Read this memo."

Felix handed him a piece of paper.

It was a memo from Alexander Exeter. "To the *Tomorrow* staff. Parker Johnson, former *Tomorrow* advertising director, has been appointed publisher of the magazine. Winston Gates joins *Tomorrow* as editor-in-chief. Winston, forty, was editor of the *Sydney Sentinal* in Australia. An outstanding journalist, he helped to double the newspaper's circulation. I know you will give Parker and Win your fullest cooperation."

"Fast work," Nicoletti said. "But what does this have to do with murder?"

"Old Alexander Exeter killed his son in a power struggle over the Exeter empire," Felix said. "A Greek tragedy. The new editor, Winston Gates, is the illegitimate son of Alexander Exeter, a love child who will finally achieve his place in the sun. Gates will be a short drink of water with an enormous head, a commanding manner, and pouchy green eyes. His fists will be notoriously tight. He'll clamp down on expense accounts and insist that all interviews be done over tuna fish sandwiches at the counter in Woolworth's." Felix lit a thin cigar.

"Some scenario, Felix," Nicoletti said.

"Winston Gates has arrived on the scene," Felix said. "He's called an editorial meeting. Come along and you'll see that I'm right."

Felix was wrong.

The man behind the desk flashed a dazzling smile at Nicoletti and

Felix as they joined the others in the editor's office. He was of medium height and built like a prizefighter, with slender hips and broad shoulders. His shirt collar was open, his sleeves rolled up to reveal muscular arms.

His square-jawed face was black and beautiful; black eyes snapped with life.

Winston Gates slapped a copy of *Tomorrow* on the desk.

"All right, staff," he exhorted. "I'm your new editor. I'm not a formal person. Call me Win. I don't plan to fire anyone. I'm not going to cut down on expense accounts or cramp your life-styles." He looked around the room at the editorial staff arranged on chairs, the couch, the floor, and leaning against the walls.

Nicoletti stood by the door, observing Gates's performance. He envisioned the man in satin trunks and boxer's gloves, going for the title.

Gates sat down on the edge of his desk.

"Any questions?" He had a lilting, Jamaican accent.

Papers rustled. Cigarettes were lit and ankles recrossed.

"Okay," Gates said. "In some ways we maintain the status quo. But there will be changes. See this magazine?" He waved a copy of *Tomorrow* aloft. "It is well written. Yes. The reporting is excellent. Yes. But do you know what I see? A magazine that is dull, middle-of-the-road, safe, unexciting. I want a magazine with punch." He thrust his fist out for emphasis. The other fist was raised. He boxed at the air. "Sock. Pizazz. I want the magazine to walk off the stands in supermarkets. I want people waiting by their mailboxes when it's delivered. I want to blow America's mind with the 'new' *Tomorrow*. Dig?"

He looked around at the dazed faces, cigarette smokers, pipe puffers, and finger twiddlers. A muffled yawn came from the back of the room.

"And how do we accomplish this?" Gates looked from person to person. "I want everybody off their asses, out there digging, digging, digging, coming back with color and first-hand reportage. I want the people in our foreign and domestic bureaus turned on. No more sitting on their hands and filing one cable a week. Are you with me?"

The editors were going down on the count, their heads about to hit the mat. They looked punched out.

"I don't want an elitist magazine. I want everyone to read the 'new' *Tomorrow*," Gates said. "We will follow the late Mark Exeter's blueprint for the magazine." Gates's ebony head swiveled. "Questions? Questions?"

The Politics editor cleared his throat and piped up in a midwestern twang. "Win, have you given any thought to *Tomorrow*'s hard-core reader? A member of the middle-class intelligentsia? We don't want to lose the loyalty of that person."

"We need not lose the loyal *Tomorrow* reader," Gates said. "But let us bring new readers into the fold." He stretched his arms out. "The young reader. The housewife. The truck driver. The newsstand salesman."

Byron Manos doodled on a piece of paper.

Felix blew up a storm of cigar smoke. He stood up to address the editor. "Gates, aren't you talking about a mass-circulation magazine for middlebrows or lowbrows?"

Parker Johnson, the new publisher, answered the question. "Wrong-o, Felix. Win is talking about America's vast, educated middle class now come to maturity."

"Why don't you let Gates answer himself?" Felix said heatedly.

"There's no place in a journalist's vocabulary for terms like *middlebrow* or *lowbrow*," Gates said. "I think in terms of human curiosity, as the late Mark Exeter did." Gates waved the magazine aloft again. "And speaking of my good friend Exeter, *Tomorrow* is sitting on the hottest story in America, his murder. I open the magazine and what do I find? A brief bio of Exeter and a three-graph story. Dignified. Yes. In good taste. Yes. But will it sell magazines?" He tapped the cover, his voice rising to a shout. "No!"

Gates paused, as though waiting to hear the response of "Amen."

"This week I want a major takeout on Exeter and the murder. I want every department in the magazine involved." Gates pointed to the Art editor. "You will do a piece on Exeter's Oriental-art collection." Gates went around the room, handing out assignments in rapid-fire delivery. "I want that reporter Theo Marlow to write a first-person account of finding the body."

"I don't think that's legit," Felix said. "The police won't like it."

"It will make great copy," Gates answered.

Nicoletti removed the revivalist's frock coat and replaced it with the khaki uniform of a general.

Gates looked at his watch.

"I know we'll work well together."

The troops were dismissed.

Nicoletti stayed behind and introduced himself to Gates.

"Please sit down," Gates said, smiling wickedly and gesturing with his thumb. "You hear them grumbling. They're out there taking me apart limb by limb and saying my ideas are a crock. I think I'll like them."

"I'm investigating tne murder of Mark Exeter," Nicoletti said.

"Yes," Gates answered. "Old Alex Exeter told me about you, that Mark hired you to track down a practical joker. Then Mark was killed. The old man thinks Eli Patterson was the joker and the killer. Do you agree?"

"The joker, no. The killer, maybe," Nicoletti said. "What was your opinion of Mark Exeter?"

The black eyes snapped. "I was one of the few men in the world who actually liked Mark Exeter." The white teeth flashed. "I was thousands of miles away the night he was killed."

"You got along well with Exeter?"

"We worked well as a team. We doubled the circulation of the *Sydney Sentinal* in three years. It was a ball. I love to see circulation go up, up, up. It gets me where I live. I have orgasms over it." His tone was mocking. "I like to shock people by talking like a black man instead of an Oxford graduate. But I am a black man *and* an Oxford graduate."

Nicoletti recalled Exeter's doodling the night before he was killed, crossing out the initials E.P. and replacing them with W.G., Winston Gates. "When did Mark Exeter appoint you editor-in-chief of the magazine?" Nicoletti asked.

"He called me two weeks ago in Sydney," Gates said. "I didn't hesitate. I jumped at the opportunity."

"So even if Patterson hadn't quit, he would have axed him."

"Exeter told me they had philosophical differences," Gates said. "I let it drop at that. We didn't discuss Patterson."

"Patterson quit Friday night after Exeter killed the cover story, an exposé of Brandon Motors."

Muscles moved in Gates's mobile face. "Yes," Gates said. "Supposedly Mark Exeter sold his soul to the Brandon devil for one hundred thousand dollars."

"Was Brandon's advertising that crucial to the magazine?" Nicoletti asked.

Gates leaned back in his chair and put his hands behind his head, dropped them, and leaned forward for emphasis. "I'll share a secret with you, Nicoletti," Gates said. "The magazine was going under financially. Old Exeter wanted to sell *Tomorrow*, sell it or close it. Kaput. Gone the way of *Collier's* and *Look*. The Brandon advertising was crucial."

"So you sympathize with Exeter's action?"

Gates threw his hands up. "How do I answer that question? I'm a journalist. Great exposés are to my liking, all well and good. But a magazine must make money, and to make money a magazine must attract advertisers. That job is getting harder and harder, because every magazine published today is in competition with a most attractive monster."

"Which is?"

"The tube, man, television," Gates said. "Quick and easily digestible, the favorite of millions. Magazines must change to compete. I want *Tomorrow* to survive."

"How does Alex Exeter feel about selling the magazine now?" Nicoletti asked.

"Iffy," Gates said. "He's superstitious. Thinks *Tomorrow* is bad luck. Regardless of what happens, I probably won't lose. I have a firm foothold in Exeter Enterprises."

"One of the lucky, or unlucky, few," Nicoletti said. "Will you be making any changes in the staff here? Any kind of reorganization?"

"No," Gates said. "I believe in encouraging competition. People won't be fired. They will fall of their own weight."

"Good luck," Nicoletti said.

Nicoletti left Gates's office, called his office, and talked to Rocko: "Check and see where Winston Gates was on Friday night."

Theo Marlow rested her feet in Emmy Kaufman's wastebasket as Emmy poured water from the electric teakettle into flower-sprigged cups. No cracked coffee mugs for Emmy. Her office was a model of domesticity.

If Theo opened the bottom drawer of Emmy's desk, she knew she would find Kleenex, Bromo-Seltzer, aspirin, instant soup, bottled Italian salad dressing, sugar, hand lotion, Band-Aids, a sewing kit, a makeup kit. A plant, lovingly tended, flourished on Emmy's desk; sharpened pencils were ensconced in a ceramic holder. A mottled watercolor over the desk testified to Emmy's night-school art classes.

Byron Manos's desk, placed against the opposite wall, was stark and bare. A plastic cover shrouded the typewriter.

"Blahs, that's what I've got," Emmy said, handing Theo a cup. Emmy's carrot-colored hair blazed next to her purple blouse. "This morning Byron gave me a copy of his book of poetry, *The Antic Wine*. For a moment, I thought he cared." Emmy plunked the tea bag up and down in the hot water. "But he was just doing it to be nice. He doesn't see me as a woman." Emmy sighed. "Next to Byron, everyone looks drippy. If only I could get him to *notice* me." Emmy glanced nervously at Theo, her round eyes wide. "Look, Theo, I shouldn't be telling you my problems. It's surreal, Theo, you and Bryon as murder suspects. I think you have a lot of guts to come to work and act as if nothing's wrong."

"I don't think I have a choice," Theo said. "How would it look if I didn't?"

"Guilty, that's how," Emmy said. She took a sip of tea. "I'm worried about Byron. He's supertense. And I don't think his devotion to Vanessa Wills is helping. I've known about their affair for months. Do you think she'll marry him?"

Theo emptied a packet of sugar into the tea and stirred it. "Unlikely," Theo said. "Byron lacks the two qualities I think she needs in a man. Money and power. And underneath that butterfly facade, I think she's a shark."

Emmy reached for a tin of cookies on the corner of the desk, opened it, and offered it to Theo. "You might be right, Theo. I've only seen her a couple of times—except for in the movies—but she does have a bitchy quality about her."

Theo bit a cookie. "She's a throwback to an enchantress in some ancient myth. It's hard to imagine her doing ordinary things, like going to the supermarket or getting cavities in her teeth."

Theo and Emmy sat silently, sipping tea, looking out the window, absorbing the peculiar Monday-morning mood of the magazine. The writers and editors were at a meeting with the new editor, Winston Gates. Even in the aftermath of shattering events—Eli Patterson's disappearance and Exeter's death—a listlessness hung in the air. The twilight zone. The weekend over, Friday too far away to contemplate. Story lists were incomplete; assignments yet to be made. Limbo.

Emmy broke the silence. "Anyway, Byron needs space. I don't know if Wills would give it to him." Amber beads rattled around Emmy's neck as she got up to pour another cup of tea. "I've discussed Byron with my therapy group," Emmy said. "They say that I have a need to be rejected dating back to my father's liking my brother better than me. And that the reason I get along so well with Lotte Van Buren is because I relate to her as though she were my mother and seek her approval."

Down the hall the television set in the TV department gave a low hum. Buses and cabs honked on the street.

Theo took another cookie. "How was your Saturday-night date, Emmy?" Rehashes of the weekend were a ritual Emmy and Theo shared, like reading the leaves in a cup to gain a sense of past, present, and future events.

"Strictly a bummer," Emmy said, relaxing as she confided in Theo. "You remember the lawyer, the one who asked me to marry him, the one I didn't like? I thought I should give him another chance. So I went out to dinner with him. All he talked about was his torts. I was glad when he went home to his mother in Queens."

Theo, usually ready to plunge into a minute analysis of the character, personality, and potential of the current man in Emmy's life, cut off the exploration. "At least you tried," Theo said.

"If I could lose ten pounds, I think my life would change," Emmy said. "You're different, Theo. You attract glamorous men."

Theo's hand shook slightly as she reached for the cup. "Don't be ridiculous, Emmy."

Emmy put her cup on a red tray. "Theo, do you think we'll be sitting here ten years from now, reporters on our way to middle age, sipping tea?"

"Not me, Emmy," Theo said. "I plan to be leading an exciting life. And if I'm still here, I'll be a writer."

"I don't really have a career goal," Emmy said. "I'd like to get married. How about yourself, Theo?"

"Maybe," Theo answered. "But he would have to be perfect. Not a perfect person but perfect for me. His idiosyncracies would have to mesh with mine."

Down the hall Emmy and Theo heard footsteps, voices; the editorial meeting was over. The phone rang in Personalities across the hall from Emmy's office. "Thanks for the tea, Emmy," Theo said, standing up. "By the way, you look thinner."

"Two pounds," Emmy said. "Thanks for noticing."

Theo walked across the hall and answered the phone, taking down the details of an upcoming press conference where a basketball star would give away candy bars to orphans. More hype.

Felix walked in energetically, sat down in the swivel chair, and whirled all the way around.

"Theo, your dream of becoming a writer is coming true," Felix said. "Winston Gates wants you to write a firsthand account of finding Mark's body for the next issue."

"Write about finding Mark Exeter's body?" Theo said. "For *Tomorrow?* Great. Yes. Maybe I'll even get a by-line." Theo touched the notebook that sat by the side of her desk, then looked pensive. "I'm just not sure if I'm ready for it yet, right now, this week."

Felix lit a cigar and waved it for emphasis. "It's easy, Theo." Felix stuck the cigar in his mouth and sat with fingers poised over the typewriter. Moving them in the air, he started talking. "It was 6:30 A.M. A hushed stillness lay over the magazine as I walked down the back stairs. Mark Exeter, publisher of *Tomorrow,* lay on the floor of his office, his head in a pool of blood. His silk, Liberty of London tie . . . ta ta, ta ta ta. I reached immediately for the phone and dialed the policy emergency number, 911. Ta tum, ta tum, ta tum. See? Simple."

Felix turned to Theo with his ever-cheerful grin.

Her face was red and her mouth tense.

"Something wrong, Theo?"

"There was no pool of blood when I found Mark's body. The blood had seeped into the carpet."

"You know the facts, Theo," Felix said.

"Mark Exeter was a human being, Felix, not just a piece of copy," Theo spluttered.

"Tsk, tsk, Theo, musn't look at it that way. The next issue is going to be a monument to Exeter."

"A monument in the *Reader's Guide to Periodical Literature,*" Theo said. "I want to be a writer, but I must admit that I'm occasionally sickened by this intellectual sausage factory."

"Sausage factory?" Felix said.

"Yes," Theo huffed. "Getting the facts, grinding them up in a rehash, and churning them out like something new and savory and original."

"So that's the way you feel about your job?" Felix sounded deflated. "Lunch at '21.' Interviewing the exciting celebrities of our time."

"Sure, sure. Lunch at '21' and tuna fish for dinner, if there's time to open the can. For instance, I put in four hours trailing Frank Sinatra around in the rain for a dumb quote," Theo huffed. "This job is about a hundred miles removed from reality."

"That's why you love it," Felix argued. "Who needs reality?"

"Being a journalist isn't always such a big, romantic deal, Felix."

Felix lit a fresh cigar. "Theo, a man or woman becomes a journalist for salvation. To keep from going mad. A journalist can pick life up and put it down as he sees fit. You organize reality at your typewriter."

"So that's the secret to this madness!"

"Anyway, the Exeter story is not my idea," Felix said. "It's the brainstorm of Win-the-War Gates."

"Win-the-War?"

"Win the circulation war," Felix said.

"You never give up, do you, Felix?" Theo said. The moment of crisis passed. "I'll write about finding Mark Exeter's body, Felix. And I'll do it in grand *Tomorrow* style."

" 'Atta girl, Theo," Felix said, reaching over to pump her hand.

Theo looked down the hallway. Lotte Van Buren was walking towards the Personalities office. Unlike her usual crisp self, Lotte moved slowly, with faltering steps.

Theo stood up.

Lotte reached the Personalities office and put a hand out to the wall to steady herself. Her eyes looked glazed. Her face was chalky white, covered with fine drops of perspiration. She struggled for breath.

Theo slid her chair over so Lotte could sit down.

"Theo," Lotte began. She collapsed on the floor.

As Theo felt Lotte's weak pulse, Felix dialed the police emergency number. Lotte started to move her head up and collapsed with a sigh into a deep faint as Emmy rushed over from across the hall, carrying aspirin and smelling salts.

Eddy O'Brien, scampering down the hall, stopped and stared at Lotte. "Hell's bells," Eddy said. "Lotte Van Buren's never had a sick day in her life."

Theo grabbed a clean handkerchief from her handbag and hurried down to the water cooler to moisten it and put it on Lotte's forehead. At the water cooler, she almost walked into Nicoletti, coming up the corridor.

"Something's happened to Lotte," Theo said.

"Lotte?" Nicoletti looked anxiously at the crowd gathering at the end of the hall, started to walk down, then turned back to Theo. "Theo, this might be the wrong moment to ask, but can you meet me tonight at Mark Exeter's apartment building?"

"Why?"

"You said you were there Thursday night, in his apartment. I want to see if anything is different than when you left."

"Yes," Theo said. "All right."

"Eight o'clock," Nicoletti said. "In the lobby." He walked down the hall towards Lotte.

Theo moistened the handkerchief, then leaned over the water cooler, taking deep gulps of cold water. Sirens, the persistent shriek of ambulance and police car crying of mortality in the midst of New York's commercial traffic, roared towards the magazine. Hearing the sirens, Theo experienced the sickening feeling that this had happened before and could happen again.

•14•

IT was 7:30 P.M. The glaring, burnt-orange walls on the eighth floor of Lenox Hill Hospital shimmered at Nicoletti as he approached Lotte's room. A young cop with a ruddy complexion stood outside the door watching for intruders and eyeing the nurses for diversion.

"She's awake," the cop said, checking Nicoletti's name off on a list of people permitted to see Lotte.

Propped up in the white hospital bed, a glucose-feeding tube attached to one arm, Lotte gazed into a hand mirror as she applied mascara to her long, heavy eyelashes.

"How do you feel, Lotte?" Nicoletti asked, entering the room.

"Sick," Lotte said slowly, putting the mascara and mirror down on the nightstand. "I am surprised to see you." The words came with effort. Lotte's face was pale; without makeup she looked at least ten years older.

"You don't think I have the proper bedside manner for hospital calls?" Nicoletti said.

"Don't play games, Nick," Lotte said. "Somebody tried to poison me. A crazy person who hates me. I'm sure it was the prankster, the person you're allowing to run loose around the magazine."

Nicoletti pulled a chair up next to Lotte's bed. "It wasn't the prankster, Lotte."

"Do you have proof? Evidence?"

"That person's jokes are over," Nicoletti said.

"I thought I could trust you, Nick," Lotte said wearily.

"You can."

"My husband is flying back from Texas. That's a relief."

"You're going to be all right, Lotte," Nicoletti said. "You were lucky."

"Poison, a barbiturate that was supposed to put me to sleep for-

106

ever," Lotte said. "What a horror. I brought chicken salad for lunch. It tasted odd. I felt queasy but ignored it. The next thing I remember is waking up in this room."

"You collapsed on the floor of the Personalities office," Nicoletti said.

"I don't remember," Lotte said, eyelashes fluttering. "Ugh. Grotesque."

"Where did you get the chicken salad?"

"I brought it from home. Always bring my lunch on Monday Keep it in the small refrigerator. Everyone knows about it."

"It was loaded with Seconal. But the dose wasn't lethal," Nicoletti said.

"What are you trying to tell me, Nick? That somebody simply wanted to scare me to death?"

"No," Nicoletti said. "I'm suggesting your would-be attacker is inept, or confused." Nicoletti got up, walked over to the window. "Exeter's murder appeared unplanned, done in a fit of rage. But this? The murderer thought about it."

"Madness," Lotte said.

"But what's the link? First Exeter, then you," Nicoletti pondered out loud.

"You are the investigator," Lotte said. "I am merely the victim."

Lotte picked up a copy of the afternoon paper from the nightstand and showed it to Nicoletti. Her picture was on the front page. The headline blared: "MAG EXEC POISONED." Lotte scanned the front page and put the paper down wearily. "I'll read the story tomorrow. That picture was taken of me ten years ago. Flattering, isn't it?" She picked up the hand mirror, looked at it, and winced. "I'm nothing without lipstick. My face is all out of proportion. My eyes take over. The lipstick gives it balance." She stopped and put the mirror down. "I don't think you came here for a course in cosmetics, Nick."

"No," Nicoletti said. "I'm looking for a killer."

"Any brilliant new insights?" Lotte asked, her voice labored, yet the tone acidic.

"Seconal is an easy drug to obtain," Nicoletti said. "Regularly prescribed for people with sleeping problems."

"It's too baffling," Lotte said, gazing around the hospital room. "Don't you abhor hospitals? What a dump."

"Will you go back to the magazine, Lotte?" Nicoletti asked.

"I'm going back as soon as they let me out of this bed," Lotte said. "I'll tough it out."

"Gutsy," Nicoletti said.

"Compulsive," Lotte answered heavily. Lotte's hyperthyroid eyes started to droop. "My head feels foggy. I think I will sleep now. What else are hospitals good for?" The words tapered off. Lotte closed her eyes and fell into a raspy doze.

Nicoletti left the hospital and walked down Lexington Avenue.

On the corner of East Seventy-fourth Street, a peroxide blond with tight black pants chewed gum as her poodle peed delicately against a tree. She smiled at Nicoletti, but he didn't steam up with ardor.

New York. Billed as the most exciting city in the world, the toughest, the loneliest. Always in superlatives. The best. The biggest. The city that bred people for survival and offered everyone a second chance. In New York you could lose and then win and maybe win and lose at the same time because people were plugged into more than one circuit, winning at careers, losing at love, or the other way around.

In Bloomingdale's window, mannequins with jet-setters' faces modeled clothes for the emaciated. Nicoletti hailed a cab and gave the driver the address of the late Mark Exeter's apartment.

Theo Marlow was waiting for him in the lobby.

"How's Lotte?" she asked.

"Alive," Nicoletti answered. They walked to the elevator.

"When is she coming back to work?"

"As soon as they'll let her out of bed," Nicoletti said.

"Lotte loves that brave *Dark Victory* scene," Theo said, "Conquering all odds."

"You and Lotte don't appear to be the closest of friends," Nicoletti said.

"She was wonderful when I first went to *Tomorrow*," Theo said. "Played mother hen. Told me where to get my hair cut, about places that sold clothes at discount prices. She even helped me find an apartment. I live right in back of her."

"And what happened, Theo?"

"I don't know. She thinks I'm an upstart, too ambitious," Theo said. "I counted the number of pairs of shoes in the closet of a woman named to the 'best-dressed' list, for which I was thrown out of the woman's apartment. The best-dressed lady also called Lotte to express her outrage. Lotte was scandalized.''

"How many pairs of shoes?" Nicoletti asked.

"One hundred and forty-five."

The elevator came. Theo and Nicoletti got on.

"Did the shoe count add to the story?" Nicoletti asked.

"Definitely," Theo said. "That's the famous *Tomorrow* formula, looking for that extra bit of color that brings a story to life."

They got off the elevator and walked to Exeter's apartment. "Theo, I want you to look around the apartment and tell me if you notice anything unusual, different from the last time you saw it," Nicoletti said. "Everything has been left exactly as it was when Exeter was murdered."

After trying several keys, Nicoletti opened the door to Exeter's apartment and switched on the lights. A scent that recalled the late publisher hung in the air: expensive cologne mingled with fine wine and leather. Nicoletti and Theo walked around the living room together. The fireplace was swept clean of ashes. A few glass-stain rings on the coffee table gave evidence of parties ended.

"It looks exactly the same," Theo said, shivering slightly. "Chilly. He liked fires. Told me he never turned on the heat."

They walked into the bedroom.

The king-sized bed was rumpled and unmade. Theo walked over to a chair festooned with a pair of torn black lace panty hose. "Mark must have had company Friday afternoon. He told me that the maid came every morning," Theo said.

Nicoletti watched Theo as she walked stiffly around the room, a frozen look on her face. She opened a closet door. Exeter's clothes, neatly hung and perfectly arranged. Shoes polished, gleaming, lined up on the floor. Soft, elegant suits draped from hangers. Shelves of sweaters, shirts crisply stacked. Hatboxes. Silk ties. Ascots. Belts. Coats. Theo closed the door of the cavernous closet.

She opened the door of the adjoining closet and stood staring at the contents. Filmy lace negligees, a riot of color. Magenta. Fuschia. Blue. Costumes. She picked one hanger off the rod and held the costume up to herself. It was a short black maid's uniform with a white apron. She put it back and reached for a low shelf, picked up a pink and green spangled garter belt, then blue crotchless underpants. Theo's face was a bright red.

"Did you set me up for this?"

"No, Theo."

"I didn't know Mark's taste ran to the bizarre."

"Let's call it vaguely kinky," Nicoletti said. "I didn't know about Mark Exeter's private rituals. It's the first time I've been in this apartment."

Theo reached back into the closet and came out with what appeared to be a small red leather diary. She started turning the pages. "Names," Theo said. She read aloud from the book. "Helen of Troy," "Orphan Annie." "The Queen of Spain." Theo stopped and stared at the page. "Tiger," she read, "With a question mark next to it." She looked at Nicoletti but didn't see him. "How could he?" Theo seethed. "These names, he must have kept a log of the women he slept with. I appear to have been next on the list. He called me Tiger, said I had tiger's eyes."

Theo's hands trembled as she started to tear at the book, rip out its pages. "It's so ugly, shabby," she said, tears streaming down her face.

Nicoletti reached over and tried to pull the book from her hands. "Don't, Theo," he said.

"He's a monster," Theo shouted, sobbing.

"He's dead, Theo," Nicoletti said, pulling the book away from her. "Over. Done. Finished."

Theo looked up helplessly at Nicoletti, tears streaming down her face. "Oh, Nick," she said. "What's wrong with me?"

"Nothing," he said. He put his arms around her and held her, feeling the tension finally leave her body as she sobbed against him.

Theo pulled away from him and sat down on a chair by the window. Nicoletti handed her a handkerchief.

"Thank you," she said. "Right now I hate Mark Exeter. I thought he had some sensitivity. I really didn't believe all those rumors about him and his absolute strings of women. I suppose I had to see for myself."

"You're a journalist, Theo."

"I didn't know I was being set up to be a name on a scorecard," Theo said. "I dislike him and I hate myself for losing control, for that rage." Theo pushed her damp hair back from her face. "It's awful."

"Don't apologize to me for having feelings, Theo," Nicoletti said.

He put Exeter's diary back in the closet and closed the door. "Use your feelings, Theo. Use your own experience. It's all any of us has got."

Theo took the notebook out of her handbag, the notebook with "Exeter" scrawled boldly on the cover. "I suppose it will make wonderful copy," Theo said. "But I won't bother counting."

"Counting what?"

"The number of anything in the late Mark Exeter's closets."

"Let's go, Theo," Nicoletti said.

They left the apartment building and Nicoletti hailed a cab going downtown. In the taxi Theo rested her head on his shoulder as the radio played an old, sad blues song. An early spring breeze floated through the window. During the past few days, Nicoletti felt something start to break up inside him, a hard emotional shale. The scent of Chanel and Theo's hair floated up to him.

He put his hand over hers.

The cab stopped in front of Theo's brownstone. He walked with her up the steps. Nicoletti looked down into Theo's face and saw sensuality and confusion.

He took her hand, held it tight, and let it go.

"Good night, Theo."

"Good night, Nick." Theo ran in the door.

Theo's hand was strong and warm. But was it strong enough to heave a lethal blow from a bronze statue against Mark Exeter's head? Nicoletti dug his hands in his pockets. The night was turning chilly. He walked to the Lion's Head bar, where he had an appointment to keep with novelist Samson Cody.

•15•

SAMSON Cody leaned against the bar in the Lion's Head, his elbow draping over the bar as he waved a glass aloft. "Ginger ale," he said to Nicoletti. "On the wagon. Drinking's the curse of the writing class. Or at least of old ink-stained wretches like me." Cody's sensual mouth drooped.

Standing at the bar, Nicoletti sipped a beer. "Congratulations on your new book," he said. "Number one on the best-seller list."

"It helps to buy shoes for the kids. And pay all the exes' alimony," Cody said. He looked like a prizefighter gone slightly to seed. Muscular. Paunchy face. Broken nose. The silvery gray ringlets surrounding his face, the longish hair, were a pixie, almost whimsical, touch. "I've spent my life shattering icons, breaking china, getting into trouble. I suppose that's why I'm so fascinated by the criminal mind."

"I called you," Nicoletti said, "Because I read in the *Post* that you're writing a piece on Mark Exeter."

"Yes. Yes," Cody said. He leaned more confidentially towards Nicoletti, then grabbed a barstool behind him and slipped it under his solid rump. "I find nonfiction restful between novelistic bouts. You're working on the case. Curious. An artist turned detective."

"You find that unusual?"

"Somewhat," Cody said. "Not really. Artists are like detectives, digging through the detritus of life, looking for clues, trying to create a new order." He swallowed the ginger ale in a gulp and waved to the bartender for another. "Mark Exeter fascinated me. He was a total paradox. He was a great appreciator of art; witness the famous Oriental-art collection. But he was also a coldhearted businessman, almost chillingly so."

"You were a friend of Exeter's."

"In a sense," Cody said, chortling. "Exeter didn't mind having one

112

foot in the literary establishment. And he liked parties. I give great parties, or used to. And he liked women. I know a lot of beautiful women. Of course, Exeter liked men, too. He would fuck any gender if it appealed to him. Yet he had taste."

"When did you last see Exeter?"

"Wednesday. We had lunch. Not the most cordial meeting."

"What happened?"

"I retain a certain warm spot in my heart for *Tomorrow* magazine," Cody said. "In fact, you might say that *Tomorrow*'s book reviewer helped establish me. He gave me a first-rate review when I was totally unknown. Over the years *Tomorrow* has remained a friend of belle lettres. God knows, they even review poetry."

Sipping the beer, Nicoletti watched Cody, who occasionally glanced in the mirror over the bar at his own self-pleasing image.

Cody continued. "Old Blair, the book reviewer—a sweet old guy—hardly goes into the office, stays home poring over the new tomes and brings his reviews in once a week—he was planning a cover story on me."

"And Exeter shot it down?"

"Not quite," Cody said. "He was enthusiastic. Said I was perfect fodder for the 'new' *Tomorrow*, a literary hero who had broken through to have mass appeal."

"So what was the problem?"

"Old Blair was working on the story, what you might call a serious literary piece, tracing my career from the beginning, discussing my work in a serious vein. I was totally charmed by the idea, as you can imagine. It traced my growth as a literary giant, rather than as a literary lion roaring to the crowds."

"And?"

Cody fingered his ginger-ale glass, looked in the mirror, and turned back to Nicoletti. "Exeter wanted to boil that down to a few paragraphs. He wanted to do a story on the *personality* Samson Cody, send reporters over to my home, talk to the new wife, take pictures of the kid . . ."

"Humanize you," Nicoletti said.

"I'm too human already," Cody said. "And, as I told him, almost everything has been written about me. Furthermore, I'm sick of having my life an open book. Furthermore, beyond that, I'd like to save a few nuggets of fresh material for my autobiography."

"And?"

"I know the power of the press, Nicoletti. Sooooo, I considered Exeter's idea. Then I told him: Do both. Do a color piece, and keep Blair's essay."

"What was Exeter's reaction?"

"Exeter said no. Said it was impossible and, anyway, he was planning to give Blair the ax, in a civilized way, of course. Keep him on retainer to write an occasional book review."

"And you said?"

"Told him to forget it. I was number one on the best-seller list already. Did I need him and his new *Tomorrow*? Absolutely not."

"Was that the last time you saw Mark Exeter?"

"Yes," Cody said.

"Did you like him?"

"He interested me. A strange bird. Loved the racetrack, but when he went, he bet on every horse. He wasn't so interested in gambling, only in having a winner," Cody said, shifting on the barstool. He looked in the mirror and back at Nicoletti. "I assume his wife killed him."

"What makes you think so?"

"Women are murderous," Cody said. "Nobody would know any better than I. A favorite wife of mine once tried to stab me. Strange, as I felt the knife pierce my arm—we were surrounded by people at a party—I was almost touched. I wanted to weep. I thought, gee, this woman must really love me. We remain good friends."

"But Vanessa Wills wasn't at the magazine the night Exeter was murdered," Nicoletti said.

"Don't underestimate Vanessa Wills," Cody said. "Wills would find a way."

Sipping champagne, Rocko leaned back in the brocade chair. He dipped the silver knife into caviar and spread it on crisp, buttered toast. As he took a bite, a few of the tiny black eggs dripped down on to his bare leg.

Vanessa Wills reached a finger over, picked up the eggs, and licked her finger.

"Musn't waste it, darling. It's the best," she said.

Seated naked on the floor, auburn hair cascading over her, Vanessa

Wills appeared perfectly poised. She was the first woman in Rocko's experience who was totally at home without her clothes. Most women were self-conscious about a scar, a sag, too fat legs. But Vanessa Wills's body was perfect. She had nothing to hide.

"This will be the last champagne and caviar party for a while, Rocko," she said. "On a stringent fifty thousand dollars a year left to me by Mark, I will have to alter my life-style." She leaned back against a velvet cushion. "I don't mind. I'll devote myself to my career. I was offered a film role yesterday, playing Meg in a remake of *Little Women*. Isn't that a howl? My playing that prig? Still, the shoot will be in California, and I know a charming group of people in Malibu." She stretched her arms back. "You would adore it, Rocko, swimming naked in the Pacific and then racing back to a party. Marvelous. Heady. Sex in California has a free, healthy feeling about it."

"How would you say it compares with sex in New York?"

"Mmmn," Vane nibbled at the toast. "An interesting concept, Rocko, how sex differs according to geography. I suppose you might say sex in New York is more cerebral. There's a great deal of chatting up on serious topics before you get down to it. And a lot of brooding psychology thrown in. After making love, a man is likely to stare at the ceiling and say something like: 'Why must I always be in competition with my brother?' Takes a bit of the edge off things. That's why I adore you, darling. You're a completely sexual being."

Champagne bubbles popped against Rocko's nose. Vane Wills was an intriguing woman, but he was beginning to feel like a sex object. One of those guys who posed flexing their muscles in magazines.

Vane looked up at him soulfully. "Rocko, you've helped me over a hard time. I won't forget it. I'll be flying back to London shortly for the funeral. Probably stay for a fortnight or so."

"And look up old friends? Like the psychiatrist who introduced you to swinging London?"

"Don't be crude, Rocko. It doesn't become you." She rubbed her forehead. "I'm beginning to feel the need for changes in my life. For sanity. Perhaps, even for a real marriage."

"To Byron Manos?"

"Byron would be a wonderful husband."

Rocko examined the bubbles in the champagne glass. "After indulging yourself in the trio of yourself, Manos, and the late Mark Exeter, wouldn't you find Manos alone dull?"

Violet eyes serious, she stared at Rocko, then erupted in laughter. "You are devilish, Rocko." Her voice had a hard edge. "How did you find out?"

"A little discreet gumshoeing." Rocko put the champagne glass down. "Why did you do it, Vane, make love with your husband and your lover? Did you have a warped childhood?"

"I had a glorious childhood," Vanessa Wills said, stroking Rocko's leg. "The threesome was my idea. I don't know why I did it. Byron hated it. Mark loved it. Mark liked Byron. It was a turn-on for him. Maybe I was trying to kick sand in both their faces. I'm not proud of it." She reached for a yellow silk robe, put it on, and tied it around her.

"Why did Manos tolerate the situation?"

"Initially, he hated the whole thing." Her face was stark white and her voice was low. "But maybe he began to like it. Strictly from a practical point of view, he wanted to keep his job. I think Mark exerted his deadly spell on Byron." Her voice was a whisper. "Byron killed Mark. I'm sure of it."

"But you told Nicoletti you were sure a woman killed Exeter."

"I wanted to divert suspicion from Byron."

"Talk to me, Vane. I'm all ears."

"I told you I was at an all-night party the night Mark was murdered."

"Yes. We checked it out. So did the police."

She took a delicate puff of a cigarette and exhaled a thin stream of white smoke. "Not quite true. Everyone at the party was, shall I say, preoccupied. About a quarter after two, I slipped out the back door, walked down the stairs, and left the building."

"Didn't the doorman see you?"

"Of course, but he didn't recognize me." She massaged the calf in Rocko's muscular right leg. "You know how I love to play dress-up. I was disguised as a boy, wore a false mustache, carried my clothes in a tote bag, and slipped them on in the stairwell. Remember the messenger who arrived at *Tomorrow* about 2:30? That was me." She began massaging the calf in Rocko's left leg with practiced hands.

"Why the Halloween bit, Vane?"

She hesitated, then plunged ahead. "My costumes turned Mark on, excited him." She stopped massaging and crumbled a piece of dry toast in her fingers. "I called Mark and told him I was coming. The

116

night watchman sent me upstairs immediately. I found Mark in his office. He was terribly preoccupied, said he was expecting someone."

"Who?"

"He didn't say." Wills rested her head against Rocko's thigh. "I started crying. I went to Mark to make a last-ditch attempt to keep our marriage together. He led me to one of the sleeping rooms upstairs and told me to wait for him. On the way we passed Byron's office door. It was closed. Mark came back in about ten minutes. I pulled out all the stops. Told him I knew he loved me. Why couldn't he be the Romeo to my Juliet?" She played with Rocko's toes.

"Get your act together, so to speak."

"He said it was too late, that it was over. He said, 'I'm sorry.' He walked out and closed the door. I wept, silently, alone in that silly sleeping room, and remembered all the times Mark deserted me. Could I go through that again? Hardly, darling." Wills reached up and pulled Rocko down next to her on the fur rug on the floor. "I'm not that much of a masochist. I dried my eyes and decided to go downstairs, shake hands, and say good-bye. The gentlemanly, or rather, ladylike, gesture."

"Were you still wearing the mustache?"

"No. I had pulled it off. Why?"

"I can't imagine you with a mustache."

"I passed Byron's door. It was open. He wasn't there. I went down the back stairs. Byron was in Mark's office. He had Mark pinned against the wall. He was slamming Mark's head from side to side, enraged, shouting."

"What was he shouting?"

"Poetry. T. S. Eliot. Calling Mark 'the hollow man.'"

"What did you do?"

"Nothing. Neither of them saw me. I went down the back stairs. I left. I put a scarf over my mouth to hide the missing mustache, walked past the night watchman, and went back to my party."

"Didn't your messenger-boy getup surprise the partygoers?"

"Don't be naive, darling," Vane Wills said with a sniff and a giggle. She kissed Rocko's shoulder. "I didn't wear a stitch at the party. It all went back into the tote. A swingers' party is the perfect alibi. Nobody remembers whom they were with at any given moment." She pecked at Rocko's ear.

"But why do you think Manos killed Exeter, because of you?"

"I don't know. It seemed the inevitable climax of the scene."

"Vane, real life is not the stage. Did you actually see Manos bean Exeter with the statue?"

"No."

"Parker Johnson talked to Exeter after that. But Byron didn't leave the magazine until 4 A.M. He could have gone back later and killed Exeter." Rocko put down the champagne glass.

"Oh, I wish we had more bubbly, darling," Wills said. "I want to laugh and drink and not think about murder. Damn Mark Exeter and his posthumous stinginess." She gracefully spread the last bit of caviar on toast and bit down with white, even teeth. "At least Mark left me the town house in London. And the Paris apartment. When Mark and I made love, we spoke French. I can teach you French, Rocko."

Rocko squirmed. He was a reluctant gold miner, collecting little nuggets about Mark Exeter, the after-shave lotion he used, his tailor, his favorite restaurants, his weakness for his mother's steak and kidney pie, that he slept in the buff on striped sheets with two pillows, that he spoke several languages fluently, that he possessed extraordinary powers of concentration. Compared to Exeter, Rocko felt he must look pretty dumb. Nevertheless, Exeter was dead and he was alive.

Rocko reached over and untied Vane Wills's yellow robe.

Gratefully, she dropped it from her shoulders.

"Let's play, Rocko," she said softly. "I'll be Shirley Temple and you'll be the old grandfather who rescues me. It will all be a lovely voyage on 'the good ship *Lollipop*.'"

Opening the door to his loft, Nicoletti found lights blazing and Rocko waiting for him in the large, dilapidated chair.

"Hi, boss," Rocko said. "I broke into your loft, the old plastic-card trick. I didn't think you'd mind."

"I wish you wouldn't call me 'boss,' Rocko. It makes me feel like a gangster," Nicoletti said.

"It's a reflex, something I picked up from my relatives," Rocko said.

Nicoletti changed into chinos and a well-worn blue shirt. "Drink?" Nicoletti said, pouring himself a healthy tumbler of brandy.

"You know I don't drink," Rocko answered. "Anyway, I've had

my share of booze. Champagne with Vanessa Wills. That's one reason I'm here. I need to talk with somebody. Being with that woman makes me crazy. Besides, I learned some new things."

Nicoletti explored his refrigerator and found a hunk of cheese and crackers as he listened to Rocko repeat Vane Wills's story about dressing up as a messenger boy and visiting Exeter at the magazine, about the fight between Manos and Exeter, about Manos's pounding of Exeter's head against the wall.

Putting a large hunk of cheese on a small cracker, Nicoletti shook his head. "It's amazing, the amount of movement that went on that night at the magazine. And nobody noticed anybody else. Almost like a slapstick comedy in slow motion."

"Beats me," Rocko said.

Nicoletti stared at the murky green eye on the canvas. "Do you believe Vanessa Wills's story?" he asked Rocko.

"Why would she lie?"

"If she killed Exeter herself. Went downstairs, checked out, then went back upstairs, hid in the sleeping room, and then returned to Exeter's office."

"I believe Vanessa Wills," Rocko said. He got up and walked restlessly around the loft, picking things up and putting them down. He paused by a mirror over Nicoletti's bureau and looked at his reflection.

"You know some guy tried to pick me up in Times Square yesterday?" Rocko said. "He told me I had a surreal transvestite beauty." Rocko threw himself into the chair. "I was with Vanessa for hours today. I thought maybe Wills and I had a relationship, a man-woman, yin-and-yang thing."

"Why?"

"She told me about her childhood. To me, when a chick talks about her childhood, it's like waving a red flag that says 'meaningful relationship.' Sex, that's not always so intimate. But when a girl tells you about her first ride on the merry-go-round, you're getting to her."

Nicoletti refilled his brandy glass. "I told you it's a mistake to get involved with women on a case, particularly murder suspects."

Rocko gave Nicoletti an appraising look. "And who visited the scene of the crime with reporter Theo Marlow?" Rocko got up and paced restlessly. "I checked up on the new editor, Winston Gates,"

Rocko said. "He wasn't in Australia the night of the murder. He landed in San Francisco Friday morning. He could have flown to New York and zapped Exeter just like that." Rocko snapped his fingers.

"Then he lied," Nicoletti said.

"For murder, I'll put my money on Manos," Rocko said. "A guy in love with Vanessa Wills is crazy enough to do anything."

"Gates fascinates me," Nicoletti said. "His drive, his intensity—his almost manic need to succeed." Nicoletti walked to the window, brandy in hand, and looked out on New York's skyline.

Rocko paused by the window, looking out with Nicoletti. "Nicoletti, do you think marriage could work between a younger man and an older woman?"

Nicoletti stared out the window. "That's the problem with this case. Any one of them *could* have done it."

"Nicoletti, have you ever considered marrying again?" Rocko asked.

Nicoletti turned around and looked at Rocko. "Do you want to become a detective, Rocko, or would you rather sign on as an assistant to Dear Abby?"

Rocko grinned. "Love is torture," he said.

"Go home, Rocko. We'll talk tomorrow."

After Rocko left, Nicoletti stood by the window gazing out at the cityscape, the Brooklyn Bridge, the city lights, New York's neon dream, a city as various as snowflakes, a city of doors and windows, a city that turned in toward itself with people fretting over their dreams and fears in private hells and heavens.

And how far would a person go to realize a love, a hope, a dream, a hate?

Nicoletti opened the window and stood gulping in the cold night air. He knew how far he would go. He was ready, anxious, to go the distance to find Mark Exeter's killer.

•16•

TUESDAY morning. At *Tomorrow* a controlled hysteria clutched the staff in its sweaty grip. Editor Win Gates's directive to get out and "dig, dig, dig" for sensational material struck greater terror in the hearts of writers and reporters than Mark Exeter's death or Lotte Van Buren's attempted poisoning. What would they dig for?

Tomorrow came by its tag, the "think" newsweekly, honestly. The majority of the staff spent their time thinking—about paying the rent, love affairs, a novel in progress. A small amount of time was devoted to writing or reporting.

Personalities was one exception; public-relations special events and celebrity visits to New York provided Felix Magill and Theo Marlow with a steady stream of material for their Tiffany-gilt gossip column.

"Yucky," Theo spluttered at Felix. "That's what I think about doing an item on an ancient burlesque dancer's revelations of her affair with America's most famous novelist, Samson Cody."

"Perhaps," Felix replied, holding a glossy photo to the light. "Still, this isn't a bad picture of Bubbles Peck and Cody on a burro. Never published before. And the publisher said they'd give us a break on quotes from Peck's book."

"I don't believe the item or the picture," Theo reported. "It's probably trick photography."

"Theo, you must learn the difference between cynicism and healthy respect for a good story. We'll do the item." Felix thought for a moment. "Peck's revelations aren't too juicy. We'll beef up the book with some fresh quotes from her. And we'll run a current picture of her next to the old one. People love that 'gee whiz' kind of item."

"Gee whiz?"

"Yeah. Gee whiz, doesn't Bubbles Peck look ugly. Or, gee whiz, she must have had a face-lift."

Theo scribbled on a long yellow pad. "Okay, Felix, item one: Bubbles Peck and macho writer."

"Peck is in New York for her book promotion. Take her to lunch. Ask her if she did her famous tassel dance for Cody." Felix scratched his head. "Also, cable our Los Angeles bureau and ask them to get some quotes from the neighbors where they had adjacent houses."

Theo and Felix continued putting their story list together, twenty items that, by the end of the week, would be pared down to ten pungent paragraphs. The items would pop out at the reader, lending the appearance that *Tomorrow* was on intimate terms with the high and mighty. Felix frequently pointed out that Personalities was the most popular department in the magazine. Readers turned to the spicy hors d'oeuvres first, before digging into the magazine's more intellectual contents.

The effortless quality of the column was the result of endless research and digging. Theo and Felix read and clipped the daily papers, local and foreign, searching for items to titillate *Tomorrow*'s readers; talked with press agents; attended public-relations hooplas; followed elusive stars around town; routed people out of bed in the middle of the night for a pithy quote; spent hours on the telephone. In toto, they were relentless.

Felix paused in making up the story list to examine a bunch of copies of letters to the editor that had popped into his in basket. "Tsk, tsk, Theo," Felix said. "Here are three letters saying that the little Broadway moppet we did an item on last week is thirteen years old, not ten."

"Ridiculous," Theo sniffed. "I checked two sources and talked with her mother. Anyway, I saw her. She looks ten."

"One can never be too sure," Felix said. "Particularly with stage mommas around. The kid's mother probably burned her birth certificate."

After Felix completed the writing of the items, Theo checked every fact and underscored it, citing at least two sources to prove its accuracy. An actress's age, for instance, would be checked in her biography, *Who's Who in America*, and *Celebrity Register*. If the dates did not jibe, Theo would call the actress on the phone and ask her age. Depending on the actress's love of the press or her state of inebriation, the actress might answer Theo, curse her, or slam down the phone.

If a fact proved wrong, Theo rather than Felix would be brought to task.

The hour wore on, with Theo and Felix batting ideas back and forth. A baseball star was lending his name to a "natural" breakfast cereal and Toasto Bostos would be served at a champagne breakfast for the press. A rock star was posing in a department store window in an astronaut's outfit to promote his new album, *Spaced*. On the occasion of her ninetieth birthday, America's most famous hostess would be asked to name the ten guests she loved the most and loathed the most.

Felix pulled a pile of photographs from his drawer. It was the week's harvest from publicity agents promoting everyone from wet-behind-the-ears comedians to statesmen. He kept the scantily clad cheesecake shots on top of the pile and took an occasional look to refresh himself.

Felix looked through the photos. He stared down at one shot. "Here's one we should do, Theo."

"Who's that?"

Felix looked at Theo over the photo. "Vane Wills. She's going to play Meg in a remake of the film *Little Women*. Here's a snap of her in Victorian garb."

Theo glanced over at the photo. "It's not particularly newsworthy, Felix."

"Of course it is, Theo," Felix said, waving his cigar in the air. "Brave widow, left in relative poverty by millionaire husband, fights back with film role."

Theo looked at the photo again. "We'll do it," she said. "I'll interview Wills."

"Good girl, Theo," Felix said. The Vane Wills item was the last one on the story list, which, when completed, would be typed, photocopied, and circulated to all the magazine's departments.

Theo typed up the list and took it to the mail room to be copied and distributed. She stopped by the cable desk, where the editor, a masochist whose wife tortured him by putting shells in his egg salad sandwiches, was gulping Valium.

Following Gates's directive, every department was sending double the usual number of cables to the magazine's bureaus. The cable editor, who practiced creativity by translating everything into "cable-ese" ("Send immediately" became "Soonest send"), was being denied this pleasure by sheer volume.

Theo left him to his harried devices and went back upstairs. She poked her head into the newly annointed Isms, formerly Religion, office. A piece of yellow paper Scotch-taped to the door declared "Isms" in red grease pencil. Underneath, someone had inked "Or isn't 'ims" and sketched a cooing baby.

Emmy was reading the *The Orthodox Observer*. Byron Manos, his back turned to her, read a book of poetry.

Walking in, Theo sniffed the air. "Incense?" she asked.

Blushing faintly, Emmy looked up. "Byron gave me a copy of his book *The Antic Wine*, so I reciprocated with the incense burner."

A small brass incense burner sat on Manos's desk. As Theo entered, he turned and smiled at her. "Come in, Theo, and tell us what scandal you and Felix are brewing up for *Tomorrow*'s readers."

Theo perched on the edge of Emmy's desk. "We're resurrecting Bubbles Peck, the burlesque dancer, who tells all about an affair with Samson Cody in her memoirs. The publisher is giving us a break on the story."

"Wicked, Theo," Manos said. "Well, old Bubbles Peck could probably use the publicity."

"And what's happening in Isms?" Theo asked.

Manos's expression was melancholy. "Gates wants us to do a piece on a witch's coven in Washington, D.C. Supposedly the wives of several senators belong to it."

"Are you doing the story?" Theo asked.

"Yes," Manos said. "This place used to remind me of a library. Now it feels like a hash house at rush hour. Slap some parsley on the food. Make the dish look appealing even if it doesn't taste good."

"Yucky," Emmy said.

"Emmy, how did we start using the word *yucky*?" Theo asked. "We're falling into the jargon trap."

"Jargon's all around us," Emmy answered. "Last night at my group therapy meeting this fellow said to me, 'I don't know where you're coming from.' I said, 'I'm from Scarsdale,' and he said, 'I mean, where are you coming from?' " Emmy raised her eyebrows. "Yucky."

"Superyucky," Theo answered.

Felix appeared in the doorway, his voice sounding strangled, his face red. "Theo, an emergency." Felix clutched a crumpled copy of the newly copied Personalities story list in his hand.

Theo left Manos and Emmy and followed Felix across the hall. Felix closed the door before he exploded. "Win Gates rejected half the items on the list," Felix huffed. "He said to forget Bubbles Peck. He says she's too *old* for the *Tomorrow* reader."

"I told you it was a crummy item," Theo answered.

"Crummy!" Felix exclaimed. "It's news. Doesn't Win Gates know *news*???!!!"

"Maybe Bubbles Peck's fame hasn't spread to Australia," Theo said. "Maybe Gates isn't interested in old tassel dancers."

"I'll quit," Felix said. "I won't put up with being shot down by Win Gates every week."

"Oh, Felix," Theo said. "First you hated Exeter. Now you're down on Gates. Give him a chance."

"*Tomorrow* is just dog-eat-dog," Felix said. His bald head was red, a magenta dome, a sure sign that his temper had been pushed to the limits.

Nicoletti walked in.

"Felix, could I talk with you for a minute?" Nicoletti asked.

"Why not?" Felix said. "Everyone else is offering their views."

"I'll be across the hall," Theo said, leaving the office.

"Something wrong?" Nicoletti asked.

"Nothing unusual, Nose," Felix said. "What do you want to talk about?"

"Friday night, there was a lot of traffic at the magazine, people coming and going, yet nobody saw anybody else. Can you explain that?"

"Sure," Felix said. "I had my door closed because I was writing the new cover story. And everybody else closed their doors—those who stayed behind—because they were indulging in *Tomorrow*'s favorite pastime, gossip. About Exeter. About Patterson, and so on. So nobody saw anybody."

"What time did you go into the sleeping room, Felix?"

"About 3:30. I conked out right away. I didn't wake up until the police arrived to tell me the good news about Exeter."

"You didn't hear anything?"

"Hear? I was dead to the world."

125

"And just you and Theo were in your office working on the new cover story?"

"That's right." Felix picked up the magazine and turned to the story on America's ten top models. "I wrote a lead-in about the modeling industry, et cetera, and then gave each model a separate copy block, just the way I write Personalities. Theo checked the story. Earlier Emmy Kaufman and Lotte Van Buren had helped check some of the facts, but they had left."

"Do you remember anything unusual about Friday night?"

"Unusual?" Felix said heatedly. "Everything was unusual. I locked myself in the office to avoid the zoolike atmosphere and Mark Exeter. It was a sick night. Theo was in a rotten mood. And Theo and I got little or no cooperation from the rest of the staff. The two of us were like shipwrecked sailors on a desert island."

Felix twirled his thumb. "I still feel that way."

"How's Gates as an editor?" Nicoletti asked.

"He's a bitch," Felix answered.

Felix's phone rang.

Felix picked up the phone. Nicoletti could hear the squawking in Felix's ear, with Felix responding, "Yes? Yes? What?" in tones of growing anger. Felix's bald head turned a darker red. He slammed the phone down and jumped up from his chair. "That was the *Wall Street Journal* calling," Felix spluttered. His voice sounded strangled. "Brandon Motors wants to buy *Tomorrow*. They can't do this!"

Eddy O'Brien hurried down the hall in sneakered feet, waving a piece of wire service copy. "The Brandon bandits are after *Tomorrow*, hot damn," Eddy said.

Striding through the magazine's corridors to Win Gates's office with Felix, Nicoletti heard buzzing, dark laughter, stoical response to fresh alarms.

"Treat us like prostitutes," a reporter said.

"Brandon, they're corrupt," an editor exploded.

"No wonder Eli Patterson murdered Exeter," an intern sulked.

"I was just getting used to the Exeter Enterprises gang," the Politics editor muttered.

"At least they're newspeople. Of a sort. But Brandon Motors? The ugly marriage of big business and news," the Foreign editor said.

Publisher Parker Johnson was in Winston Gates's office, with Gates talking on the phone. As Nicoletti and Felix walked in, Gates slammed down the phone. "Son of a bitch, it's true," Gates said. "Why didn't old man Exeter tell me. Brandon Motors wants to buy *Tomorrow*." Gates turned to Johnson. "Parker, you're the Brandon liaison man. You must have known. You probably negotiated the deal."

Johnson puffed his pipe. "Wrong-o, Win. My hands are clean. I'm as surprised as you are."

"Damn, damn," Gates shouted, slamming things around on his desk. "I can't stomach it." His ebony face took on a purplish hue.

Johnson continued to puff quietly on his pipe. "Win, try and take a broader view. Brandon is a socially responsible organization. They practically support public broadcasting on TV single-handed. They sponsored the Mark Twain series." He looked earnestly at Gates.

"You're boring me, Johnson," Gates said.

"I believe you're overreacting, Win," Johnson said.

Gates leaned across the desk. "I'm a newsman, not a car salesman. I want this magazine to survive. But I draw the line at Brandon. Their big-business attitudes will color everything we print." Gates pounded his fist against his hand.

"*Why* does Brandon want to buy *Tomorrow*?" Nicoletti asked.

"They claim for diversification," Gates said. He sat down.

"Diversify!" Felix spluttered. "They want Patterson's cover story exposé on Brandon Motors. Little do they know that the material's vanished along with Patterson."

Gates turned to Parker Johnson. "What was *in* that Brandon story?"

"Six of one and half a dozen of the other," Johnson said. "I don't know."

Gates looked over at Nicoletti. "I'd like to talk with Nicoletti alone for a few minutes," he said, turning to Felix and Parker Johnson. "Reassure everyone that old man Exeter will *not* sell to Brandon. I'll be sending around a memo to quash the story."

"Right-o," Johnson said. "Keep things on an even keel."

"Pfffft," Felix muttered.

Felix and Johnson left Gates's office.

"What's really happening?" Nicoletti asked.

Gates lowered his voice. "The old man told me he's definitely selling *Tomorrow* to Brandon. I begged him to hold off on the decision. He gave me until Friday to try and change his mind."

"And what could sway old Exeter?" Nicoletti asked.

"Two things," Gates said. "Exposing Brandon for the rotten bastards they really are. And finding the person who killed Mark Exeter."

"By Friday," Nicoletti said. "A tall order."

"A desperate order," Gates answered.

"On the subject of murder, Gates, you told me you were in Sydney, Australia, the night Exeter was killed," Nicoletti said. "You lied. You landed in San Francisco that morning and came directly to New York."

"I was up all night talking to the top men at *Newsweek*," Gates said. "They wanted me to join them, but I always take the best offer, the highest salary and the most perks."

"I thought you showed signs of being a human being, Gates," Nicoletti said.

"Call me a pragmatist," Gates answered. "I like to keep my idealism in reserve."

"I think maybe I believe you," Nicoletti said.

Nicoletti left Gates's office, walked to his gray cubicle, closed the door, unlocked the desk drawer, and took out the notes he had made on the *Tomorrow* case. Underneath the notes sat the pencil box, Eddy O'Brien's farewell gift to Eli Patterson. Nicoletti took it out of the drawer and opened it to gaze at sharpened pencils and fishing hooks. He called Eddy in the mail room and asked him to come down to his office.

Eddy scampered in looking cheerful. "Looks like they're going to sell the joint, Nicoletti," he said. "Might be headed for Mexico sooner than I thought."

"Eddy, why did you put fishing hooks in the pencil box you gave Patterson? In the note you said: 'Catch the Big One.' I assumed you meant Exeter. Was I right?"

"Of course not," Eddy said. "I thought you knew. Patterson is a great fisherman. Fishing was his favorite relaxation. He told few people, but, of course, I was his confidant. Ran into him when I was fishing in Okrakoke."

"Where is Okrakoke?"

"It's a teeny, tiny island at the tip of Cape Hatteras, North Carolina. Not a lot of people know about it."

"Did Patterson go there frequently?"

"Certainly did. In fact, I believe he stayed on Saint Helena, which is an even smaller island, off the shore of Okrakoke."

"How do you get to Saint Helena?" Nicoletti asked.

"Fly to North Carolina, drive to Okrakoke. Then you have to know one of the boys on Okrakoke, get them to take you over on a boat. I know them well."

"Would Saint Helena be a good place to hide?"

"Perfect place," Eddy said.

"Eddy, how would you like to go on a fishing expedition?"

"Delighted," Eddy said. "In fact, I even have a new rod I bought to take south of the border."

"Grab your fishing rod, Eddy," Nicoletti said, "And then we'll go straight to the airport."

It was a hunch, Nicoletti thought, taken on the information of a semisenile copy "boy," but maybe it was a hunch that would work.

•17•

NICOLETTI watched Eddy O'Brien with annoyed amusement as they stood on the deck of the ferry carrying them from the tip of Cape Hatteras to the island of Okrakoke, North Carolina. Madness, Nicoletti said to himself. A plane trip to Washington, D.C.; then to Newbury, North Carolina; the breakneck-speed drive down Cape Hatteras in the rented car. He and Eddy were the only passengers on the late-afternoon ferry. Eddy stood by the rail blithely tossing popcorn to the gulls flying alongside them, the gulls crying out as they caught white pellets in their beaks.

"Look at that, Nicoletti,' Eddy said. "Amazing the way they snap that popcorn up." The popcorn exhausted, Eddy took deep breaths of air, stretching his arms up like an aging Nature Boy. "This is God's country, to be sure."

"Enjoying the trip, Eddy?" Nicoletti asked dryly, watching Okrakoke get closer and its wild horses dancing by the shore.

"Heh, heh," Eddy cackled. "You're a sport, Nicoletti."

As the ferry creaked into the dock, Nicoletti and Eddy got back in the car. Seated next to Nicoletti in the front seat, Eddy rubbed his hands together.

"We're getting warm. I feel it in my Irish bones," Eddy said. "Now, when we get off the ferry, we drive down the main road to the dock. I'll find Clem Jakes and he'll run us to our destination."

Nicoletti drove past Okrakoke's small pastel houses and parked the car on the dock by the crescent-shaped bay. Eddy skipped off to knock on the door of a pink house and emerged a few minutes later with a muscular man with a long, weathered face.

"Clem's the name," he said. "Climb aboard." He pointed to a power motorboat. As they got in, he lit a pipe and revved up the engine, and, spray flying in their faces, they were off to the tiny island the natives called Saint Helena.

"Don't see many folks this time of year," Jakes chatted. "Too early in the season. Only visitors we get is maybe a couple from Washington, D.C., pretending to be man and wife. Don't fool me. Don't approve of it. Of course, you take Saint Helena. Nobody goes there never. Just three people live on the island, year round. Nothing there but a few dead turtles. You fellows going there for any particular reason?"

"Just fishing," Eddy said, holding the fishing rod firmly.

"We're looking for a friend," Nicoletti answered.

"Funny place to find him," Jakes mused. "Haven't taken anyone there in months."

As the boat pulled up to the shore of the small island, Nicoletti handed Jakes fifty dollars and said: "Wait for us. We won't be long."

The island looked deserted. Nicoletti could see from one end of the scrubby place to another. A huge turtle shell sat marooned on the beach. Nothing stirred or moved in the waning sunlight. Except for the lapping of the waves, silence.

Nicoletti walked up the sand dune. Over the rise, behind the dune, was a small gray weathered house. Nicoletti walked towards the house, Eddy behind him. As the sun dropped lower, a chill filled the air. Dilapidated wooden steps creaked under Eddy and Nicoletti as they approached the door.

Nicoletti knocked on the door. No answer. He knocked again. Wind whipped through his jacket. "Anybody home?" Nicoletti called.

"Yoo hoo," Eddy chimed in.

Silence.

Nicoletti pounded on the door.

The door opened. A skinny woman with short, iron-gray hair and straight bangs poked her head out. "Breeze must have blown away the No Trespassing sign, fellow," she said flatly. Her eyes were framed by pale blue, rhinestone-studded glasses.

"Sorry to disturb you," Nicoletti said. "We're looking for a friend."

"Ain't no one around here, young man," she said. "Hardly a soul."

"Can we come in?" Nicoletti asked. "We'll just warm up for a few minutes."

"If I was you, I'd head back to Okrakoke and have me a hot supper at Whistling Bill's. Real nice Virginia ham and grits. Least he had them ten years ago. Come to think of it, don't know if Whistling Bill is still alive. If he ain't, I'm sure his son is minding the store."

She started to close the door. Nicoletti held it open with his hand. He got out his card and gave it to her. "We'll only take a few minutes of your time," he said.

The woman examined Nicoletti's card, brushed her finger over the raised surface. "Private investigator," she said. "Fancy."

"Bring them in, Jane," a woman called from inside the door. "We ain't had a visitor in more than five years."

The woman with iron-gray hair reluctantly opened the door. "Come in, if you must. There ain't much to see."

Nicoletti and Eddy stepped into the house.

An elderly black man sat in a rocking chair by a potbellied stove and read a Bible by a kerosene lamp. An enormously fat woman, with cotton stockings rolled up around her knees, sat on a couch knitting, her chubby hands flying, her clicking needles the only sound in the sparsely furnished room.

Nicoletti introduced himself and Eddy, who stood next to him shuffling from foot to foot.

The woman who opened the door responded by pointing to the man in the rocker. "That's my husband, Tom Jones. Tom and I married many years ago, back when a black and white together was a problem. Came to Saint Helena to live." She pointed to the fat woman. "That's my sister, Ruthy. Together we make the fat and the lean. She knits sweaters and sells them to the tourists on Okrakoke. I'm Jane Jones."

The black man nodded a grave greeting and returned to his Bible. The fat woman waved her knitting at them. "Hello, handsome," she said to Nicoletti, offering him a toothless grin.

"Don't mind her," Jane Jones said. "She's a little cracked."

Nobody asked them to sit down.

"We're looking for a friend," Nicoletti said.

"We are alone here on the island," the black man responded.

"You want to be my friend, good-looking?" Ruthy, the fat lady, giggled.

"Hush up, Ruthy," Jane Jones hissed.

The trio stared silently at Nicoletti and Eddy.

132

A primitive painting of a horse hung over the ash-swept fireplace. It was the room's only decoration.

"Nice painting," Nicoletti said.

"Tom does those," Jane Jones answered. "Only knows how to paint one thing, wild horses. Sells them in Okrakoke. Five years ago a big art man came here and wanted Tom to come to New York. Said he'd give him a show, get his name in the papers. Tom didn't take to that, nor did Ruthy or me. We'll stay put where we are."

Nicoletti looked around. Two doors opened onto bedrooms, revealing neatly made beds and clothes hanging on pegs. The kitchen and living room were one, with an old black stove in the corner next to the sink.

"A cozy place," Nicoletti said. "Are there any more rooms?"

"What you see is what there is," Jane Jones said. "We manage."

"Do you mind if I look around?" Nicoletti asked.

Tom Jones looked up from his Bible. "We do not welcome snoops on Saint Helena," he said.

"Tell it like it is, Tommy," fat Ruthy giggled.

"May I trouble you to use your bathroom before I leave?" Nicoletti asked. The trio exchanged glances. The black man pointed to a closed door. Nicoletti went into the bathroom and ran water in the sink. There was no place for a person to hide here, not even under the claw-footed bathtub. Frustration. The trio were in cahoots, hiding something, somebody. But where?

"Are there any other houses on Saint Helena?" Nicoletti asked, coming back into the front room.

"That's a laugh," fat Ruth crossed her chubby knees. "What do you think Saint Helena's is? The Howard Johnson Motel?" She rocked with laughter.

Jane Jones held the door open for them.

"Thanks for the hospitality," Nicoletti said. Nicoletti and Eddy walked out of the house. The door slammed behind them.

"Wild-goose department, Nicoletti," Eddy said. "Too bad."

They started to walk up the dune and back to the boat. Nicoletti stood still for a moment, listening. Faintly, very faintly, he heard a rat-a-tat, rat-a-tat. He turned around and walked back behind the gray house, Eddy trailing along. Almost hidden by the bush, old wood blending in with it, was a weathered shack. As Nicoletti moved towards it, trailed by a reluctant Eddy, the sounds became more distinct. Clickety-click, pause. Clickety-click, pause. A typewriter in slow, staccato motion.

"Help!" Eddy O'Brien screeched. Nicoletti turned quickly.

Eddy was on the ground, flailing with his fishing rod, as fat Ruthy attacked him with her steel knitting needles. Tom Jones was moving up on Nicoletti with a rock in his hand. Jane Jones was in back of him, holding a small fire ax, menace in her eyes.

The hoarse voice came from behind Nicoletti.

"It's okay, Tom, Ruthy, Jane. Leave the bastards alone."

Ruthy got off Eddy. Tom dropped the rock.

Nicoletti turned around.

Eli Patterson, wiry hair in wild disarray, eyes bloodshot, leaned in the doorway of the shack. He wore rumpled slacks and a navy-blue sweater out at the elbows. His chin showed the beginnings of a beard and, even from where he stood, Nicoletti caught the aroma of Scotch. Patterson's mouth tightened in a thin, straight line.

"What brings you two oddly coupled gentlemen to the island of Saint Helena?" he asked, swaying in the doorway.

"A special fishing expedition," Nicoletti said.

"Don't let these guys give you trouble," fat Ruthy shouted to Patterson. "This guy may be cute, but I don't like him."

"Looks like you made some friends, Patterson," Nicoletti said. "And friends are something you definitely could use at the moment."

•18•

"HOW did you find me?" Patterson asked.

"Eddy," Nicoletti answered. "You told him you come here to fish and get away from it all."

"Stuck in my mind," Eddy said.

Patterson's bloodshot eyes focused on Eddy.

"Can we come in and talk?" Nicoletti asked.

Patterson swung open the door to the shack. "My castle," he said with a sweep of his hand. "All the amenities." The shack was furnished with a sagging cot, a small table that held a typewriter, and a wooden chair. A suitcase and shopping bag sat on the floor.

"The gin supply seems to have dwindled," Patterson said. "Will you have Scotch?"

Patterson rounded up a chipped cup, a jelly glass, and a water glass and poured Scotch from a half-gallon bottle that was three-quarters empty. He handed the drinks around. He took the chair by the typewriter, Eddy sat on the cot, and Nicoletti stood by the door.

Patterson took a healthy gulp of his drink. "Do you bring news from the great Mark Exeter?" he asked acidly.

"You live an isolated life here," Nicoletti said. "Haven't you heard?"

"Heard what?"

"Mark Exeter was murdered," Nicoletti said. "You're suspect number one. The police are looking for you."

Patterson stared silently at Nicoletti. Suddenly he was out of the chair, springing across the small floor space to Nicoletti, his strong hands pressing around Nicoletti's neck. "Liar," Patterson shouted. "Slick private eye looking for a victim. Accusing me of murder."

Nicoletti felt blood pulsing in his head. He reached up with one hand and shoved at Patterson's chin, pushed his right fist into

135

Patterson's stomach. Patterson sprawled on the floor, landing against the chair. He shook his head, dazed.

Nicoletti stood over him. "Simmer down, Patterson. You'll disturb the neighbors."

Patterson pulled himself up, sat down in the chair, and reached for his drink. "Cute," he said. "A sick joke. So somebody finally killed the son of a bitch and the police are looking for me." Patterson's eyes glittered. The harlequin mouth turned down at the corners in a grimace. His laugh was an angry bark.

"His skull was bashed in with a bronze Chinese statue," Nicoletti said. "Your fingerprints are all over it. The police matched them up with the prints on a glass on your desk. The night watchman saw you go into the magazine at 3 A.M., drunk and raging for a fight."

"I'm glad Exeter is dead," Patterson said hollowly. He poured more Scotch from the rapidly depleting bottle. "He bought me out along with the magazine. The day he arrived at *Tomorrow*, I walked into his office and resigned. He offered me more money. I stayed. I'm a bum." Patterson sloshed his drink.

"Why did you try to resign?" Nicoletti asked. "You didn't like Exeter's brand of publishing?"

Patterson's voice was bitter. "If it weren't for Exeter, my wife would still be alive."

"Ah, yes," Eddy said. "A beautiful girl, a sad story."

"We were living in Turkey," Patterson continued. "I was a correspondent for *Tomorrow*. Yvette was a free-lance photographer. She went to London for a month on assignment and met the great womanizer, Mark Exeter. She had an affair with him."

"And?" Nicoletti asked.

"She came back and told me about it when we were driving through the Turkish mountains. True confessions. My blood boiled. I raced the car. Yvette begged me to slow down. I smashed into a truck on a curve. She was killed instantly. I survived." Patterson stared into space. "For nothing. Dumb. A waste."

"I'm sorry," Nicoletti said.

Eddy tsk-tsked softly.

"Patterson, tell me what happened Friday night," Nicoletti said "Why did you go back to the magazine?"

"None of your damned business." The freckles stood out on Patterson's pale skin.

136

"Did you go back to pick up the background on the Brandon Motors story? The file is missing."

"I'm not that nuts, Nicoletti. Why would I want the background on the Brandon story? Didn't it cause me enough grief? Do you think I wanted to lug it around with me, an old magazine souvenir?"

"What did you take out in the shopping bag?"

Patterson snorted. "If you must know, it was the unfinished manuscript of my novel." He pointed to a stack of paper by the typewriter. "Call it a work in progress."

"The night watchman at *Tomorrow* says you looked drunk Friday night when you came back to the magazine."

"Sure I was drunk, and in a black rage," Patterson said. "If I saw Exeter, I was planning to sock him in the jaw. He wasn't in his office. I picked up the Chinese statue and weighed it in my hand, thinking it would be great to heave Exeter's prize possession through the window.

"But I took pity on the poor slobs who might be passing on the sidewalk and get clunked on the head. I put the statue down. I left without seeing Exeter or anyone."

"The doorman in your apartment building said your right hand was bloody."

"I smashed it against the wall in the men's room in a bar on Third Avenue." Patterson was sunk in drunken gloom. "So instead of writing a story, I'm part of a story. I hope the papers get the facts straight."

Nicoletti poured the Scotch from his glass into Patterson's cup. The former editor drank it gratefully.

"Exeter," Patterson mumbled. "The British creep. Killing the Brandon Motors exposé. Story of a decade."

"Patterson, what was the Brandon Motors exposé about?"

Patterson's head wobbled as he shook it from side to side, his voice slurring. "Top secret," he said, wiping his mouth with his hand. He picked up the Scotch bottle and poured the last trickling drops into the chipped cup. "I could use a drink."

Nicoletti reached into his jacket's inside pocket and produced a thin pewter flask. He held it out to Patterson.

"I'll swap you a drink for a story," Nicoletti said.

Patterson continued to shake his head from side to side. Then he reached out an unsteady hand for the flask. "What the hell," he said.

"Story never see the light of day, anyway." Patterson opened the flask and took a healthy slug of brandy.

"It's like this," Patterson went on. "Brandon Motors has an intricate system for monitoring their own employees, bugging offices, keeping tabs on their home life."

"Big brother is watching you," Nicoletti said.

"That's not the worst. They also spy on other companies."

"How's that?"

"They have well-placed spies in development laboratories, working to find out if there's anything new in the world of cars. Suppose Brandon hears that some guy at Ford is developing a new substance that goes into oil and lowers engine friction. They'll go to that guy and offer him double the salary to come to Brandon."

"The American system of free enterprise," Nicoletti said. "What's so shocking?"

"The guy goes to Brandon at double the salary he made before. He buys a bigger house, sends his kids to better schools, dines out at the country club. American upward mobility. Then Brandon shelves the new development because Brandon doesn't want to lower engine friction. Brandon wants cars to wear out. They'll sell more cars. See, Nicoletti? All dollars and cents. A crock." Patterson poured brandy into the cup.

"You learned that Brandon's holding out on some new development?" Nicoletti asked. "A new invention?"

A sudden gust of wind made the shack rattle. The three men sat in shadowed, rapidly fading twilight. Patterson stood up slowly, walked unsteadily to the corner, and, after fumbling in his pocket for matches, lit a gasoline lamp suspended from the ceiling. In the lamp's glow, Patterson's face was gaunt and drawn.

"Yes, I interviewed one of the poor slobs who works for Brandon." Patterson sat down heavily.

"Who?"

"No names, please," Patterson held up a hand. "A little guy who has a hard time getting his socks on in the morning. But he's a genius." A wan grin spread across Patterson's face. "He's perfected a solar-energy car, a car that gobbles up sunbeams instead of gasoline. And it could be manufactured for peanuts. It would blow the Arabs and their oil business right off the map, change the face of civilization.

Good-bye, energy crisis! Hello, fume-free America!" Patterson raised the flask and gulped; brandy trickled down his chin.

"Has the car been built?" Nicoletti asked.

"Sure. I rode in the damn buggy. It's surreal. It's silent. You purr down the road."

"And what happened to it?"

"Brandon was going to put it into production. Then they decided to shelve it. And they put a tight security lid on it. The inventor built his own prototype and keeps it in his garage under wraps."

"Why doesn't the inventor go to another car manufacturer?"

Patterson laughed. "For a detective, you're pretty naive, Nicoletti. He's scared. Brandon is paying him a lot of money to keep quiet."

"Why did the inventor talk to you?" Nicoletti asked.

"Because underneath that sappy, paid-for soul is a fat, healthy ego. He wants the world to know about his invention."

"Wouldn't Brandon stand to make a fortune on the solar-energy car?"

"Ha!" Patterson barked. "Someday, but right now they have millions of gas guzzlers they want to unload on the public. Money. It's the name of the game, Nicoletti."

"Can you back up what you just told me?"

"It's all in the research file. Names. Dates. Quotes. Transcribed interviews."

"But the file is missing," Nicoletti said.

"So it's in my head."

At the moment Patterson's head didn't seem like a safe place. The former editor gulped the last swallow of brandy. "Think of the public outrage. The story would be bigger than Watergate." Patterson's voice slurred.

Patterson stood up, staggered to the door. "Excuse me," he said, and wove out the door.

Nicoletti looked around the shack. A jacket hung on a peg. Nicoletti looked through the pockets. A wallet with credit cards, $250 in cash, a photograph of a dark, lovely young woman. A clipping was torn from yesterday's paper: "Police Seek Editor."

Patterson walked wearily back into the shack.

"I always feel better after I throw up," Patterson said.

Nicoletti handed him the newspaper clipping. Patterson took it from him, crumpled it into a ball, and threw it on the floor. "I went into Okrakoke this morning," he said. "That's when I found out I was on the 'most-wanted' list."

"Your friends tried to protect you," Nicoletti said.

"The neighbors and Clem Jakes know me as Grant James, the novelist, not Eli Patterson, the editor. We made a pact years ago that I'm not here. No visitors. No dogs allowed."

Patterson swayed towards the cot and collapsed on it.

"Tired," Patterson said.

"Patterson, what's the name of the inventor, the one who keeps the solar-energy car in his garage?"

"Archie K-E-R-R, pronounced *car*, as in Deborah Kerr. Isn't that a gas?" Patterson passed out.

A full moon beamed down on the silvery sands of Saint Helena Island as Nicoletti and Eddy walked down to Clem Jakes and the waiting boat. Nicoletti carried Eli Patterson slung over his shoulder while Eddy toted the suitcase and shopping bag filled with Patterson's manuscript.

Through the lit window of the gray house on the dune, three faces watched. Nicoletti was sure he saw fat Ruthy wave good-bye.

•19•

NICOLETTI read the newspapers on the plane to Detroit. New York's leading tabloid carried a full-page picture of a haggard Eli Patterson walking into police headquarters with Eddy O'Brien by his side. "EDITOR PLEADS INNOCENT," the headline said, followed by the subhead "Tells Fishing Story." The paper quoted Patterson on his quitting the magazine, retreating to Saint Helena to "work on a book," and being unaware of the murder of Mark Exeter until he "ran into" Eddy O'Brien. In the body of the story, Eddy managed to drop a few quotes, including the information that he was Eddy of the famed "Little O'Briens."

Spurning the plastic-looking eggs offered by a drowsy-eyed stewardess, Nicoletti settled for a cup of black coffee. Surrounded by gray-suited midwestern businessmen, he experienced the disorientation of a New Yorker out of his habitat.

In the Detroit airport, Nicoletti found a phone booth, dialed Brandon Motors, and asked for Archie Kerr. The phone rang ten times before someone picked it up.

"Mr. Kerr is not in the office. Can I take a message?"

"No, thank you." Nicoletti went through the suburban phone directories. Archibald Kerr, Grosse Point. Nicoletti hailed a cab and gave Kerr's address.

The cab pulled up in front of a palatial-looking residence of brick, stone, and glass, a castle replete with turrets. All it lacked was a moat. Nicoletti rang the bell, then pounded on the brass knocker. No answer. He stood back from the door and looked up at the house.

A pale face appeared at the first-floor window, then vanished. The door opened. A slender woman in denim overalls answered the door. She gave Nicoletti a worried look. "Who are you looking for?"

"Is Mr. Kerr at home?"

She peered through thick glasses. Her straight, wispy hair was held back by barrettes. On first appearance she looked about sixteen, but on second look Nicoletti realized that she was at least thirty.

"I'm sorry. Mr. Kerr is ill. He can't see anyone."

"It's important," Nicoletti said. "I'm a friend of Eli Patterson. Mr. Kerr knows him. Patterson interviewed him for a story on Brandon Motors." Nicoletti took out his card and handed it to her. "I'm a private investigator, Nick Nicoletti."

Her face went white. She started to close the door on Nicoletti when a small man with large glasses, looking like her brother, stepped out of the shadows behind her.

"It's all right," he said, putting a hand on the woman's shoulder. "This is my wife, Matilda, Mr. Nicoletti. I'm Archie Kerr. Come in."

Kerr led Nicoletti into a vast living room. In contrast to the luxurious surroundings, the inventor wore old chinos and a frayed shirt. His pale eyes behind the bifocals looked soft and sad. His voice was high and squeaky. "I'm on temporary leave of absence from Brandon," he said, rubbing his small hands together. "I read about Patterson in the papers. I know he's suspected of killing the publisher of *Tomorrow*."

"Patterson was planning to run the exposé on Brandon. At the last minute Mark Exeter killed the story," Nicoletti said. "Patterson quit. Exeter was found murdered. And all the background on the story is missing. Including the material on your solar-energy car."

Kerr rubbed his skinny knees, as though trying to hold himself in the chair. "Yipes," he said. "If that material gets into the wrong hands, it could put me in a pretty pickle with Brandon. I was sworn to secrecy. How did *you* find out?" His voice rose an octave.

"Patterson was drunk and upset. I dragged the information out of him," Nicoletti said. "You can trust me. The only people who know about your invention are you, me, my detective aide in finding Patterson, and Patterson himself."

"And whoever has the background material on the story," Kerr said. "What could have happened to it?"

"Exeter might have destroyed it," Nicoletti said. "Unlikely, though."

"It's the crime of the century," Kerr said, "Suppression of the solar-energy car. I call her Sunbeam. Will she ever see the light of day?"

"Sunbeam isn't the first solar-energy car. What's so special about this one?"

"All the other cars cost a fortune. About thirty thousand dollars each. I developed a device to gather the sun's energy that is small, inexpensive, and totally efficient. Sunbeam could revolutionize transportation. She's a dream."

"If Sunbeam is your brainchild, why do you have to keep quiet about her?" Nicoletti asked.

"Look around you," Archie Kerr said. "This house is why. I gave my brain to Brandon. Not just for a huge salary and this house . . . I never lived in a palace before . . . but they also gave me all the facilities I needed to develop Sunbeam. A wonderful laboratory, perfect secrecy. I felt like a genius, going in there every day to putter and work. Oh, yes. I got the pats on the back, too. All the encouragement in the world. I was able to build a wonderful prototype, a slick working model of Sunbeam. And Brandon loved the car." Kerr's eyes watered. "Then, suddenly, they said they were shelving her production for a future date. They took all the plans, paid me a vast sum of money to keep quiet, and put me on a leave of absence." Kerr took off his glasses and wiped them with a handkerchief.

"Patterson told me you keep the prototype of Sunbeam in your garage," Nicoletti said.

Kerr looked nervously around the huge room. "Sssh. Nobody is supposed to know about that."

"I'd love to see the car, take a ride in her," Nicoletti said.

"Extremely risky," Kerr squeaked. "I only take her out after dark. If you stick around until tonight, I'll take you for a short spin."

Nicoletti's eyelids felt weighted down. He had been up most of the night. "If you have a place where I can take a nap, that's a bargain."

Nicoletti spent the next hours sleeping in a mahogany four-poster in a room with tapestry draperies and old oil paintings on the wall.

Matilda Kerr woke him up. "Come down and have supper," she said. "Then Archie will take you for a ride."

Matilda Kerr served ham, corn, salad, and apple cobbler in the kitchen, a comfortable room with beat-up furniture and a resident cocker spaniel who lapped up kibbled bits in the corner. The formal dining room was ignored.

"Archie and I never really got used to this place," Matilda said.

143

"We're planning to sell it eventually and move to something homier."

"True," Archie agreed, reaching for his second piece of apple cobbler. "The fantasy of living here beat the reality by a mile."

After dinner, the sun long set, Archie Kerr picked up a flashlight and took Nicoletti out the back door, leading him down a long path to the garage. He opened the garage door, closed it behind him, and turned on the flashlight. Then he removed canvas covers from what appeared to be a chunky, oversized box, and flashed the light on Sunbeam.

At first glance, it looked like any small foreign car, a Volkswagen Beetle or the French Deux Cheveaux. It was small, chubby, and yellow. Then Nicoletti noticed the small dome at the front of the car that capped a transparent roof. The dome looked like the kind of accessory a teenage automobile enthusiast might add to give his car an individual touch. Kerr pointed to the dome. "That's where she collects sunshine," he said. "She's all charged up. The last time she was out was when I took Eli Patterson for a ride."

Kerr opened the doors, and Nicoletti and he got into the car. With headlights darkened, they drove around the estate, the car purring silently down the tree-lined lanes through the moonless night.

"I'm proud of this car," Kerr said. "I consider it my life's work. When Matilda and I move away from here, I plan to take Sunbeam with me." He sounded like a jealous lover eager to keep his woman by his side.

"Why do you think Brandon's blocked the car's production?" Nicoletti asked.

"Too big a backlog of gas guzzlers they want to unload on the public. The world, and Brandon Motors in particular, does not seem ready for Sunbeam," Archie said. "Certainly the oil companies aren't. Frankly, I think the oil big shots are in cahoots with Brandon, that they're paying Brandon a mighty pile of dough to keep the car off the market."

"What makes you say that?" Nicoletti asked.

"The oil biggies have been flying out to Detroit quite a bit, of late," Archie said. "The word came down the grapevine to me, even though, it seems, Brandon was trying to keep it hush-hush."

They drove back to the castlelike house in silence. As they approached the garage, Nicoletti gave startled thanks they had not taken their joyride any later. Nearing the garage, he saw flames lick the corner of the building. Archie slammed on the brakes. With a roar the garage exploded in a mass of flames that reflected in the bifocals of the stunned inventor.

Archie hugged the steering wheel of the car. "Good grief," he cried. "Holy cats! I didn't have any explosives in the garage, not even a drop of gasoline." He hurriedly backed up the car.

Nicoletti watched the flames leaping toward them. "Archie, it looks like you've been sabotaged."

"It's Brandon," Archie said. "They're trying to blow up Sunbeam. Brandon Motors won't get away with this. I could have been in that garage. I might be the little guy, but the little guy can fight back."

Nicoletti opened the window and felt the heat from the fire on his face. "Brandon must have read about Patterson's turning himself in. Maybe they thought he spilled the story about your car, Archie."

"Brandon creeps," Archie said bitterly. "Just because they contribute to the Home for Retired Auto Workers, they think they can get away with anything."

Matilda Kerr came running out the back door, the dog, Edison, behind her. Archie got out of the car and put his arms around his wife. "We have to leave here, Matilda," he said.

"Do you think Sunbeam could make the trip to New York?" Nicoletti asked.

"She sure can try," Archie said.

"Then let's go," Nicoletti said. "Now, before the fire department and police show up." The Kerrs grabbed their coats and cocker spaniel, locked the doors of the house, and they headed out of Grosse Point in the dark of night. Nicoletti shared the backseat with the dog, a quiet beast who occasionally licked his face.

The group was silent until they were on the thruway past Detroit.

"The price for being a tinkerer at Brandon Motors is too high," Archie said. "Matilda, I'd like to go back to university life. That's where I belong. Teach a few hours and putter around the rest. That's the ticket."

"How about a college in the country?" Matilda said, "with an old house and a place for the dog to run."

"Perfect," Archie said.

Scrunching up his long legs, Nicoletti patted the cocker spaniel on the head. "Archie, would you and Matilda be willing to stay in New York for a few days, under cover, so to speak?"

"I suppose," Archie said. "But why?"

"You want the story about Brandon Motors and Sunbeam to hit the press, don't you?" Nicoletti said. "I think *Tomorrow* magazine might find its way clear to do it, with a splash."

"But how? Why?"

"Trust me," Nicoletti said.

"You saved Sunbeam's life, and maybe mine," Archie said. "We'll do it for you. We owe you."

"Where will we stay in New York?" Matilda Kerr asked. "I'm certainly not dressed for the Plaza."

"I have a downstairs neighbor, a sculptor, Germaine, who has a huge loft and loves visitors and dogs," Nicoletti said.

"And Sunbeam?" Archie asked.

"We'll put her in a garage I use in SoHo," Nicoletti said. "I know the owners. The car will be safe."

"I feel better already," Archie said, as a pale gray light showed on the horizon. "And I think we've run into another bit of luck; today is going to be sunny. As soon as the sun comes up, we'll stop and collect some rays. Even so, we don't have to worry. We've got plenty of energy stored up for the trip. People like myself might eventually run out of gas, but never my Sunbeam."

·20·

IN the SoHo garage in New York, Nicoletti plucked cocker-spaniel hairs from his sleeve while Archie Kerr fussed and fidgeted. Sunbeam was parked in a far corner of the garage, securely covered with canvas. "Don't worry, Archie," Nicoletti said. "The car will be safe. This place has top security, and they know me."

"I guess I'm just a country boy," Archie said, as they left the garage. "The city gets to me."

The Kerrs, their cocker spaniel, Edison, and Nicoletti walked the two blocks to Nicoletti's loft building, where Germaine greeted her guests with open arms. "You're a godsend," Germaine said. "You can pose for my new sculpture series on couples."

Leaving Germaine and the Kerrs and dog, Nicoletti returned gratefully to his loft. His legs ached from being scrunched up in the backseat of the car, against the dog's nose during the thirteen-hour drive from Detroit.

Nicoletti pushed a pile of books off a chair, sat down, and stretched his legs. Rain trickled down the window. The time was 6 P.M., Thursday. It was a blue, rainy day with a London-Whistler mood, the kind of day he usually savored. But today Nicoletti seethed with frustration. Found: Eli Patterson. Learned: the heart of the Brandon exposé, the shelving of the solar-energy car. Missing: background on the Brandon story. Still in question: the identity of a murderer.

Nicoletti looked at the murky green eye, glaring and garish on the canvas. He felt he was standing in front of a new piece of canvas, slashing on paint with a palette knife, attempting to wrest symmetry from chaos, reaching for the connecting element—the red center—to make the painting hang together.

Nicoletti poured a brandy. The phone rang. It was Eddy O'Brien, calling from his room at the Wentworth.

"Looks like I may be breaking the slave chains at *Tomorrow* once

147

again," Eddy said with his usual cheerful cackle. "I thank the power of the press."

"I notice you slipped in a few facts on your dancing career to the reporters who covered Patterson," Nicoletti said.

"Yes, and I've gotten several calls from TV variety shows," Eddy replied. "In fact, I'm tap-dancing on the Joe Franklin Show tomorrow. Who knows? Next week it might be Johnny Carson. An agent wants to take me on as a client."

"In between tap dances, could you do something for me?" Nicoletti asked.

"Always try to oblige," Eddy said.

"Try and remember if somebody who works, or worked, at *Tomorrow* has the initials B.D. I'm not sure if it's a real name. It could be a nickname used by Mark Exeter."

"Does this have to do with murder?" Eddy asked.

"It might," Nicoletti said.

"Tsk, tsk, tsk. I'll ponder it, look through my *Tomorrow* scrapbook, and see if it jogs the memory."

"Thanks, Eddy."

Nicoletti hung up the phone and turned the TV set on, low. An interviewer smiled and chortled as he talked to a famous husband-and-wife team of sex researchers, both of them pudgy and gray-haired, beaming with amiability. Nicoletti could guess what the woman was saying: "Sex is communication. Couples must work at it." From the bland expression on her face, she could have been addressing a garden club. Modern sex: safe and sanitized, uncomplicated by passion.

Switching to the TV news, Nicoletti turned the sound up. Garbage strike imminent. Flu epidemic. A new, battery-operated sled for kids. "Insiders say that Alexander Exeter will definitely sell *Tomorrow* magazine to Brandon Motors. America's 'think' weekly, currently undergoing a revamping, has steadily lost money in recent years . . ." Nicoletti turned the TV off and drank the brandy in a gulp, staring at the murky green eye—enigmatic, waiting, demanding—on the canvas.

Two hours later Nicoletti headed for the subway. Steady rain plopped down on the sidewalks of New York, sending derelicts seeking shelter into doorways and filling the city's subway cars with cranky passengers, steamy, wet, and packed against each other.

At *Tomorrow* Parker Johnson's office looked like headquarters for the commander in chief of an army. A huge map hung on the wall. It was covered with pins, Johnson's circulation targets.

Nicoletti's arrival jarred Johnson out of his revery over special inserts, tie-in promotions, and other schemes to advance *Tomorrow*'s circulation and profits.

Speaking through clenched teeth, Johnson attempted to sound cordial.

"Well, well, burning the midnight oil, too, Nicoletti?" Johnson's voice boomed with false heartiness. "Glad to see it. I myself find it hard to get things done during the daytime. Once the phones start ringing, I simply can't get back to the paperwork."

"I'm not burning the midnight oil," Nicoletti said, pushing aside a pile of promotional brochures and sitting down on the couch. "I came here to talk with you about Brandon Motors."

Johnson puffed on his pipe. "Ah yes, Brandon. They sent a beautiful bouquet of flowers to Exeter's mother. They're what I call 'real people.' 'People-people,' in fact," Johnson replied with a low chuckle. "They're also contributing to the Mark Exeter Scholarship Fund for journalists."

"I suppose Brandon should be eternally grateful to the late Mark Exeter," Nicoletti said.

Johnson's expression soured. His teeth clenched more firmly on the pipe. "Are you still hammering at Exeter's postponing the Brandon Motors exposé? That's a water-over-the-dam issue."

"Not water over the dam," Nicoletti said. "I wonder what happened to the background on the story. Could it have gone up in flames in a fireplace in an eighteenth-century house in Princeton?"

Johnson took the pipe from his mouth and tapped it on the ashtray. His face was beet-red, his voice impatient. "I've been over all this ground with the police. More than once. I didn't take the file and I didn't burn it. If you're trying to pin Exeter's murder on me, you're in the 'wrong-party' department."

"Did I mention murder?"

Some of the wind seemed to go out of Johnson's sails. He sounded calmer.

"Why would I burn up the background on the Brandon Motors exposé, Nicoletti?"

"To cover up a scandal involving yourself, Mark Exeter, and Brandon Motors."

"I'm considering suing you for defamation of character, Nicoletti."

"Save your money," Nicoletti said. "The scandal is Brandon's shelving production of the solar-energy car."

Johnson's face was motionless, a study in blandness. "Solar-energy car? News to me, Nicoletti."

"I met Archie Kerr, the inventor," Nicoletti said. "Brandon's suppressing something that could change the world, for the good. It's criminal." His eyes unwavering, Nicoletti looked straight at Johnson.

Johnson offered Nicoletti a tense smile. "You're all wet, Nicoletti," he said. "Wrong-o. Brandon isn't shelving the solar-energy car." He puffed his pipe and declaimed sonorously. "The car is on the drawing board, but it's under wraps until it's perfected."

"And when will the solar-energy car hit the market?"

"At some future date," Johnson said.

"Meanwhile the price of gasoline will continue to soar."

"The way the cookie crumbles. People don't *have* to own cars. Why don't they use public transportation?"

"So it wasn't your clever presentation that sold Brandon Motors advertising in the magazine. It was a lousy, crooked deal."

"Nicoletti, you don't understand the ABC's of the publishing game. Exeter was a genius. He told Brandon he'd hold off on the story. Then, when Brandon does put the car on the market, *Tomorrow* will do a major cover piece. Brandon, in turn, will take out four-color advertising in the magazine worth a million dollars . . . a huge insert."

"Not legit," Nicoletti said.

"Call it what you want, Nicoletti. I was brought up to carry the ball. To win for my team. Exeter was the coach."

"The true-blue executive," Nicoletti said, standing up.

"You can laugh and smirk at me, Nicoletti," Johnson huffed. "I was raised to believe in old-fashioned values. The home. The family. Raising my kids and supporting and loving my wife. I've never looked at another woman. I'd do anything for my family, and solar-energy cars be damned." Johnson pounded his desk for emphasis.

"I'm a freak, a dinosaur, but it's people like me who keep America glued together."

"Corrupt," Nicoletti said. He turned and left Johnson's office. The door slammed behind him.

Nicoletti walked past empty offices, desks awash with pencils and paper. The magazine felt empty, like a stage setting waiting for the actors to bring it to life. Around him Nicoletti sensed ghostly echoes of people.

The door to the mailroom was closed, but a light seeped under it. Nicoletti pushed the door open.

The lifeless body of Eddy O'Brien was sprawled over the old wooden desk he used to sort mail. Eddy's purple face was turned to the side, his blue eyes popping grotesquely. Knotted tightly around his neck and neatly tied at the back was the piece of mail-room twine that had been used to strangle him.

Instead of his usual T-shirt, Eddy wore a gray suit, white shirt, and green tie. Dressed for the kill.

A final sick and bizarre touch: a piece of brown tape, used to secure packages, was stuck over Eddy's mouth.

Eddy's right hand was stretched out towards a pair of scissors. His left hand formed a fist. Nicoletti opened it and found the torn fragment of a photograph. He looked at it. He saw oversized polka dots on what could have been a blouse, a shirt, a clown's costume. An empty white envelope, Wentworth Hotel stationary, sat on the desk next to Eddy's fist.

Nicoletti put the torn photograph back in Eddy's hand. Touching the still-warm palm, Nicoletti felt his own hand grow cold; his face flushed with hot anger.

Nicoletti went out to the bull pen and switched on the lights. Nobody. He went to the stairway leading to the back-of-the-book department and heard footsteps. Pursuing the footsteps, he ran upstairs, down the pitch-black corridor, the figure in front of him. By the clip desk, they circled, the other person gasping, breathing heavily. Silence. Then movement, the breathing again. Nicoletti moved quietly through the dark and lunged out, bring the figure in front of him down on the floor.

He felt a woman's body under him and smelled, in the dark, Chanel Number 5.

"Theo," he said.

"Nick!" Theo gasped.

Nicoletti stood up and switched on the lights.

Rubbing her shoulder, Theo glared up at him, tears in her eyes. "What are you doing here?" Theo said. "Why are you chasing me?"

"Why were you running?"

"Because it was dark, and I heard footsteps behind me."

"What were you doing downstairs?"

"I picked up a story from the copydesk, an advance. I was coming back upstairs and I heard these footsteps pounding behind me. I was scared." Theo stood up. Her cheek was smudged, and a ball-point-pen mark streaked across her yellow sweater. "I work here, remember? Why are you looking at me like that, as if I were a criminal?" Theo reached down and picked up the copy scattered on the floor.

"Eddy O'Brien is dead, Theo," Nicoletti said. "He was murdered."

Theo shivered, dropping the copy to the floor again. "Oh, no. Not Eddy. How?"

"Strangled to death. In the mail room," Nicoletti said. He walked to the phone on the clip desk and dialed the police number, talking with Sergeant Ajax.

Theo looked blankly at Nicoletti, her body trembling. "How horrible. Eddy." Nicoletti hung up the phone and took off his jacket and put it around Theo's shoulders.

"Was anybody here with you tonight, Theo?"

"No. I didn't see a soul. Nobody." Her teeth were chattering. "What was Eddy doing here, tonight?"

"Coming to meet somebody, I suppose."

"Why in the mail room?"

"Maybe he was meeting somebody who worked at the magazine."

Theo pulled Nicoletti's jacket tighter around her.

"Let me get you a shot of Felix's bourbon, Theo," Nicoletti said.

"I don't want a drink," Theo said, holding her hands out help-lessly. A bright red gash ran across her right palm.

Nicoletti took her hand. "How did you do that?" he asked.

Theo's gold-flecked eyes were black.

"I scratched my hand on the edge of the filing cabinet this morning," Theo said. "No, no, no, I didn't strangle Eddy O'Brien." She sat down on the chair by the clip desk and wept.

152

Nicoletti put his arm around her shoulder. "Cry, Theo," Nicoletti said. "Cry for both of us. If it weren't for me, Eddy might be alive now."

•21•

LOOKING at Eddy's body sprawled across the desk, Sergeant Ajax shook his head. "An outrage, an absolute outrage," he said. "You found him, Nicoletti?"

"Yes," Nicoletti said.

"Look at that," Ajax fumed. "Tape over his mouth. What kind of nuts work at *Tomorrow* magazine? This place is going to drive me to the bin."

A police photographer and medical examiner followed behind Ajax. "Shame," the photographer said as he focused his camera on the late Eddy O'Brien. "I hear the old boy was going to make a show business comeback, tap-dance on the Joe Franklin Show tomorrow night."

Ajax motioned Nicoletti outside.

"Anyone else around here tonight?" Ajax asked.

"Parker Johnson, the new publisher, and Theo Marlow," Nicoletti said. Theo sat in a chair in the bull pen. She looked up from the notebook she was writing in as she heard her name.

"The boys will find Johnson," Ajax said. "I'd like to talk to you and Miss Marlow, Nicoletti. Miss Marlow, first."

Calmly Theo answered Ajax's questions. "I was in my office working on a story. I came downstairs to pick up some copy and then went upstairs. I heard somebody behind me, chasing me. I was scared, so I ran. It was Nick."

She lapsed into silence.

"Please go on, Miss Marlow."

"I liked Eddy. We shared an interest in electric trains. At Christmastime we went to F A O Schwarz to look at the new models."

Ajax listened to Theo patiently. He was tired. Furthermore, cheese was congealing on a half-eaten pizza back at the station. Cocaine was transforming the town's disco crowd into troublemakers who kept him busy all night. Streetwalkers were out looking for problems. Why couldn't they operate out of safe apartments and save him aggravation and the taxpayers, money?

"Yes, Virginia, there is a Santa Claus," Ajax said.

"That's a condescending remark, Sergeant Ajax," Theo said. "I am not crazy."

"Sane people commit murder, Miss Marlow," Ajax answered. "Our prisons are full of them."

"What's your position on capital punishment, Sergeant Ajax?" Theo asked.

"Just answer the questions, Miss Marlow."

It was going to be a long night.

While Theo talked with Ajax, Nicoletti paced restlessly around the bull pen. When he had talked to Eddy earlier, the old man was soaring, feisty, planning his move into the big time of show business. There wasn't a hint of threat or anxiety. Now he was dead, and not in a pretty fashion. Why the tape—a seemingly bizarre touch of symbolism left by a sick killer—over his mouth? Why the meeting in the mail room? Had Eddy turned his back to reach for the scissors—to defend himself—as the strong fingers wound the cord around his neck?

Theo walked over to Nicoletti. "Ajax is through talking with me," she said, giving Nicoletti a cool glance. "You look rotten, Nick."

"I feel worse."

Theo took Nicoletti's jacket off her shoulders and handed it to him. "Thank you," she said.

"Are you all right?" Nicoletti asked.

"I suppose," Theo said. "Eddy. Well, he was a part of the magazine, a part of my life here. Murder. It still doesn't seem real to me."

"It will be when you read about it in the paper tomorrow," Nicoletti said.

"I'm not a total media freak, Nick," Theo said. "All of life doesn't have to be in black and white on page one before I'll believe it."

"That's a good sign," Nicoletti said.

They had been talking in whispers; the spell was broken.

"Good-night, Nick," Theo said crisply. "Good-night, Sergeant Ajax." She walked out to the elevator.

Ajax came over to Nicoletti. "A beaut, that one," Ajax said. "A beautiful girl, but a little crazy, like the rest of the *Tomorrow* crew. That bunch is a real mystery to me."

"In what sense?" Nicoletti asked.

"I'm a student of psychology. You have to be in this business," Ajax said. "I've talked to the whole gang at *Tomorrow*, and there's one thing they have in common. Paranoia. They all feel persecuted. I'd say any one of them is capable of murder."

"But which one would have the nerve?"

"The chutzpah? I'll put my money on Patterson. He's the most paranoiac of all," Ajax said. "I'm getting to know the man fairly well. For instance, we're talking about the novel he wrote under the nom de plume of Grant James. Suddenly this guy breaks into a long-winded diatribe. About how the publishing house didn't do enough publicity on the book. And how he was robbed when a movie company optioned the book for a film and never made it."

"All book authors are crazy on those subjects." Nicoletti said. "At least from my experience. Writing and show business—they're not so far apart."

"Well, this is the last killing at *Tomorrow* magazine," Ajax said. "I'm putting a ring of security around the magazine so tight a fly won't be able to get in the door."

As Ajax talked, Parker Johnson walked into the area accompanied by a cop. Sitting down to wait for Ajax, Johnson opened up the briefcase he carried with him and began going over papers inside it. Spotting Nicoletti, Johnson flashed him a hostile look and returned to his paperwork.

"Looks like the next customer is here, Nicoletti," Ajax said, going over to Johnson.

Nicoletti walked to the elevator, passing Johnson, who was checking his watch, anxious to leave. Nicoletti gave him a bare nod.

Down on the sidewalk, a fat lady in sagging stockings stood on the corner shouting about Franklin D. Roosevelt and Jesus Christ. Rain settled into a fine mist, melting last week's snow, now black slush. Cabs hissed up the avenue towards East Side dinner parties, fine wines, and elegant conversation—"in" New York talk about the latest book and play and maybe even the latest murder.

Lost in thought, Nicoletti almost bumped into a slightly intoxicated executive, who moved laboriously down the street towards a suburban train.

Hands thrust in his pockets, Nicoletti walked towards the Wentworth through Times Square, where cab horns blared in the traffic slowdown caused by the rain. Out-of-town tourists walked past Nicoletti in firm clutches.

Eddy O'Brien's old stone heap of a hotel was still standing, and the receptionist of the sausage curls, heaving breasts, and lollipop was seated at the switchboard. Today she wore a bright red dress and an extra coat of mascara on her eyelashes.

"Mr. Nicoletti," she pouted at him as he approached the desk.

"You remembered my name," he said, smiling and leaning over her switchboard. Her breasts puffed up at the gesture.

"I always remember a handsome fellow," she said coyly. "Wonderful about Eddy, isn't it? Going back to show business. Yesterday I said to him, 'Eddy, I always knew you were gonna be a star.' "

"I was wondering, Miss . . ."

"Millie," she said. "Millie Stark." The eyes batted. "I used to do some dancing myself in the old days. In the chorus line. That's why I work here. Lots of show business people live here and I say it's good to be among your own kind."

"As soon as I saw you, I knew you were engaged in the arts. It shows."

"Well, there's life in the old girl yet," she tittered with delight.

"And the show must go on," Nicoletti said. He took out his private investigator's card and handed it to her, his voice dropping to a conspirator's whisper. "Millie, I need to take a quick look around Eddy's room. I'm a friend of his. He's worried that someone might be bugging his room."

"Listening in on him?" Millie almost swallowed the lollipop. She took it out of her mouth.

"Yes," Nicoletti said.

Millie looked carefully at Nicoletti's card. She scanned the empty reception area, then reached for a key, and gave it to Nicoletti with a wink. "A detective, like Humphrey Bogart in *The Maltese Falcon*. Sexy," Millie said.

"Thanks, Millie."

"Not to worry," Millie answered. "I don't approve of bugging rooms. Gives the hotel a bad name."

Nicoletti took the creaky elevator up to Eddy's room, recalling their earlier phone conversation. Did Eddy know anyone with the in-

157

itials B.D. at the magazine? Eddy had possessed an intriguing mind that operated like an old junk shop, full of odd bits and pieces of information.

Eddy's room was neat as a pin, his clothes hung, the bed made, the cymbal-clanging toy monkey dusted. An arrangement of red carnations decorated the top of the bureau. A card propped up in front of it read: "Congratulations, Gramps, on your comeback. We're cheering from the wings."

Nicoletti searched through the bureau drawers and found bunion pads, a pile of girlie magazines, leopard print shorts, two flannel nightgowns, a pile of handkerchiefs.

The bottom drawer held a large, worn leather scrapbook. Nicoletti took it out and sat down on the wooden chair to look through it.

The earlier pages held yellowed, crumbling clips from newspapers about the Five Little O'Briens, then progressed through Eddy's career as a headliner, his marriage, the bank robbery that sent him to jail. After that, pictures of the grandchildren and photographs taken at *Tomorrow* magazine staff events. A picture of Eddy cutting a birthday cake, surrounded by early members of the *Tomorrow* staff . . . a Christmas party . . . a company picnic.

The last two pages of the scrapbook showed a group of pictures taken at a farewell party for the old publisher just three months ago. At the top of the page, Eddy had written: "So long, Mr. Hendricks, my finest friend." Glossy snapshots caught almost every member of the *Tomorrow* staff, and all in costume: Theo as a dancer, in a short skirt; Lotte Van Buren as a forties' movie star; Emmy Kaufman as a cheerleader; Byron Manos, pirate; Eli Patterson, football player; and Felix Magill, clown.

One snapshot was missing from the page, taken out of the gummed folders, leaving a pale spot on the page. Nicoletti remembered the piece of photograph clutched in the murdered Eddy's hand: a fragment of a person wearing polka dots. Nicoletti looked at the pictures, at Felix Magill, splendidly dressed in a clown's polka-dotted costume, cavorting next to Theo. Felix was the only person dressed in polka dots.

Felix was at the magazine all night when Mark Exeter was writing the cover story. What did he once tell Nicoletti? He couldn't kill, it would be like making love to two women at once, ludicrous, out of scale.

Nicoletti put the scrapbook back in the drawer, turned off the light, and locked the door behind him. Could a missing snapshot point the way to murder?

He returned the key to Millie, who winked him a good-bye. "Keep your powder dry," she called after him as he left the Wentworth Hotel.

On Times Square the gaudy Walpurgis Night of New York was slowing down. A few drifters meandered down the street. A drunk held his hand out to Nicoletti. Nicoletti gave him a quarter.

Nicoletti stopped at a phone booth, put in a dime, gave the operator his credit-card number, and called Felix on Long Island.

Felix's wife answered the phone. No, Felix wasn't home. He was staying in New York for the night, she said. In fact, Felix told her he might be seeing Nicoletti.

Nicoletti thanked her and put the receiver down. Then he kept walking, all the way home.

Nicoletti needed to think, to separate his feelings from the knowledge that when he finally identified the murderer, he might do it with regret, even sorrow. But he could not turn back, could only move forward, piecing together a strange collage. An image sprang to mind: a large painting composed of a Chinese statue, a bloody head, a strangled man, and all through it, the dark purple hues of a man or woman in murderous desperation.

·22·

NEW York's scandal rag carried the story about Eddy on the front page Friday morning:

JIG'S UP FOR MAG'S EDDIE
MAIL ROOM "BOY" MURDERED!

FOR THE THIRD TIME IN A WEEK, A SADISTIC KILLER STRUCK *TOMORROW* MAGAZINE. LAST NIGHT AT 9:10 P.M., EDDY O'BRIEN, 69, MAIL ROOM "BOY" WHO TAP-DANCED HIS WAY TO FAME IN THE TWENTIES, WAS FOUND STRANGLED TO DEATH WITH A ROPE AROUND HIS NECK IN THE MAGAZINE OFFICES.

SEVERAL MEMBERS OF *TOMORROW'S* STAFF WERE AT THE MAGAZINE WHEN THE KILLING OCCURRED. POLICE HAVE NOT YET RELEASED THEIR NAMES AS QUESTIONING CONTINUES.

O'BRIEN, A ONE-TIME VAUDEVILLE STAR, WAS ABOUT TO MAKE A THEATRICAL COMEBACK WITH A NIGHTCLUB TOUR SPONSORED BY TALENT LTD.

SATURDAY MORNING, PUBLISHER MARK EXETER WAS FOUND MURDERED IN HIS *TOMORROW* OFFICE. MR. EXETER DIED OF A CEREBRAL CONCUSSION AFTER HIS HEAD WAS BASHED IN WITH A STATUE.

ON MONDAY CHIEF REPORTER LOTTE VAN BUREN WAS CONFINED TO LENOX HILL HOSPITAL, SUFFERING FROM POISONING.

BRANDON MOTORS HAD A BID IN TO BUY *TOMORROW* MAGAZINE FROM EXETER ENTER-

PRISES. NEITHER BRANDON NOR ALEXANDER EXETER, CHAIRMAN OF EXETER ENTERPRISES, WAS AVAILABLE FOR COMMENT ON THE LATEST MAYHEM AT *TOMOROW*.

TOMORROW EARNED A REPUTATION AS AMERICA'S "THINK" NEWSWEEKLY BUT, DURING THE PAST DECADE, HAS FALLEN ON HARD TIMES, WITH SEVERE DROPS IN CIRCULATION AND ADVERTISING REVENUES.

THE BRUTAL KILLINGS APPEAR TO HAVE PIQUED INTEREST IN THE "DOWAGER OF THE NEWS WORLD." ACCORDING TO SPOT CHECKS IN THE NEW YORK AREA, *TOMORROW* IS SELLING OUT ON NEWSSTANDS.

In his cube at *Tomorrow*, Nicoletti tossed his coat on the rack and put the newspaper down on his desk as Lotte Van Buren appeared in the doorway.

"Nick, how can you read that paper?" Lotte asked, picking it up. Wearing a tweed skirt, beige jacket, and green cashmere sweater, Lotte looked trim and in command, but the large hyperthyroid eyes batted rapidly.

"You don't approve of terms like *sadistic murderer*, Lotte?" Nicoletti said, gesturing to a chair. Lotte remained standing.

She held the paper at arm's length as she scanned the front page. "I object to all of it, the hype, the distortion, and the inaccuracy," Lotte said. "For starters, the paper spelled Eddy's name two different ways. He was seventy, not sixty-nine. He was *not* making a comeback tour; Talent Ltd. merely hinted at the possibility. He was not strangled with a rope, but with twine. And I further object to *Tomorrow*'s being called the 'Dowager of the News World,' " Lotte said, putting the paper down.

Nicoletti tossed it in the wastebasket. "The paper belongs in the round file," he said. "*Tomorrow* will miss Eddy."

"Yes, Eddy counted," Lotte said. "In light of this newest tragedy, somebody has to maintain a semblance of sanity, and I suppose I have been elected." Lotte mustered a smile. "There's an issue to get out, and copy is piling on my desk. We'll talk later, Nick."

Lotte left his office, heels clicking resolutely. Alone in his cube,

Nicoletti became aware of a new sound coming from the office next door to his, which had been empty. A typewriter was pounding at lightning speed. Thrum, rattle rattle, bang. Nicoletti walked outside and saw that the formerly vacant cubicle next to his was now occupied by the novelist Samson Cody. Cody sat at a desk behind an old-fashioned manual typewriter. Around him, paper and magazine files were piled high. Cody stared at the ceiling while engaging in a loud tête-à-tête with Lotte Van Buren.

"No, no, woman, I say and say again. I will not have my copy checked by *anybody*! The only person who sees my copy is Win Gates, my editor."

"Mr. Cody, it is an established policy of *Tomorrow* that no story runs without being thoroughly checked for fact," Lotte said, her voice rising. "You're doing the profile on Mark Exeter. It's important that it be right, that I check the copy."

"My dear girl, I'm telling you, I'm writing a personal remembrance, not a news story," Cody said, mopping his forehead with a damp white handkerchief. "Check that! Check out stories written about me. Check out my reputation, but leave me alone. Do you people go through this nit-picking every week?"

"If it is not a news story, why is your desk heaped with clips and files?" Lotte demanded.

"God only knows," Cody said. "Looks like every bureau in the world filed on Mark Exeter, all stunning and titillating stuff, I'm sure, of which I may salvage two lines."

"I'll discuss this with Winston Gates," Lotte said, leaving Cody's office, flashing him a look of contempt, and hardly glancing at Nicoletti as she walked out the door.

"You do that, dear, amen," Cody said.

Nicoletti walked into Cody's office.

"This place is a hellhole," Cody said. "Reminds me of the time I spent doing a story on a guy convicted for murder. Hung around the prison a lot. At least their air conditioning was better than *Tomorrow*'s," he added, mopping his forehead again.

"So you're writing the cover story, Cody?"

"Gate's brainstorm. He heard I was doing a piece on Exeter and asked me to do it for *Tomorrow*. It's a remembrance, America's most famous novelist writing about the world's most notorious publisher.

It's an extremely personal story, and this chick Van Buren wants to check it out. What's to check?"

"Checking the facts is a time-honored *Tomorrow* magazine tradition," Nicoletti said.

"This Van Buren has to get off my back," Cody said. "She's a tyrant, attractive but manipulative. I was once married to a woman like her."

"And what happened to your wife?"

"After divorcing me, she became a psychiatrist, the better to understand the sick literary mind," Cody said.

"I'll leave you to your agonies at the typewriter."

"I never agonize," Cody said. "Spills from the gut. I write it like I see it, and this piece is no whitewashing."

"Oh?"

"It is a real profile of the man as I knew him, highlights and dark shadows, with the more sensational stuff merely alluded to, of course. It will win high points for *Tomorrow* on objectivity and courage."

"Do you think Alexander Exeter, father of the late Mark Exeter, will find it appealing?"

"Alex Exeter's opinion doesn't mean anything to me," Cody said. "Yes, as a matter of fact, he will adore it. It's got class." Cody went back to his typewriter, the keys clacking vigorously away.

Nicoletti went up the back stairs. Walking through the magazine's corridors, Nicoletti felt engulfed by the anger and anxiety radiating from the magazine's staff. The place was alive with cops and plainclothesmen, keeping their eagle eyes peeled for trouble.

Phones rang. Typewriters clattered. Like a bunch of crack troops, the *Tomorrow* team worked to get out the issue, all in an atmosphere of quietly contained hysteria.

The magazine felt like a submerged submarine. A bomb might explode outside the building, an ocean liner crash, without altering the Friday mood. The period of intense concentration, of getting the magazine out, had arrived. Heaps of paper littered desks. Weary-looking writers hunched over their typewriters. Like practiced lovers reaching for a climax, writers sought the precise fact, the pithy phrase, the colorful detail.

Ten years ago Nicoletti was part of the *Tomorrow* team. Now he was an outsider.

As Nicoletti approached the Personalities office, Felix hurried past him, pieces of paper clutched in his hand. "The whole thing sucks, Nicoletti," Felix said, continuing his rapid march past Nicoletti.

The door to Personalities was open. Theo looked up, gestured Nicoletti in, and closed the door behind him. "This place has become freak city," Theo said.

"Eddy O'Brien's murder really hit home," Nicoletti said. "I can feel the anger in the air."

"Ha!" Theo said. "Nobody gives a hoot about poor Eddy. Eddy-schmeddy. It's Byron Manos who has them enflamed."

"Manos?"

"Haven't you heard?" Theo said. "Manos resigned today. He's gotten a job as a TV anchorman at ninety thousand dollars a year. Everyone's in a rage, calling him a sellout. I call it green with envy."

"Manos is still a murder suspect," Nicoletti said.

"The blue-shirted pooh-bahs at the local TV channel don't seem to mind," Theo said. "They think Manos's bedroom eyes and voice will lure the ladies away from their cocktails to watch the six-o'clock news while their husbands are slogging home on commuter trains. Raise the ratings."

"To say nothing of Manos's salary," Nicoletti said. "He must have been angling for this job for a while. Anchormen don't get hired overnight."

"Maybe his instant notoriety at *Tomorrow* was a help," Theo said. "TV people adore a known quantity." Theo drummed a pencil on her desk. "And if that's not enough, Gates goes and brings in an outsider to write the cover story on Exeter."

"At least that gets the staff off the hook—including yourself," Nicoletti said.

"Yes," Theo said. "I'm not sure if that's a positive thing." Theo's hair was disheveled and her lipstick worn off. "I suppose I'll see you at the party later."

"Whose party?" Nicoletti asked.

"The farewell party for Byron Manos. It will be over by the clip desk tonight, after the magazine closes."

"I wouldn't miss it for the world," Nicoletti said. "In fact, I think I'll walk across the hall and offer Byron Manos my congratulations on his new job right now."

Nicoletti opened the Personalities door and crossed the hall to

Isms. Byron Manos was correcting a piece of copy. His beard was neatly trimmed and the usual turtleneck was now replaced by a silky pale-blue shirt and a striped tie, melding magnificently with a dark-blue blazer.

"Congratulations, Manos," Nicoletti said. "I hear you're joining the world of electronic journalism."

Manos turned his Byzantine face to Nicoletti. His black eyes gleamed like coals.

"I had my final interview this morning, signed a contract, and handed in my resignation," Manos said. "Everyone says I'm a sell-out, becoming a talking head, leaving behind the wonderful world of magazine journalism."

"But you think the whoredom of TV could not be worse than *Tomorrow*."

"Putting words in my mouth, Nicoletti."

"From pulpit to prime time," Nicoletti said. "I didn't know your ambition was TV."

"It wasn't," Manos said. "They came after me. It's nice to be wanted."

"Manos, you play things pretty close to the vest," Nicoletti said. "You didn't tell me about the argument you had with Mark Exeter the night he was murdered. What were you fighting so violently about?"

Manos looked uncomfortable. He fiddled with a letter opener and stroked his beard. His eyes were haunted. "None of your business, Nicoletti."

"You beat Exeter up, maybe killed him," Nicoletti said. "It could be the business of the cops."

"I didn't kill him," Manos said. "Don't think I wasn't tempted."

"What happened that night?" Nicoletti asked.

Manos was silent, his coal-black eyes glowing.

"Exeter wanted to have an affair with me," Manos said weakly.

"I wonder if you'd kill Exeter for making a pass at you," Nicoletti said.

"I'm not that thin-skinned, Nicoletti."

"Was Exeter expecting anybody when you left his office?"

"I didn't ask." Manos fingered the copy on his desk. "I wanted to get far away from Exeter and his corrosive personality, the stinking soul that after-shave lotion and fancy suits couldn't disguise."

"You're in love with his wife."

"Vane will always be the central woman in my life, but I can't hold her. She's a butterfly," Manos said. "A lost soul, lost to me."

"What does she want?"

"Why don't you ask her?"

"I might," Nicoletti said, walking out of Isms. He collided into Theo Marlow, notebook in hand.

"I'm on the run," Theo said. "I have a last-minute interview with Vanessa Wills."

"Just where I was headed," Nicoletti said. "Let me grab my coat and I'll go with you."

"I'm not sure if that's legit," Theo said. "Interviews are private."

"I'm sure Vanessa Wills won't mind."

Nicoletti rang the bell four times before Vane Wills came to the door. Her long red hair was wound into corkscrew curls. She wore pale makeup and a flower-sprigged Victorian dress and looked innocently lovely.

"What a surprise," she said. "Theo *and* Nick. Please come in." No love was lost between the two women as they greeted each other, Nicoletti could see.

"I'm playing fly on the wall," Nicoletti said. "I'll wait until the interview is over, Vane. I just want to talk to you for a few minutes."

"How divine," Vane Wills said, walking towards the library.

Theo and Nicoletti followed her. Vane Wills sat down and casually draped a leg over the arm of her chair. "I decided to wear my *Little Women* outfit for you, Theo. I like costumes. Can I get either of you anything? Coffee? Tea? A drink?" She shot Nicoletti a sultry look.

"No, thanks," Nicoletti said, walking around the library.

"Thank you, but no," Theo said, opening her notebook. She glanced across at the actress, whose fingernails were chewed to the quick, in incongruous contrast to her glamorous, polished appearance. Theo made a note of it. "I can't stay long. We're on deadline at the magazine."

"What can I tell you?" Vane asked.

"Did you read *Little Women* as a child?"

"Read it? I was raised on it. Jo was my favorite character . . . I admired her rebel's spirit."

"You usually play saintly characters like Meg. Do you feel you're being typecast?"

"No, when I complete the film, I'm going to play Lady Macbeth in a modern stage version of the classic. I like the role of Ophelia, too. I couldn't imagine playing Sadie Thompson in *Rain*, the tarty woman who brings the minister to his knees. It wouldn't be *me*." Vanessa Wills smiled radiantly at Theo.

Nicoletti moved around the library, listening to the interview and studying the nineteenth-century etchings.

"Is the costume you're wearing authentic?" Theo asked.

"Every inch, darling. And the waistline didn't have to be taken out. I have a twenty-two-inch waist."

Theo scribbled down details on the dress's fabric, number of buttons, fine stitches.

"Do you feel anything in your background qualifies you for the role of Lady Macbeth?" Theo asked, pen poised.

"Is that a zinger, darling?"

"What do you mean?"

"You lull me into a tranquil state by discussing Victorian dresses, then throw me a curve."

"You haven't answered the question."

"Do I have blood dripping from my hands? No."

Theo snapped the notebook shut.

"I was curious to talk with you," Theo said.

"And I was interested in meeting you, Theo." Vane Wills leaned back in the chair, her ample bust tugging at the Victorian dress, her foot wagging over the chair arm to reveal ruffled pantaloons. "You are interesting looking, and intelligent. My husband did have good taste in women. His casual affairs were never the tacky types."

Nicoletti leaned forward to study a Tintoretto.

"Mark and I were not having an affair," Theo said icily. "And if we were, I know it would not have been casual."

Nicoletti moved on to a small Picasso etching.

"How foolish, darling," Wills said, her voice trilling, her foot waving more vigorously. "None of the women Mark was involved with thought the affair was casual. He made every woman feel she was the only one who counted. He even gave each woman a special name. He called me 'Vanity.' " Vane Wills's laugh rang out. "He had a special thing for journalists, women writers and the like. At the paper in Sydney, Australia, it got to be a joke. Somebody who had not slept with Mark was considered an E.V., an Exeter Virgin."

"Really," Theo said, biting off the word.

"He was an outrageous person, wasn't he?" Vane said.

"In some ways," Theo answered.

Hands in his pockets, Nicoletti looked out the window.

"Well, darling, we both miss him, I know," Vane said to Theo. "I didn't mean to be catty. I'm sure Mark thought highly of you."

"You seem to have kept up with your late husband's social life rather well. Was he involved with anyone else at *Tomorrow*?" Theo asked. "Besides the Medicine reporter and the new reporter in the Foreign department?"

"I didn't know about the last two," Vane Wills answered. "That blond mouse in the Medicine department? I met her. Don't think she was Mark's type."

"They spent an evening together. That's all," Theo said.

Nicoletti turned around. Theo was sitting forward on the edge of her chair, hands clutching her notebook.

"A one-night stand. Gets a bit sordid, doesn't it?" Wills said. "There was somebody else at *Tomorrow*. At any rate, the affair was over. Dead as a doornail."

Nicoletti cleared his throat.

"I'd better get back." Theo stood up and put on her raincoat. Both women acted as though Nicoletti were not in the room. "What do you think of Byron Manos's leaving the magazine to become a TV anchorman?"

Vane Wills registered surprise. "I didn't know about it, darling."

"He gave in his resignation this morning," Theo said.

"I think that's utterly divine." Vane Wills smiled brilliantly, extending a cool hand to Theo. "I must call and congratulate him. Byron's so marvelous in bed. I'm sure he can do anything."

Theo shook Wills's hand briefly. "I'll find my way out," she said, leaving the library.

After Theo left, Vane Wills flung her arms wide at Nicoletti. "And now, darling, let's have a brandy," she said to Nicoletti. "Interviews exhaust me."

She poured brandy into two snifters, handed one to Nicoletti, and swirled her glass around. Nicoletti sat down in the chair vacated by Theo. Vane Wills, seated on the arm of his chair, plumped the soft pillow in back of him.

"How can I help you in your private eye—or rather, tec business—as we say in Britain?" Wills asked.

"Just a point of curiosity," Nicoletti said. "Your husband gave nicknames to women. Did he do the same with men?"

"Of course, darling, although never in person. But in our little chit-chats, he usually referred to people by tags, some less charming than others."

"Anyone at the magazine he called B.D.?"

Wills was silent for a moment. She took a deep sip of brandy, leaned back, and suddenly exploded with laughter. "Yes, yes," she said. "But it was silly. I don't know if I should repeat it."

"Don't be shy, Vanessa."

"He called Byron B.D.," Wills said. "Byron DeSade. Isn't that gross? Mark said he could imagine Byron's torturing him, pictured him with leather whips and the like." Wills's giggles died down.

"Your husband seems to have been a man of many dimensions," Nicoletti said.

"Waste, waste," Wills said, refilling her glass.

"And who was the other woman at the magazine he had an affair with?"

"Haven't the slightest, darling," Wills said. She turned to Nicoletti. "Does Victorian dress appeal to you, Nick? I thought it might."

"You look beautiful, as always, Vane," Nicoletti said.

"I have other costumes," Wills answered, lowering her voice.

Nicoletti put his brandy glass down. "I can't stay," he said. "But there's going to be a farewell party tonight at the magazine for Byron. After closing time. Perhaps you'd like to come."

"How divine of you to invite me, darling," Wills said, doing a pirouette. "I adore parties. Of course, too bad we can't have a private one."

"The fantasy will keep me alive," Nicoletti said charmingly. "We'll see you tonight."

Nicoletti left Wills's town house and walked back towards his office on Madison Avenue, the private-eye lair. He wove through crowds, which, even in the rain, were rushing off to banks, to cash paychecks, to head for the Friday lunch: young women in the office sharing Chinese food; junior executives having one-too-many martinis. T.G.I.F. Thank God It's Friday.

Nicoletti passed an open stand where hot dogs sizzled. (New York, a city of smells: hot dogs, flowers, ozone, piss on the sidewalk, Chanel Number 5, glue and paint, the foot-trod, dusty smell of theaters and offices; murky river smells and fresh ocean breezes.) Fine wines and stale beer. Sweat and cologne.

Back in his Madison Avenue office, he drank a chilled bottle of Heineken's as the rain dripped down the window. Then he called Winston Gates and suggested a few more guests to round out Byron Manos's farewell party at the magazine that night.

Watching the rain, seeing streetlights turning green, yellow, red, hearing cars and cabs hiss along the sidewalk, Nicoletti thought about Rembrandt, the great artist who probed into men's souls. He thought about human need and ambition that could lead to love, glory, triumph—or murder.

•23•

FRIDAY night. Rocko, *Tomorrow*'s temporary mail-room boy, dragged Mohammad Dakar, the new "intern," around the magazine with him. Mohammed, enormously overweight, wore an immense pale-blue suit and blue suede shoes. His thin mustache was waxed into a villainous arc. He reeked of hair tonic, garlic, and cologne.

Rocko paused with Mohammed by the Foreign department. "Okay, Mo, here's where the international news is written. That's the European desk, there's Latin America, that's the Far East," Rocko said, disposing of a large part of the world's surface with a point of his finger.

"And the Middle East?" Mohammed asked gravely, fingering his mustache and ogling a saried Indian beauty eating an ice-cream sundae as she read the *London Observer*. "There is no desk?"

"Sure there is," Rocko said, gesturing to the end of the room. "See, there it is."

Mohammed wheezed and sighed, rolled his eyes heavenward. "The Middle East desk. Yes. Perhaps I will sit there someday."

Rocko moved along down the corridor. "Don't get overly ambitious, Mo. Just get the right mail to the right person. René de Goncourt, the Foreign editor, goes crazy when his mail is late or misplaced."

"Crazy? He goes mad?" Mohammed asked, padding beside Rocko.

"Yes. He's a French count. He challenges people to duels."

They returned to the mail room, where Mohammed immediately eased his form onto a chair.

"Can't be sitting down on the job," Rocko said. "Do you realize that if you don't get the mail or the A.P. clips delivered on time, *Tomorrow* could miss an important story? Your job is vital, Mo."

Mohammed pulled himself up and joined Rocko in sorting

through an enormous pile of mail.

"It is a privilege to be here," Mohammed said gravely, gazing at an address on an envelope. "I hope someday to pursue a journalistic career. I am taking courses at Columbia."

"So I hear," Rocko said, whipping through the mail.

"And what are you studying at the New School, Rocko?" Mohammed asked, slowly going through a pile of papers.

"Me? Girls. It's a great place to meet women."

"But what of your future?"

"I'm studying different things, film, philosophy. I'm finding myself, Mo."

"If you wish, I will attempt to teach you Arabic."

"I'm no good at languages. The only thing I can say in Italian is pastafazool."

"You Americans. Such a casual approach to scholarly pursuits." Mohammed unbuttoned his voluminous jacket.

As Rocko sorted the mail, he watched Mohammed out of the corner of his eye. Mohammed went laboriously over each piece of mail, testing it with his fingers, examining it. At this pace, Mohammed would never move the mountain.

Rocko tossed the neatly sorted piles of mail and paper into the rolling cart. "I'm off on the delivery round now, Mo. Hold the fort." Rocko pushed the mail-room cart through the halls of *Tomorrow*. The magazine was beginning to present a pattern of familiarity to Rocko. The writers—calm, cool, collected, cerebral—reminded him of athletes sitting on the bench, waiting to apply their fingers to the typewriter. The reporters were birds of varying plumage: chirpy wrens; exotic flamingos; cheerful red-breasted robins; cawing black crows; wise, motherly owls. For Rocko, getting out a magazine was alchemy, mysterious, the transforming of words into print, print into opinion, opinion into action.

He returned to the mail room. Softly chewing, Mohammed was eating an éclair—its cream coating his mustache—from the coffee wagon as, his rump overflowing the chair, he studied a copy of *TV Guide*. "I love TV," Mohammed said. "I think maybe I would like to be an anchorman, a TV pundit like Dan Rather. He is so dynamic."

"How do you like Barbara Walters?"

172

"I don't approve of her asking Presidents questions about their sexual habits. She is immodest."

"To each his own."

"Tonight they are showing *Charade* on the late TV show," Mohammed said solemnly. "I must choose between the film and Johnny Carson."

"Tough choice, Mo," Rocko answered. "But one you won't have to make. We'll be working late. It's Friday, deadline night, at the magazine."

"Ah, yes. Deadline," Mohammed said. "The word that takes its origins from the line drawn within or around a prison that a prisoner passes at the risk of being shot. The day by which something must be done. The time after which copy cannot be accepted for publication. I do find the English language amusing."

"You'll have fun tonight, Mo. Friday nights are never dull. That's when everything happens. When it all comes together, at last."

Nicoletti locked his office door behind him, went down the elevator and into the street, and walked over to the late Mark Exeter's apartment. On the elevator, a tiny lady with a hunchback, blue hair, and a silver-mink coat clutched a small mesh sack filled with cans of cat food while a young couple, expensively dressed in matching brown leather outfits, stood entwined in the corner.

The little lady twinkled at Nicoletti as she got off the elevator, and he held the door open for her. "Have a nice evening," she said.

Nicoletti walked down the hall to Exeter's apartment, unlocked the door, and walked in, switching on the lights. Viewing the enormous luxurious bed, the elegant and solid furniture, the rich Oriental rugs, Nicoletti felt the tug of mortality and breathed in the personality of the man—the late Mark Exeter—sensualist, loner, bon vivant, whose freshly laundered shirts awaited tomorrows that would never be.

Opening the closet that held Exeter's collection of women's clothes and playthings, he sniffed a whiff of English lavender perfuming the black satin garter belts and negligees. Nicoletti went slowly through the clothes hanging in the closet: a short waitress uniform with a frilly white apron and a backless skirt; a belly dancer's outfit; a skirt woven

173

of fine mesh chains; a 1940s dress with shoulder pads; a grass skirt; a long red satin dress with a full, flowing skirt and plunging neckline; a black leather G-string studded with nails, mated with a thin string top whose small black leather cups were barely large enough to cover a woman's breasts.

From the bottom shelf in the closet where he had placed it, Nicoletti retrieved the diary of Mark Exeter, the sensualist. Nicoletti took the book out and turned backward through the pages. First "B.D.," then "Tiger?", the tag that enraged Theo. "Salome . . . Helen of Troy . . . Belinda Delight . . . Marvella . . . Vanity . . . Bette D. . . . Marina . . . Stardust . . . Angel Face . . . Wanda . . ." No dates. Name after name, some repeating, some punctuated (!) or (!!!!!!) or (*).

No verbal comments marred the roué's memory gallery. Did Exeter sit up on lonely nights, if he had lonely nights, reading over the names, savoring the experiences? Nicoletti put the book back and closed the closet door.

Nicoletti turned off the lights and stood, for a moment, looking out at the full moon shining down on the East River. The Fifty-ninth Street bridge was aglitter, and a chubby, cheerful tug floated down the river fourteen stories below the late Mark Exeter's elegant pad. The same river that ran like an elegant ribbon past New York's poshest area also witnessed suicides, murder, bodies found bloated and floating down its stream.

Nicoletti thought about Exeter—who had combined the subtlest appreciation of art with a closet full of girlie costumes—a man who had been consummately charming and brutally ruthless, a man whose own desires had come first. Other people were merely minor players in Exeter's game, characters to be pushed offstage at whim. Exeter had pushed one person too far.

Nicoletti closed the door to Mark Exeter's apartment behind him and walked the six blocks to *Tomorrow*, moving almost at a saunter, half-wanting to delay the confrontation.

When Nicoletti got off the elevator on the fifth floor, the party for Byron Manos was in full swing. The gray workaday area by the clip tables had been completely transformed. Bright balloons hung from the ceiling. A stereo played ragtime music. Bottles, ice, and plastic glasses, along with mountains of hors d'oeuvres, sat atop the clip desk.

A new poster hung on the wall under the aegis of the art department—a cartoon of Byron Manos on a TV screen, being watched by a woman in curlers and a housecoat, sitting in her living room with a cocktail glass in hand and exclaiming: "My Lord—Byron!"

As the music changed to a disco tune and *Tomorrow* staffers danced to the thumping, twanging beat, Nicoletti gave the room a quick survey. His guests had arrived: Vanessa Wills, resplendent in a flowing maroon velvet dress; Archie and Matilda Kerr, quietly seated on the sidelines; Eli Patterson, out on bail, surrounded by his fans, and obviously the star attraction of the evening.

"Amazing, utterly," Samson Cody said to Nicoletti as he walked in. Cody shook his curly head at Nicoletti and took a healthy slug of ginger ale. "Bodies falling around them, the magazine about to be sold under their feet, and this crowd just keeps on partying like there's no tomorrow. Forgive the pun."

"You're a writer," Nicoletti said. "You must understand the syndrome."

"I suppose they like the action," Cody said, waving his glass aloft. "One thing for sure, I certainly know what the pecking order is here. America's greatest novelist stands by the sidelines while Eli Patterson gets the limelight." Cody looked over at Patterson, who, slightly intoxicated, was holding an animated conversation with a group of goggle-eyed staffers.

Archie and Matilda Kerr smiled shyly at Nicoletti as he continued his conversation with Cody, who moved his pudgy form to the disco beat. "Good-looking women here," Cody said. "But having been married five times, and with twelve kids, I no longer indulge myself in the occasional tryst. By the way, Nicoletti, I've completely revised my opinion of Lotte Van Buren. She's dynamite."

"She charmed you?"

"No, her checking system did. Fantastic. I didn't have to worry about facts, only words. For instance, I could write Mark Exeter, born in T.C., and she would fill in the date."

"T. C.," Nicoletti said, "That's newsmagazine-ese, standing for 'To Come.' "

"Fascinating," Cody said. "I'm living out my Clark Kent fantasy. I hear you were a top Art reporter here, Nicoletti. What made you leave?"

"Playing the complete observer isn't my role," Nicoletti said.

"Well, *Tomorrow* is a wonderful place. It's wonderful to write a story and only have to think about my superlative prose, while somebody else worries about the details."

Rocko moved across the room to Nicoletti and Cody, Mohammed trailing behind him. Wheezing and pulling on his mustache, Mohammed nodded gravely as he was introduced to the two men.

"How are the Kerrs?" Nicoletti asked Rocko.

"Shy," Rocko said. "And under cover. I introduced them as relatives of yours from out of town."

Emmy, playing the gracious hostess, walked towards them with a tray of rounds of pumpernickel bread covered with pâté. Mohammed, reaching a paw out delicately, took two.

"Delicious," he sighed.

"Thank you," Emmy said, "I made the pâté myself."

As she walked away, Mohammed said, "Beautiful."

"You mean her?" Rocko said, looking towards Vanessa Wills, who flashed him a radiant smile as she leaned towards Byron Manos.

"Oh, no, that woman is too skinny," Mohammed said gravely. "She is the one," nodding towards Emmy, who had moved to a cluster next to them.

"A little plump," Rocko said.

"Voluptuous," Mohammed said, breathing the word with a wheeze and a sigh. "I must get to know that woman."

As the disco beat accelerated, Nicoletti looked around at the crowd. Theo and Felix danced together; Lotte Van Buren, her head thrown back in laughter, talked with Winston Gates. The sari-robed Indian researcher pulled Byron Manos towards the dance floor.

Nicoletti started walking towards Archie and Matilda Kerr when the music stopped. Winston Gates climbed up and stood on top of a chair, raising his arms for silence, his white teeth sparkling. As the room quieted down, he held up a dummy copy of the magazine, with a photograph of the late Mark Exeter on the cover. A bold and simple block headline read: "MARK EXETER: A REMEMBRANCE BY SAMSON CODY."

Gates's voice was resonant. "I want to congratulate everyone on getting out this issue. You're all pros and I'm proud to be working with you." Applause. "I know how hard this week has been on everybody," Gates said. "But I think we have a great issue here, and the piece written by Sam Cody is nothing short of brilliant. Let's hear it for Cody." Applause. Cheers. Whistles. Cody acknowledged the good feeling by clasping his hands aloft like a prizefighter.

"More congratulations are in order," Gates said. "We all wish Byron Manos good luck in his new television career. Please come up here, Byron, to receive a farewell gift from your friends at *Tomorrow*."

Manos walked up to Gates, who handed him a package decorated with silver paper and bows. Manos opened it slowly. He lifted the lid off a black box filled with powders, paints, and brushes.

"A makeup kit," Manos laughed, displaying it to the crowd. "Thank you. Thank you, everybody, for the present and for your good wishes."

More cheers.

"And now let's have a ball," Gates said, stepping down from the chair. Gates grabbed Vanessa Wills and broke into a dance as Frank Sinatra's "New York, New York" came on. Partygoers started singing and clapping to the rhythm as Wills and Gates held center stage.

Suddenly the music stopped. Heads turned as Alexander Exeter walked into the room, trailed by publisher Parker Johnson. Exeter's off-the-rack, double-breasted suit hung on his tired frame as he moved ponderously across the floor, the crowd parting to make way for him. Winston Gates, unaware, continued to move over the silent floor with Vanessa Wills, swooping and gliding.

Exeter boomed out the command: "Gates, I want to talk with you."

Turning, Winston Gates let go of Vanessa Wills, who stood next to him, smiling at Exeter.

"Darling Alex," Vanessa said. "How marvelous to see you."

"This is an unexpected surprise," Gates said. "Will you join the party, Alex?"

"Party?" Alex Exeter fumed, staring at Gates and Vanessa Wills "And what, may I ask, is the occasion?" Exeter clenched and unclenched his fists.

"It's a farewell party for Byron Manos," Gates said. "He's leaving *Tomorrow*. He has a new job as a TV anchorman."

Exeter looked over towards Manos, then glanced around at the gathering with his hard eyes. The *Tomorrow* staffers stood quietly, waiting.

"I don't mix work and play," Exeter said. Exeter motioned Gates aside and whispered a few words to him, causing Gates's expression to darken.

Exeter started to walk away, but Gates put a restraining hand on his arm.

"Alex Exeter has something to tell you," Gates said to the waiting crowd.

Exeter's mouth sagged. "I didn't come prepared to make a speech," he said impatiently.

"Speech! Speech!" an exuberant and slightly tipsy reporter cried out. Alex Exeter shot her a sour look.

"I'll be brief," Exeter said, his cockney tones pronounced. "I am selling *Tomorrow* to Brandon Motors. The final papers will be signed in the morning."

A moment of deadly silence followed Exeter's pronouncement.

Then Felix Magill, standing by a bunch of brightly hued balloons, reached up with his lighted cigar and popped one, two, three balloons. Crack, pop, bang. More balloons popped around the room in a mutinous burst. Voices erupted in excited chatter, tears, swears, groans, moans. A rowdy chorus in the back of the room broke out in "So long, it's been good to know you."

"Quiet," Win Gates shouted. "Pipe down." The room settled down to a quiet lull. Gates turned to Exeter and said forcefully: "What are the terms, Alex? Will Brandon keep the *Tomorrow* staff?"

"That remains the decision of Brandon," Exeter said. "I didn't feel it my place to dicker with them about terms and conditions. Parker is the liaison with Brandon. Talk with him."

"Right-o," Parker Johnson said. "I'll be happy to answer any questions I can."

Eli Patterson suddenly burst out of his circle of admirers, stepping forward on slightly unsteady legs. "Just for starters, Johnson, do you want to tell us why Brandon Motors has scrapped the solar-energy car?"

Alexander Exeter stared at Eli Patterson, his face going from gray to ash-gray. "What is *he* doing here?" Exeter snorted. He dropped his large hammy hands by his sides and then lifted one hand and pointed towards Eli Patterson. "Get him off the premises. I own this magazine and I order him off. He killed my son."

Patterson and Alexander Exeter stared at each other; hatred spilled out of Exeter's green eyes. Patterson moved towards him.

"If I took the rap for killing your son, would you still sell this magazine to a bunch of corporate schmucks?" Patterson said.

"Don't mix apples and oranges, Mr. Eli Patterson," Exeter spit out the words. "Brandon is the company of the working man, and I believe in the working man, not in a bunch of alcoholic, murderous journalists."

"Working man?" Patterson guffawed. "How about the solar-energy car, the car Brandon refuses to put on the market? That's the car of the working man. That's the story I wrote and the story your son killed for a few advertising bucks." Patterson swayed on his feet. "Brandon's a bunch of thieves."

"Lies, all lies," Exeter said, glaring at Patterson.

Archie Kerr stepped forth, his voice squeaking, his eyes glittering behind thick glasses. "It's true, Mr. Exeter. I invented the solar-energy car. I worked for Brandon Motors."

Every eye turned towards Archie.

"I don't know what you're talking about," Exeter said. "Car? What car?"

"The car is called Sunbeam. She uses energy from the sun, not gasoline, and she's cheap to run," Archie said. "She could put the Arabs with their oil wells right out of business."

"I'll believe it when I see it," Exeter said. "Solar-energy cars and poppycock."

"Come to the window," Archie said. "I've parked Sunbeam on the street downstairs." He walked to the window and pointed to Sunbeam, gleaming under the streetlight. "There she is, all fueled up," Archie said. "If you want, I'll take you for a spin."

Exeter followed Archie to the window and looked down. The crowd gathered behind Archie and Alex Exeter, staring down at the yellow car on the street below.

"Allah be praised," Mohammed said. "A car that runs without gasoline."

Exeter turned around and started to push his way through the crowd. "Brandon Motors and how they deal with solar-energy cars is not my affair. It does not change my decision to sell to them," he said. "My son is dead. Eli Patterson killed him. *Tomorrow* killed him."

Eli Paterson moved towards Exeter, swaying on unsteady legs. The two men were only a few inches apart. "Say it once more and I'll kill you, too, Exeter," Patterson said, "just the way I killed your son."

Nicoletti moved across the room in swift strides, getting between Exeter and Patterson, pushing the two men away from each other.

"Cut the dramatics, Patterson," Nicoletti said. Nicoletti turned to Exeter. "Eli Patterson did not kill your son."

"He admitted it," Exeter said, his hands still clawing towards Patterson.

Nicoletti stared into Alex Exeter's eyes. "I know who killed your son," Nicoletti said. "Mark drove that person to kill him, led that person to the brink of destruction. That person killed, in a way, for survival."

"It was Patterson," Exeter gasped.

"No," Nicoletti said.

"Who?" Exeter demanded. "Who?"

Turning from Exeter, Nicoletti looked quickly around the room at the tableau, frozen as if caught by a camera, no foot shifting, nobody moving. As his eyes moved swiftly from person to person, standing where his memory had positioned them a few minutes ago, Nicoletti felt the tingling sensation of danger.

Two people were missing from the group.

And one of those people was the murderer of Mark Exeter.

·24·

NICOLETTI pushed through the silent crowd and raced down to the Personalities office. As he walked in, he saw Theo standing by her desk by the window, and then a blinding light went off in his face.

Shielding his eyes with his arm, he cried out: "What are you doing, Theo?"

"Testing the camera," Theo said. "I volunteered to take pictures at Byron's party." She hurried towards the door. "I must get these pictures, Nick. This is a historic—if last—moment in the life of *Tomorrow* magazine." Theo looked at Nicoletti. "What's wrong?"

Nicoletti shook his head, left the Personalities office, and hurried down the back stairs. He pushed open the closed door of Lotte Van Buren's office. Drink in hand, Lotte sat behind her desk, smoking. "Come in, Nick," Lotte said. "I thought I'd come down and escape the melodramatics going on upstairs." Lotte's cheeks were spotted with color.

She put out her cigarette, jammed another one into the holder, put the cigarette to her lips, struck a match repeatedly, and finally lit the cigarette. "I think old Alex Exeter is having a nervous breakdown," Lotte said, inhaling deeply.

"It's not Exeter who's having the nervous breakdown, Lotte," Nicoletti said. "It's you."

Nicoletti closed the door behind him and stood in front of it, looking at Lotte, poised behind the well-organized desk, which did not have even a stray paper clip to mar its precise order.

"Have you gone crazy, too, Nick?" Lotte attempted an offhand smile that turned into a grimace.

"Lotte, the nightmare can't go on," Nicoletti said. "You killed Mark Exeter. He was destroying you, Lotte. Professionally and emotionally, he drove you over the brink."

"You must be mad, Nick," Lotte said. "Somebody poisoned me. I

181

almost died." She took quick, angry puffs on the cigarette. "Can you explain that?"

"You tried to commit suicide, Lotte," Nicoletti said. "It didn't work."

"You're insane, totally," Lotte said. "What's happened to you, Nick? You're acting most peculiar. Remember me, your friend, Lotte?"

"Yes," Nicoletti said. "But that doesn't change the facts. You also murdered Eddy O'Brien."

"Eddy O'Brien?" Lotte hissed out the name. "Don't be utterly ridiculous, Nick. Get your facts straight."

"The facts undid you, Lotte," Nicoletti said.

"I don't know what you're talking about," Lotte said, her eyelashes fluttering, her hyperthyroid blue eyes wide.

"The morning paper ran a front-page story about Eddy's murder. The story said Eddy was strangled with a piece of rope," Nicoletti said. "When we were talking, you pointed out that the paper was wrong, that Eddy was strangled with twine, not rope. Only the police, myself, and the killer knew that. The facts, Lotte."

"The facts," Lotte said, her voice quivering. "Yes, facts are important." She stubbed out the cigarette and put another one in the holder, jamming it in. She sat with the cold unlit cigarette in her hand. "Eddy, horrible little worm." Suddenly, Lotte's face crumpled and her voice was filled with anger and pain. "He didn't deserve to live." Tears ran down Lotte's face. "Slashing my phone wire was unforgivable." Lotte reached for a tissue and mopped at her eyes.

"Eddy learned something about you," Nicoletti said, "Something that made you a murder suspect."

Lotte stared coldly at Nicoletti. She poured more liquor into her glass, lit the cigarette, and took a puff, clutching the holder with trembling hand. "What is this valuable piece of information that Eddy held?" Lotte asked.

"You and Exeter were lovers," Nicoletti said. "He called you B.D., short for Bette Davis. You look like the actress, a young Bette Davis—the dark-blond hair, the blue eyes, the intense manner."

Lotte's mouth trembled as she looked at Nicoletti.

"Your name is in his book." Nicoletti said. "You met him at his apartment on Friday afternoon, the Friday he was murdered. You made love. You thought you could control him, that everything would be all right, that he would listen to you."

Lotte's face was a deadly white. "My name is Lotte Van Buren," Lotte seethed. "L.V.B., L.V.B." Lotte's face twisted. Mascara ran down her cheeks. The clock on her desk ticked insistently

"I'm sorry, Lotte," Nicoletti said, "that things didn't work out as you hoped." Nicoletti reached into his pocket and took out the piece of yellow copy paper covered with Exeter's doodling. He held it up. "Friday night, Exeter was working on a reorganization plan for the magazine. Exeter drew a pyramid at the top that stood for the writers and editors. He crossed out the initials E.P., standing for Eli Patterson, and replaced them with the initials W.G. Even if Patterson had not quit, he was planning to fire him and replace him with Winston Gates."

Lotte stared at Nicoletti with glazed eyes. "How fascinating," Lotte said caustically, exhaling smoke.

"Underneath the big pyramid he drew a smaller pyramid with a wavy line through it that canceled it out. He also wrote the initials B.D. under the pyramid and crossed them out. The B.D. stood for you, Lotte. Exeter was eliminating you from the magazine, Lotte, and he was also eliminating the entire reporter system, the smaller pyramid, the substructure of *Tomorrow*."

Lotte gasped.

"It was unjust, Lotte," Nicoletti said. "After years of dedication, he was throwing you on the ash heap. *Tomorrow* was your life, Lotte. You cracked. I started to suspect you, almost against my will, last Saturday night when you told me you were considering retiring from *Tomorrow*. That was merely a smoke screen. You were not sure if anyone else was privy to the information that Exeter was dumping you. You wanted to cover your tracks."

Lotte took a deep gulp of her drink and put the glass down on the desk. Her mouth quivered. "It was cruel, Nick, a cruel and ugly trick. Oh, Nick, you don't understand."

"Help me to understand, Lotte."

Lotte's voice was heavy with rage and despair. "On Friday night Mark called and asked me to come into his office. I went. He handed me the Brandon Motors story and all the background on it. He told me to destroy the story and the background. He asked me to come back to his office later. He said there was something he had to discuss with me, something important."

Lotte gulped, put a cigarette in the black holder, and took a deep puff. "I took the background on the Brandon exposé back to my office. Then I went downstairs, signed out, and came back upstairs when nobody was looking—that night watchman is useless—then went back into my office and closed the door."

Lotte's eyes batted rapidly. "I read the story Eli Patterson had written, the Brandon Motors exposé. It was brilliant, a *great* story." Tears welled in Lotte's eyes. "I hated to destroy it, but I did." Lotte picked up the scissors from her desk and held them up. "I used these. I cut that story into bits, along with the background," Lotte gulped. "It was like cutting out my heart. Mark Exeter made me compromise the light I lived my life by, the journalistic truth." Lotte winced. "Wasn't I the trusting fool?

"After 4 A.M., I went down to Mark's office. I told him that I had destroyed the story." Lotte paused. She looked at Nicoletti helplessly. "Please don't laugh at me, Nick."

"I'm not laughing."

"I told Mark that I wanted Eli Patterson's job," Lotte said, her mouth quivering. "Eli Patterson walked out that night. Mark *needed* a managing editor. Who knows more about *Tomorrow* than I do? I deserved the job. I *wanted* it." Tears streamed down Lotte's face.

"Mark told me the position had already been filled." She paused. "Then he told me he was eliminating my job and the entire reporter system. He said the writers could do their own reporting."

Lotte sat up straighter in her chair. "I said to him, 'Who will check the facts?' He said it wasn't necessary to document how many angels can stand on the head of a pin. He told me to get out. He said I was a 'has-been,' over the hill. He turned his back to dismiss me." Lotte shuddered. "I tried to remind him of our—passion. Just that afternoon, we had made love." Lotte put her face between her hands. "I'll never forget that moment. He laughed. I was flooded with self-loathing. He was going to toss me away like a piece of used paper." Lotte clenched her hand in a fist, looking up at Nicoletti. Her voice was dense with rage. "I picked up the statue and hit him over the head, again and again. I was wearing gloves, you see . . . hands can get rough handling paper every day. . . ." Lotte's voice wandered. "I use hand cream and get a manicure once a week. . . ."

"And so your fingerprints were not on the statue," Nicoletti said. "Where are the gloves, Lotte?"

"In a drawer in my apartment," Lotte said. Lotte's large blue eyes were dilated, the black centers small as pinpricks. She looked at Nicoletti with confusion.

"And after you killed Exeter, you put the statue neatly back on his desk," Nicoletti said.

"Yes," Lotte said. "I left his office and took the elevator downstairs. I carried the background on the Brandon story, cut into tiny pieces, in my tote bag with me. I didn't care who saw me. Nobody did. Larry, the night watchman, was asleep. I went home. The aftermath was horrible. I wasn't sorry Mark Exeter was dead, but I hated myself for throwing suspicion on other people. I tried to kill myself with an overdose of Seconal. But when I woke up in Lenox Hill Hospital, life seemed infinitely precious. I decided to tough it out."

"Then Eddy came to me with his accusations about B.D. He tried to blackmail me, wanted money to make a theatrical comeback. He heard Mark call me B.D., remembered the Bette Davis costume." Lotte's eyelashes fluttered. "He told me he was the prankster. How dare he! I wanted to fire him years ago, he was always snooping and nosing about, but Hendricks, the old publisher, wouldn't allow it." Lotte trembled. "I strangled Eddy, there, in the mail room."

"And left the string around his neck neatly tied, in the same compulsively neat way you returned the statue to Mark Exeter's desk after you murdered him," Nicoletti said.

Lotte jammed a fresh cigarette into the black holder and lit it. "I like to do things properly," Lotte said, bursting into laughter that stopped as quickly as it started. "Eddy knew about Mark and me, about the costumes, about the affair. I know he would have talked. I silenced him, for good. God, it was dreadful." Tears steamed down her face again.

"Lotte, were you in love with Mark Exeter?" Nicoletti asked.

"Love?" Lotte's voice was almost a whisper. "I despised Mark Exeter."

"Why did you get involved with him?"

"I *needed* him," Lotte said. "I needed to prove that I was attractive, interesting, appealing. But most of all, I needed to make it all count, all the years of work. I wanted *more*. I thought I could get close to

Mark Exeter, influence him. I wanted to make *Tomorrow* great. I would have done anything, anything."

Lotte looked at Nicoletti. He looked back at her, now hearing the clock ticking, the traffic on the street below.

"I think it's time to talk to the police, Lotte," Nicoletti said. "I'm sorry, Lotte, sorry."

"Don't be sorry, Nick," Lotte said. "I'm not."

She stood up and lunged at him, the sharp-bladed scissors aimed at his heart.

As Nicoletti wrestled them away from her, fighting her amazingly strong grip, he heard Lotte cry out: "Help me. Help me."

•EPILOGUE•

TOMORROW hit the newsstands with a bang. It was an instant sellout, offering the "inside" story on Mark Exeter, the most enigmatic and glamorous communications figure since Howard Hughes, and the Brandon Motors exposé.

Winston Gates pulled out all the stops, telling the story of Brandon's suppressing the solar-energy car; Eli Patterson got a by-line on the story, which also carried a four-color picture of Archie and Matilda Kerr, Sunbeam, and Edison—the cocker spaniel.

Alexander Exeter did not sell *Tomorrow* to Brandon. Brandon refused to buy, and Exeter saw the cash register jingling.

With one issue the magazine's circulation had tripled.

Vanessa Wills went to California to film *Little Women*. When a casting call went out for an angelic-looking blond man with muscular legs, she sent for Rocko. Nicoletti gave Rocko a temporary leave of absence to try a film career.

As TV anchorman, Byron Manos sent the ratings soaring. He bought a new wardrobe befitting TV stardom. Two months later he quit his job and went to a Greek island to write poetry, thus becoming, in a minor way, a "legend in his own time."

Nicoletti stopped by Win Gates's office to congratulate him on the success of the special Exeter/Brandon issue.

"Yes, I am proud of it," Gates said. "You made the Brandon story possible, Nicoletti. Archie Kerr told me that you said I would run it. How did you know?" Gates's white teeth flashed; his black eyes glittered.

"I guess I know a newsman when I see one," Nicoletti said.

"I take that as a compliment," Gates answered.

After leaving Gates's office, Nicoletti dropped off in Personalities.

Felix was leafing throught the magazine and burping. "So, Nose, you did a good job. I've already put in my order for a solar-energy car, now that Archie Kerr has given his blueprint to Newworth Motors."

"Gates really told it like it is," Nicoletti said. "The Brandon exposé."

"Yeah, Gates isn't all that bad. He promises a mixture of the sordid and the sound, as opposed to the naked and the deadly. And the 'new' *Tomorrow* has certain merits. This four-color picture of an old fan dancer shows her with all her warts and blemishes."

"What's Gates planning to do about the reporter system? Will he eliminate it now that Lotte's gone?"

"No. He grooves on it. All those pretty girls. Emmy Kaufman is taking over Lotte's job as head of reporters. By the way, that Arab intern, Mohammed, seems sweet on her. And she doesn't seem to mind him. I suppose his father's oil wells help."

"Romance blooms at *Tomorrow*."

"And did you hear what a women's lib group is doing for Lotte?"

"No."

"They've set up a fund-raising committee. They're going to get her the best defense lawyer in America. She's already become a martyr to the cause of feminist rights. She might be nuts, but she's a damned fine reporter."

"Speaking of reporters, where's Theo?"

"She's out interviewing a rock star who's seeking a sex-reversal operation, a she who was operated on to become a he and then decided he wanted to be a she again. Tough age we live in, Nose."

"It has its peculiar charms."

"Theo left a message for you if you called. She said she'll see you later," Felix said. "What are you planning to do now that this case is over?"

"Nothing for a few days," Nicoletti said.

Nicoletti went home to his loft, where he changed to a pair of chinos and an old shirt. Then he lifted the painting of the muddy green eye off the easel and carried it down to the sidewalk.

He went back to the loft, propped a new canvas on the easel, and got out paints, brushes, turps.

He would create a dramatic painting in black and white and just a few bright splashes of color.

When it was finished, he would title it *Tomorrow*.

The painting would be good, and if life followed art, there was no limit to the exciting possibilities yet to be explored.